CONTENTS

Made in the USA
Columbia, SC
26 June 2017

ACKNOWLEDGMENTS

Mahalo to: Karen & John at Autism Empowerment, Susan at
Indigo Editing, my fellow authors from NIWA and SCBWI,
everyone who has helped me spread the word about Joel's story,
and, of course, all the fans and supporters. You guys rock.

CHAPTER 1: THE COFFEE SHOP

Where the heck is she? Joel thought as he glanced down at his smartphone once again.

On my way, the most recent text message from Felicity read.

On my way? Joel frowned. *But that was fifty-five minutes ago. It doesn't usually take that long to get here from Bellevue, especially on a Saturday afternoon. Hope she's all right.*

Joel took another sip of his hot chocolate, which was now anything but hot. He thought about texting or calling, but he didn't want to disturb Felicity if she was driving.

C'mon, we're cutting it really close...

Joel glanced around. Could she have walked in and sat down at another table without him noticing? That seemed unlikely. This particular coffee shop was small and narrow, so even though he was seated near the back, he should have been able to spot her the moment she arrived.

Maybe there's traffic or something, Joel mused. He opened up the map application on his phone and swiped the phone's screen several times with his index finger. *Doesn't seem like it...*

"Boo!"

Joel jumped in his chair.

"Scared you, huh?" Felicity smirked.

"Yeah—um, I mean, no, I mean...how did you do that?"

"Do what?" she said, placing an overstuffed backpack on the ground.

"I dunno, like, sneak in, or whatever."

"Not sure what you're talking about, dude." She shrugged as she took a seat opposite Joel. "I just walked in normally. You were all into your phone, there. Playing a game?"

"No. Checking the traffic."

"Why?"

"'Cause...'cause you're late."

"Yeah, yeah, I know. Parking around this area sucks. Why'd you want to meet here, anyway?"

"It's close to my apartment," Joel replied. "And," he leaned forward and said in a lowered voice, "there's an alleyway nearby that will be perfect."

Felicity flashed him a distasteful look. "An alleyway? Are you serious?"

"No, I'm joking."

A long pause ensued, after which Felicity said with her brow furrowed, "Wait—are you trying to be sarcastic?"

"Yes." Joel grinned. "Um, I mean, no. I mean...hold on, are you talking about the 'no, I'm joking' part, or the thing about the alleyway? Because if you were talking about the—"

"Just—forget it," she interrupted, holding up her hands and shaking her head. "Why an alleyway? Won't people see us?"

"Well, it's the same place where Marshall and I did it," Joel answered. "So I figured that since it worked that time, then it's probably our best bet."

"What about your apartment? I mean, that's where *we* did it."

"We who?"

"Me and Marshall."

"You did it in my apartment?"

"No, *my* apartment. When Vicky wasn't home."

"Who?"

"You know, my sister. Victoria."

"Oh—uh, well, we can't do that. My mom and Taylor and Art are all there right now."

"Ugh, great. There's gotta be a better place, though."

"Maybe, but we're running out of time."

"Of course we are." Felicity chuckled. "I thought we had three days from the time we got back on Wednesday night?"

"It's actually a few hours less," Joel replied. "Fire-flower got Spectraland and Earth days mixed up," he added, referring to the leader of the Wavemakers—those with the ability to create musical magic—and the land that she was from.

"All right, fine. The alley it is."

The intro riff to "Slo-Mo Kikaida" by The Dambuilders sounded. It was the ringtone on Joel's phone.

"Dude, why don't you use one of *our* songs as your ringtone?"

"What?"

"Never mind."

3

Joel swiped the phone's screen with his index finger. "Hello?"

"Hey, bud," Art's voice said. "How's your coffee date going?"

"Um, good."

"Cool. Anyway, I didn't want to bother you guys, but I thought both of you might want to know about this."

"Know about what?"

"Julio called."

A cold feeling hit the pit of Joel's stomach. Julio was the record-company representative who had signed Joel's band to a contract, and he hadn't exactly been thrilled with the way things had turned out at their Halloween show three days ago. Not only did the opening band leave the stage early, but Joel and Felicity had to walk off in the middle of their own set when Fireflower needed their help, leaving Trevor, their bass player, to do an extended instrumental solo that ended up running well over twenty-five minutes. Even though Julio was one of their biggest supporters, he had warned them about the possibility of the label dropping the band if the show wasn't as successful as everyone wanted it to be.

"What, uh...what did he say?" Joel asked, bracing himself for the worst.

"Okay, well, get this—remember that tall woman with the spiky purple hair Julio was talking to after the show?"

"Yeah."

"Turns out, she used to be the manager for Biledriver—your favorite band."

"Oh." Joel grimaced. Biledriver *used* to be his favorite band, and its lead singer and guitarist, Marshall Byle, *used* to be his idol and hero...that is, until Marshall attempted to kill him and Felicity not just once, but several

4

times over the course of two convoluted and downright evil schemes back in Spectraland. "Is that all?"

"No, no," Art said, "Julio found out that now she manages Sugarblood."

"Sugarblood? Wow."

"And guess what?"

"What?"

"She wants us to open for them at their arena show next month!"

Joel's mouth dropped open. "Whoa—wait, really?"

"Really!"

"What's going on?" Felicity said.

"Is that Felicity?" Art asked.

"Yeah, um, hold on"—Joel lowered the phone and looked up—"it's Art. He said Julio called, and, uh, Sugarblood—you know, that band with the female singer who had four songs in the top ten of the modern rock chart all at the same time before they—"

"I know who they are," Felicity said.

"Well, they want us to open for them at the arena next month!"

"Oh wow—cool," Felicity said with an expression that was a little less excited looking than Joel would have expected.

"Yeah! So"—Joel put the phone back up to his ear—"is it all confirmed, then?"

"Yup," Art said. "And that's not all. Apparently, the reviews of the Halloween show were pretty incredible."

"Even—even the bass solo?"

"Even the bass solo. One blogger said that it 'bordered on genius.'"

"But Julio was all worried and stuff."

"He's always like that." Art chuckled. "I keep telling him that worrying is a waste of time, but I don't think he really listens to me."

Joel grinned. "Okay, well, that's awesome."

"Yeah," Art said, "so anyway, I'll leave you two alone. Just thought some good news might help enhance the mood."

Joel wasn't really sure what Art meant by that, but since they were pressed for time, he didn't bother to ask. "Um, thanks."

"See you when you get home."

"Okay." Joel hung up and put the phone down on the table. "Turns out people liked the Halloween show—a lot!"

"Well, that's a relief," Felicity said. "Anyway, shouldn't we talk about this later? I thought we had to get going."

"Oh—uh, yeah, we do. You brought your wavebow, right?"

"Nope. Why would I need that thing?"

"Wait—what?"

"Dude, I'm kidding." She nodded at the backpack on the ground next to her. "Got it right here."

"Okay, cool." Joel stood up and took his own backpack off of his chair. "You want the rest of my hot chocolate?"

"Ugh, no. And actually, I gotta hit the restroom real quick. Why don't you throw that away and I'll meet you outside."

"Okay."

As Felicity headed for the restroom, Joel walked over to the recycle bins.

Hmm, let's see...this one says "paper—clean and dry"...this is a paper cup, but it's not clean or dry, so where else would it go...maybe "compostables—food and food-related paper?" Or is it just "compost?" Or what about "paper, cans, and plastic bottles?" I mean, since it's technically a beverage container and it's made out of paper, it would seem to match that one...and what should I do with the rest of the hot chocolate...is that considered food?

"Joel!"

"Huh? What?" Joel spun around, nearly hitting the person behind him with his backpack.

"Whoa!" the person laughed. It was Suzi, Joel's high school classmate and former crush. "Sorry, didn't mean to startle you."

"Oh—uh, no...no problem."

"So, what are you up to?" Suzi asked with a smile. "I haven't see you in here before. Were you studying?"

"Well, no—I mean, uh, yeah, kind of. Sort of."

"Let me guess—that big physics test on Monday, right?"

"Physics? Um, yeah, sure."

"I knew it! You know, I usually come here every Saturday to study—maybe we should meet up sometime?"

Joel felt his face getting hot. "Uh...meet up?"

"Yeah, to study together. You know, since we basically have all the same classes."

"Well, I..." Joel wanted to tell her that they only had three classes together, but he couldn't quite get the words out of his mouth.

"Oh, and before I forget, congratulations on everything going on with your band! I keep wanting to tell you that at school, but you always dash out of class before I get a chance." Suzi giggled.

"Um, okay."

"I just think it's so cool that you got a record deal and you're playing all these shows and people are starting to—oh, you must be Felicity!"

Joel turned his head. Felicity was standing behind him with an annoyed look on her face.

"Maybe," Felicity said. "Who're you?"

"I'm Suzi," Suzi replied, extending her hand. "Joel's classmate. It's so nice to meet you!"

"Yeah, whatever," Felicity mumbled, thrusting her hands into the pockets of her hooded sweatshirt and looking away.

"I was just telling Joel how awesome it is that your band is doing so well," Suzi continued, unperturbed. "Especially since the two of you are..."

Felicity looked back up. "Are what?"

"You know...on the autism spectrum."

"Oh...well, so what if we are?" Felicity snapped. "What does that have to do with anything?"

"No, no, I know," Suzi said, holding up her hands defensively, "I'm sorry, I just meant that, you know, people on the autism spectrum are supposed to have trouble with social interaction, so the fact that you're in a successful band makes it—"

"We're a successful band because we rock," Felicity said, taking a step forward and nudging Joel aside. "End of story."

"I'm sure you do, I was just trying to say that—"

"Um, we really have to get going," Joel broke in, his stress level rising. He glanced at Suzi, who looked either angry or dismayed; in the moment, it was hard to tell exactly which. "I'll, uh, I'll try not to dash out of class next time. We can talk more then."

"Okay." Suzi nodded.

Joel put his head down and walked out of the coffee shop, looking back to make sure that Felicity was following him and not still verbally sparring with Suzi, or worse.

"Well, that wasn't awkward at all," Felicity exhaled once they were outside.

"What are you talking about?" Joel said as he continued walking, still feeling flustered. "That was, like, the most awkward—oh, right."

"Dude, I'm sure you've noticed this, but that girl *totally* looks like Auravine. Kinda creepy, no?"

"Yeah, I guess," Joel muttered, his anxiety level ramping up another couple of notches. Auravine was the young Wavemaker who had turned out to be assisting Marshall Byle during his second evil scheme, and it was for her trial that Joel and Felicity needed to return to Spectraland, to serve as witnesses and provide testimony. They had also agreed to help recapture Darkeye, the potion-making old native who had escaped from prison, and they needed to make it back there before the three-day window was up, otherwise it would be too late; with the way the time difference between Spectraland and Earth worked, missing the window would mean that they would end up returning months, or possibly years, later.

"They're like doppelgangers," Felicity said. "They even sound the same."

"Yeah. Anyway, there's the alley."

"Eww," Felicity said. "Looks super sketchy to me. No wonder Marshall picked that place."

Joel walked into the alley and crouched behind a dumpster. "You know, we should have done this on Thursday night, like I originally wanted to," he grumbled, his agitated mood giving him the courage to speak

9

his mind. "That way we wouldn't have run into Suzi and we wouldn't be in such a rush."

"I told you, I was busy," Felicity said as she crouched down next to him.

"Doing what?"

"Stuff."

"What kind of stuff?"

"Never mind, just—"

A soft tone rang out, like a high E note being played on an electric guitar with the amp turned down.

"What was that?" Joel asked, looking around.

"I'm sure it's nothing," Felicity said. "Hurry up and get out your wavebow."

"Are you coming?" a muffled voice said. "You only have a minute of your time left."

"What the—is there someone in your backpack?" Joel asked.

"Of course not," Felicity replied. "Now c'mon, hurry up."

Joel opened his backpack and took out his wavebow. Even more unnerved now, he fumbled the first few chords of the incantation that would send them back to Spectraland.

"Where's the sheet music?" Felicity demanded.

"I—I memorized the song, so I don't need it."

"Memorized? Sure doesn't seem like it."

"Thirty seconds," the muffled voice said.

"Who *is* that?" Joel asked.

"Just play the song!"

Joel tried again. This time, he was pretty sure he was getting it right, as the now-familiar sensation of nausea and vertigo began to set in. Halfway through, however, he could sense that something was amiss; the streams of light that usually danced before his eyes were uniformly purple, rather than multicolored, and they moved around in a slower, more deliberate fashion. Before he could do anything about it, he lost all feeling in his fingertips, and the alleyway disappeared in a dark, shrinking circular scene wipe, like the kind you see at the end of an old cartoon show.

CHAPTER 2: THE YELLOW ROCK

The next thing Joel knew, he was floating, lost in space. That is, if space were teal instead of black, and instead of stars, there were ghostly images of seemingly random objects, among them guitars, books, tablet computers, and cell phones. Some of the images appeared to be far away, while some of them were so close that he could almost reach out and touch them. He pushed himself forward and extended his hand toward a large pepperoni pizza that was hovering just a few feet in front of him, but his fingers passed right through it as if it were made of smoke.

"Felicity?" he called out. His voice sounded muffled to his own ears, like something was swallowing it up as he spoke. "Where are you?"

No response.

He was still holding his wavebow, so he tried playing the incantation once again. The correct notes emanated from the instrument, but nothing else happened.

Hmm, he thought. *I may be in a little bit of trouble here.*

Scanning his surroundings, he spotted some shapes off in the distance that resembled a group of people. So, hoping that Felicity might be among them, he strapped his wavebow around his shoulder and began propelling himself in their direction. Along the way he passed more familiar objects, some of which were not from Earth, but from Spectraland: lifepods, sleepdarts, and even a bowl of the icky soup that the Roughrock Tribe had served him at Spiral Landing.

It's like...these are all things from my own life.

That theory was bolstered as he neared the group of people, which he now noticed was made up of both Earth denizens and Spectraland natives. Some of them he recognized right away—like Julio, Fireflower, and Trevor—while others were people that he had only seen in passing, like the girl in the homemade Joel Suzuki and the Wavemakers T-shirt that he had spotted in the crowd of a Portland show they played forty-six days ago.

"Felicity?" Joel called out again. Still no response. He waved his arms, doing what he assumed was a reasonable approximation of a breaststroke, until he was up in front of Trevor. "Hey, Trevor—have you seen Felicity?"

Uncharacteristically, Trevor didn't say a word. Instead, without looking at Joel, he slowly turned and pointed to his left.

"What? No, I already looked over there, and I didn't see—" Joel stopped himself. Now, in a spot twenty-seven feet away, where there used to only be empty space, there was a familiar figure of a girl with long blond hair, floating motionless with her back turned to him. "Oh—uh, thanks." He turned away from Trevor and air-swam in the figure's direction, wondering if it was the real thing or an apparition. "Felicity!" he shouted. "I'm over here! Are you all right?"

The figure didn't turn around.

Maybe she can't hear me because something is affecting the sound in this place, he thought, trying to quell a rising sense of panic. *I'm sure that's all it is...*

As he continued flapping his arms, he noticed something strange: he didn't seem to be getting any closer to the figure. He knew that he couldn't be stuck in place, since he was passing by all the other random objects around him, but the distance between him and her remained the same no matter how hard he flapped.

What the heck?

Then, the figure started to shrink, as if it were moving away from him.

"Felicity!"

It kept shrinking. A hissing sound started up in Joel's ears.

"Where are you going?" he yelled, flapping as hard as he could. "I'm over here!"

The hissing sound got louder as the figure receded into the teal-colored nothingness.

"Felicity!"

The hissing sound crescendoed, as if a snake were closing in on him. He started to get a sharp headache. Then—

"Yo," a voice said from behind, loud and clear.

Startled, Joel whirled around to see Felicity facing him, a little over ten feet away. The hissing sound faded, and all of the ghostly images were suddenly gone.

"Second time I've scared you today." She smirked as she pushed herself forward.

"Were you—was that—where did you—" Joel stammered.

"Dude, are you okay? You look kinda pale."

"Uh, yeah...I'm fine," he replied, trying to regain his composure. What he had just seen was more than a bit unsettling, but at least Felicity was here now, safe. Figuring that the image of her floating away had been nothing more than a harmless illusion, he cleared his throat and tried to strike up a confident pose. "Um...how about you?"

"Okay, I guess." She shrugged. "At least you didn't teleport us into a wall, or a volcano, or something. What is this place?"

"I dunno," he said, looking around. The surrounding teal hue had shifted into more of a shade of turquoise. "Must be some kind of alternate plane, I think. Like where we found Marshall the last time."

"Great. Well, play the song again and get us out of here. Hopefully we're not too late."

He was about to when he remembered something. "There's, um, there's a problem, though."

"Of course there is," she sighed. "What is it?"

"It's like there's no Aura energy here. I tried playing my wavebow, but nothing happened. Did you try?"

"Hello, I just got here. I thought you did too?"

"Um, not exactly."

"How long have you been here?"

"About six minutes and thirty-three seconds. No, wait, are you talking about how long I was here before you arrived, or how long I was here before you asked that question?"

"Forget it." She chuckled. "Must've just been some kind of minor time shift-y thing. Anyhoo, so—no Aura energy, eh?"

"No. I mean, yes. I mean, right. No Aura energy."

"In that case," Felicity said, opening her backpack, "I have an idea."

"Um, okay."

She reached into her backpack and pulled something out. "We'll use this." In her palm was a small yellow rock that looked sort of like a lemon drop, which began to give off a faint rainbow-colored glow. Joel could have sworn that he'd seen something like it before—and not in the candy aisle.

"What is that thing? Where did you get it?"

"Never mind that right now. Just use it. It has some Aura energy stored up in it."

"But—how am I supposed to do that?"

"I dunno, like, I'll hold it up to your head, or something."

"Is that really gonna work?"

"It better."

Felicity gripped the rock between her forefinger and her thumb and placed it up against Joel's temple.

"Ow," Joel said.

"Oh, c'mon, that didn't hurt."

"Yeah, it did. You just, like, poked me with the pointy end."

"Don't be such a wimp. Is it working?"

"I'm not sure, I think it—" he broke off, interrupted by a sudden jolt that coursed throughout his body like a strong electrical shock. "Whoa—okay, yeah, it's working."

"Awesome. Now get us out of here before it runs out."

Joel played the transfer cast once more, trying his best to relax. As soon as he finished the final note, his surroundings shifted and swirled, and a few moments later, he found himself standing atop the islet called Crownrock, the site of the gateway between Earth and Spectraland known as the Rift. Little wisps of multicolored Aura drifted along on a warm, gentle breeze.

16

"Okay, much better," Felicity, standing next to him, remarked. "I didn't even get queasy that time."

"So, I guess that's a point for you?" Joel said with a grin.

"Eh, I stopped playing that game."

Joel's grin faded. "What? When?"

"Just now."

"Why?"

"Since I told you about it, it doesn't seem like fun anymore."

"Oh."

"Anyway, looks like we made it back in time."

Joel glanced around. It was early evening, and the twin moons were shining brightly in a cloudless sky. "Actually," he said. "I think we're late."

"How do you know?"

"If everything went as planned, we were supposed to get back here during the day. At least, that's what Fireflower told me."

"Well, hopefully we're just a little late, and not, like, a decade late, or whatever."

"Yeah, um—so, what is that yellow rock thing, anyway?" Joel asked, pointing at Felicity's hand. "And who was talking from inside your backpack?"

"I'll tell you later," she replied, opening her backpack and switching out the yellow rock for her wavebow. "I thought we were running late?"

"I know, but—"

Felicity began playing the notes of the particular wavecast that would allow her to soar through the sky like a bird. "Then c'mon, let's go."

Joel let out a little sigh of frustration before he joined her in the cast. Clouds of dark-green Aura billowed out of their instruments and surrounded them, forming sparkling, shimmering cocoons of buoyancy. Then they took off, flying through Crownrock's protective shield of Aura energy and up into the air.

"Why don't you tell me along the way?" Joel shouted after they had leveled off.

Felicity cupped her ear, not looking at him. "What?"

"I said, why don't you tell me along the way?"

"Can't hear a word you're saying, dude!" She extended her arms and sped up.

Ugh, Joel groused. *I hate it when she does stuff like this.*

It wasn't long before Joel caught sight of their destination: the village of Headsmouth, which was one of the four main settlements in Spectraland as well as the island's de facto capital. In accordance with custom, they landed about fifty yards outside of the main entrance (to fly directly into the village was considered a sign of disrespect to everyone who couldn't fly, which was everyone except for the Wavemakers), where a pair of familiar green-skinned locals met them.

"You are late," one of the locals, a tall male Wavemaker named Thornleaf, said.

"Yeah, yeah, we know," Felicity responded with a dismissive wave.

Joel noticed the diamond-shaped yellow pendant that hung from a brown band around Thornleaf's neck.

Oh yeah, now I remember—Felicity's lemon-drop rock looks just like that!

The other local, a short, thin male named Windblade who was also a Wavemaker, looked Joel and Felicity over with a concerned expression, as if he were inspecting them for battle wounds. "Is everything all right?" he asked. "What happened?"

Felicity glanced at Joel. "Why don't you tell them?" she said.

"You can explain on the way in," Thornleaf said, turning back toward the village. "Auravine's trial has already begun."

"I, uh, I just messed up the transfer cast a little, that's all," Joel said as he, Felicity, and Windblade followed after Thornleaf. "Then we got stuck in some kind of strange limbo state where there was no Aura energy. But then, Felicity had this—"

"So," Felicity interrupted loudly, "what did we miss so far?"

"Not much," Windblade replied. "Just the opening statements, mostly."

"You did miss all of Stoneroot's hearing, however," Thornleaf said. "Fortunately, the evidence against him was overwhelming enough that your testimony was not required."

"What's gonna happen to him?" Joel asked. Stoneroot used to be the leader of the Silencers, a group of Spectraland natives who were opposed to the Wavemaker Order, until it was discovered that he had been plotting to take over the Chieftain Council by means of a forbidden mind-control potion.

"He will spend fifteen years in a Headsmouth prison hut," Thornleaf replied evenly, apparently trying not to betray any lingering resentment he may have felt toward his estranged father.

"What about Marshall?" Felicity asked. "Did he get a trial after all?"

"He did not," Thornleaf answered. "The chiefs sent him and the Lightsnakes directly to the Pit of Ashes."

Felicity nodded. "Cool."

Joel considered trying to ask about the yellow rock once more, but, figuring that Felicity would just find some new way to dodge the question, he went with a different inquiry instead, one that was related to the current flow of conversation. "Speaking of the Pit of Ashes," he said, "has anyone found Darkeye yet?"

"We were waiting for you to return," Windblade responded good-naturedly. "Fireflower decided that we would simply be wasting time, looking for him without your Sight ability to aid us."

"Makes sense," Felicity said. She glanced at Joel. "With the Sight, you could probably just do a quick flyover of the island and spot him instantly, like a Where's Waldo picture."

"I am pretty good at those." Joel grinned. The Sight was his ability to spot tiny details that everyone else seemed to miss, and it had been instrumental in saving the day in Spectraland on multiple occasions. Felicity was exaggerating a bit, but it was true that it would come in handy.

"Darkeye is not all that dangerous on his own, anyway." Thornleaf sniffed. "We can start searching after the trial is over."

They entered the village. Joel hadn't actually seen Headsmouth the last time he was here, and he was anxious to discover what changes it had undergone during the long interval between his first and second visits. To his surprise, it didn't really look all that different; there were a few additional huts and tree houses, but nothing in the way of noticeable technological advancements like the flume system he had observed in the village of Bluecrest. Only a handful of natives were walking about. Joel wondered if the rest were attending Auravine's trial.

"What was that limbo state like?" Windblade asked as they all headed for the middle of the village. "Was it frightening?"

"Um, not really," Joel answered, reluctant to go into too much detail. "It was just like floating in midair."

"And there was no Aura energy?"

"Yeah."

"Then how did you get back?"

"Well, we—"

"We figured something out," Felicity said. "It's not really important. Oh, hey, look, we're here."

CHAPTER 3: THE TRIAL

The four Wavemakers had arrived at Headsmouth's central courtyard, which was packed with an eerily silent, shoulder-to-shoulder audience of Spectraland natives. Joel craned his neck to get a better look at the stage, which stood at the far end of the courtyard. Large, wooden, rectangular, and built on risers that put it several feet above the ground, it was similar to the one where he and Felicity had performed an elaborate show of wavecasting a little over six months (Earth time) or nineteen years (Spectraland time) ago. But while that particular stage supported a number of festive decorations, this one had only a long table made out of what looked like black volcanic rock, flanked on each side by a stone column topped off with a flickering torch. Behind the table sat the chiefs of the four villages: Silverfern, Twotrunk, Raintree, and Scarskin.

"Please rephrase the question to the accused," Silverfern intoned.

"Yes, my chief," an unfamiliar voice said. "Auravine, do you deny that you conspired with Chief Byle to bring about the destruction of your fellow Wavemakers?"

"They have arrived!" someone in the crowd exclaimed. All heads turned, making Joel suddenly nervous. Whispers started to ripple through the gathering.

"Please pardon the interruption," Thornleaf said, holding up his hand. "But yes, the legendary offworlders have returned, and they apologize for their tardiness."

"We do?" Felicity said.

"Let them through," Silverfern ordered.

A number of natives shuffled out of the way, opening up a path down the middle of the crowd. Thornleaf led the way to the front, and now Joel could see Auravine sitting on a stone stool on the ground off to the left of the stage. Behind her stood a pair of spear-wielding guards, and in front of her, a short, pudgy native was busy leafing through a set of parchments and mumbling inaudibly to himself. Auravine wore a sad, scared expression, and she was visibly trembling, as if she expected the guards to pierce her with their weapons at any moment.

"Over here," Thornleaf grunted.

Joel turned and followed the tall native over to the right of the stage, where they joined some other familiar faces: Fireflower, Riverhand, and Redstem. All three native Wavemakers gave Joel and Felicity silent nods of greeting, which Joel interpreted as a cue that now was not the time to be having any catch-up conversations.

"All right, Ringneck, you may continue," Silverfern said.

The short, pudgy native cleared his throat. "Thank you, my chief. So, Auravine, what is your answer?"

"I—I am sorry," Auravine said in a voice that Joel could barely hear, "but...what was the question again?"

"Do you deny," the pudgy native, who was apparently named Ringneck, sighed, "that you conspired with

Chief Byle to bring about the destruction of your fellow Wavemakers?"

"Well, no, but..."

"But what?"

"At the time, there was a very good reason for what I did," Auravine finished, a hint of resolve creeping into her tone.

"And what reason could possibly justify the restoration of Byle, one of the worst criminals in Spectraland history?"

Auravine paused for a long moment before responding. "I believed that Chief Byle would bring us peace," she finally said. "That he would end the long conflict between the Wavemakers and the Silencers that claimed the lives of my parents."

"Is that what he told you he would do?"

"Yes." Auravine nodded. "But now I know that I was wrong. I was wrong for trusting him. I was wrong for hurting my friends. And even though I regenerated most of Chief Byle's physical form, I stopped before any more damage could be done."

Ringneck squinted and looked over one of the parchments in his hands. "All right, so tell me...how, exactly, did you arrive at this—this change of heart?"

Auravine turned her gaze to Joel. He looked down at his shoes, though it was more of an unconscious reflex than an actual response.

"One of the legendary offworlders convinced me that I had chosen the wrong path," she said, "and that it was not too late for me to turn back."

A round of murmurs sounded. Joel gave the crowd a side-eyed glance and saw that a number of the natives in attendance were looking at him with what he assumed were appreciative expressions, although it was hard to be completely sure. Almost involuntarily, his lips formed a sheepish, awkward sort of half-grin that he quickly erased.

"With that," Ringneck said, "I would like to call the offworlder, Joel Suzuki, as a witness."

Joel looked around, hesitating. Even though he had been expecting this, he hadn't thought he would be called upon so soon. Unfortunately, his being late had apparently robbed him of whatever time he may have had to confer with Fireflower and decide upon what, exactly, he was going to say.

"You're up, dude," Felicity muttered out of the side of her mouth.

Auravine stood up from the stone stool. Joel could see that her wrists were tied together in front of her with binding vine. She didn't look in his direction as one of the guards led her away at spear-point.

"Please, have a seat," Ringneck said to Joel, motioning toward the stool.

Joel sat down. The seat of the stool was hard and flat, and it took a few moments of awkward shifting and repositioning before he was able to find a somewhat comfortable position.

"I do not believe we have met before," Ringneck said with a respectful nod. "I am Ringneck, the Four Villages' minister of justice."

"Um, nice to meet you," Joel said.

"I assume you are unaware of how these particular rituals work, is that correct?"

Joel just nodded.

"I will be asking you a series of questions, which you must answer completely and truthfully, to the best of your knowledge," Ringneck said, his tone somehow becoming even more formal than it already was. "While the practice of using wavecasts or potions to verify one's honesty has officially been discontinued, the Chieftain Council has agreed, in this particular case, to make an exception if, in my expert opinion, the witness—you, in this case—appears to be telling a falsehood or withholding information. Do you understand?"

"Yes," Joel replied, even though he had partially tuned Ringneck out shortly after the pudgy native had started his second sentence.

"Very good." Ringneck shuffled his parchments. "Now then, is it your belief that Auravine, here, is the one responsible for creating the Moonfires?"

Joel glanced at Fireflower and the other Wavemakers. All of them remained motionless and expressionless, except for Felicity, who, with her arms folded, gave him a barely perceptible shrug. "Um...well...I, uh—"

"A simple *yes* or *no* will suffice," Ringneck said.

"Yes," Joel said.

"And what purpose did the Moonfires serve?"

"Well, they served a couple of purposes."

A few moments passed. "Such as?" Ringneck finally asked.

"They, uh, they were a portal to the alternate plane where Marshall was living."

"What else?"

"They also disrupted the Aura and knocked people out, to make it easier for someone"—he didn't want to say Auravine's name right there—"to kidnap other Wavemakers."

"And did they not also have the side effect of creating violent storms and sickening animals all across the island?"

Joel scratched his nose as he tried to parse out what Ringneck had just asked him. *Well, I dunno if it was necessarily* all *across the island, since I didn't see the whole island every time Auravine cast the Moonfire. And what does he mean, exactly, by "and did they not?" Is he trying to say they did or they didn't? I wonder why the translation cast isn't being clearer. Maybe if I ask him to rephrase—*

"Please, just answer the question to the best of your knowledge."

"To the best of my knowledge?"

"Yes."

"Um, well, yeah, I guess so."

"Then you agree that Auravine is not only responsible for restoring Chief Byle's physical form and nearly killing her fellow Wavemakers but also for the widespread destruction suffered by almost every inhabitant of the island."

Joel took a deep breath. Fortunately, Auravine had been moved to a spot behind the stool by her guards, sparing Joel the possibility of seeing her expression. "Yes," he exhaled. The courtyard was unnervingly quiet in the wake of his response.

"Those are all the questions I have for this witness," Ringneck said, addressing the four chiefs.

"Very well," Silverfern said. She looked over to her left at Twotrunk, who gave her an affirmative nod. Then she looked over to her right at Raintree and Scarskin. Both chiefs nodded as well.

I wonder who's gonna be the next witness, Joel thought, relieved that he would be able to get off of this hideously uncomfortable stool. He felt like his entire backside was about to cramp up.

"In light of what we have heard so far," Silverfern continued in a louder voice, "I believe that no further witnesses or testimonies are required. It appears clear to this council that the defendant, Auravine of Nightshore, is to be found guilty of all the crimes of which she has been accused."

"Wait, what?" Joel said out loud.

"In accordance with Spectraland law, she is hereby sentenced to the maximum allowable punishment: lifetime imprisonment in the Pit of Ashes."

Joel looked at the natives in the crowd. None of them appeared to be surprised or disturbed by this outcome; in fact, a few were even smiling or nodding in silent approval. He looked at the other Wavemakers. Fireflower was staring straight ahead, a grim expression on her face, while the others were either hanging their heads or looking blankly at nothing in particular. Finally, he turned around and looked at Auravine. The young healer's eyes were closed, and thin streaks of tears were falling down her cheeks.

"Take her away," Silverfern ordered.

"Wait, um—you mean, that's it?" Joel said, standing up and approaching the stage. "That's the whole trial?"

"Indeed it is," Silverfern replied as the crowd began to disperse.

"Well, uh, shouldn't there be, like," Joel stammered, furiously trying to recall any details about the legal process that he had peripherally picked up from movies, TV shows, and the like, "a defense lawyer, and cross-examination, and evidence, like, you know, exhibit A, exhibit B, exhibit C—"

"I am not sure what kind of justice rituals you observe in your world," Silverfern said, descending a short flight of wooden stairs that led off the stage, "but here in Spectraland, we believe in efficiency and expediency. If it is obvious that someone is guilty, we see no reason to belabor the point."

"Well, okay, but..."

"Thank you for your testimony, by the way. Please join us for a quick meal at my residence before Fireflower briefs you on your next mission."

"Oh, I know—what if I object?" Joel pressed on, ignoring the Headsmouth chief's expression of gratitude. "I object, Your Honor! Can I do that?" He felt a hand on his shoulder. It was Fireflower, standing next to him along with Felicity and the rest of the Wavemakers.

"Joel, please," the diminutive Wavemaker leader said. "Do not question the council's judgment."

"It is quite all right, Fireflower," Silverfern said, holding up her hand. "I am actually rather interested in learning why he persists in defending someone who very nearly killed him."

That's actually a good question, Joel thought. Why did he, anyway? Was it because he believed in forgiveness, or in redemption? Auravine did, after all, change her mind in the end. Or was it because of something else—a slightly more selfish reason, one based on a murky jumble of feelings that he thought could possibly add up to...affection? A desire to see if he and Auravine shared some kind of mutual attraction that could maybe, possibly lead to—*gasp*—something more than friendship?

"I, um, I just think that we left out a lot of the story," he said, deciding to push those feelings aside for now. "You know, like how I was able to talk her out of killing us, and how she hit Marshall with rocks when the drone Lightsnakes were strangling us, and how she flew us all out of that alternate plane before it disintegrated."

Silverfern raised an eyebrow. "Do you believe that, based on those actions, we should pardon or excuse her previous deeds? That her decision to turn and help you should cleanse her hands of every evil she had perpetrated up until that point?"

"Well...sure?" Joel ventured. After all, there were many examples of that kind of thing happening in the stories that he was a fan of. Like Zuko in *Avatar: The Last Airbender*, Anakin Skywalker in *Star Wars*...

"Again, I am not sure how your world dispenses its own particular brand of justice," Silverfern said, "but here, individuals cannot make up for their past crimes with present virtue."

"She's got a point there, dude," Felicity said. "If you robbed a bank one day, I don't think they'd let you off if you gave the money back the next."

"Um, okay," Joel said, conceding. "But does she really have to spend the rest of her life in the Pit of Ashes? Isn't that kinda harsh?"

"It is a fitting punishment."

"Will she be safe in there, you know, with Marshall and the Lightsnakes?"

"Given how many of the island's villagers feel about her," Silverfern said, "the Pit of Ashes may actually be the safest place of all."

CHAPTER 4: CHROMA CANYON

Joel didn't talk much during the short meal that ensued as he contemplated this latest turn of events that, to him, was rather disappointing. Even though he was very aware of all the bad things that Auravine had done, he had harbored some measure of hope that his testimony would convince people that she should be, at the most, pardoned, or, at the least, confined to some sort of house arrest situation at the Wavemaker Temple for a temporary period of time.

Given the somber mood that followed the proceedings, no one else talked much either, with a couple of exceptions: Thornleaf informed Joel and Felicity that the swordcats—their animal allies who had been a big help in solving the Moonfire mystery—had returned to their home on Sunpeak mountain, and Fireflower told them about her initial attempts to find out where Darkeye might have gone after escaping from the Pit of Ashes. As it turned out, the two offworlders had only been gone for one Spectraland week (thanks to Fireflower's new Rift-travel wavecast that minimized the time differences between the two worlds), so there was really nothing much else to catch up on anyway.

After the meal (which Joel ate none of), everyone split up: Thornleaf accompanied a contingent of guards whose job it was to escort Auravine to prison, Windblade returned to the Wavemaker Temple to assist Yellowpetal—Fireflower's mother—with ongoing chores and routine maintenance, and Joel and Felicity flew with Fireflower, Riverhand, and Redstem to a location called Chroma Canyon, which is where they believed Darkeye had fled to.

"So you think he's hiding in here?" Joel said after they had arrived at their destination, which, while deep, was relatively small and bowl-shaped, making it seem more like a crater than a canyon. A dense cloud of bright-yellow Aura energy slowly swirled around the area as if it were trapped there, and dozens of multicolored crystal formations resembling giant ice pops jutted out of the ground at random intervals.

"Quite possibly," Riverhand replied. "According to our strongest tracking casts, this is where he went immediately after he escaped."

"And the casts appear to indicate that he has not gone anywhere else," Redstem added.

"Seems like it would be a dumb move for him to hang around here, though," Felicity remarked, taking in her surroundings. "I mean, look at it. It's just a big ol' pit. He'd be a sitting duck."

"True," Fireflower said as Joel wondered what *sitting duck* translated to in the Spectraland language. "That is why I wanted to see what he might be up to before we attempted to apprehend him. This is where Joel's Sight power will come in handy."

"It will?" Felicity asked. "How?"

Fireflower looked over at Joel. "Did you not tell her about your enhanced ability?"

Joel grimaced as Felicity shot him a glance with her brow furrowed. His Sight power appeared to have gained a new dimension—"leveled up," as it were—at the end of their previous adventure. Instead of only being able to see what was there in front of him, he could now also perceive images of events that had happened in that location in the recent past.

Felicity placed her hands on her hips. "What enhanced ability?" she demanded.

"I, uh, I can see more stuff now," Joel replied, feeling nervous. Felicity could still be quite intimidating when she wanted to be. "Like, remember when we were at the temple after we got back from Marshall's alternate plane? I was looking for Stoneroot's trail in the clearing when suddenly, I saw all these images, like moving holograms, of him and his guards fighting the Lightsnakes, Whitenose running away, things like that."

"Why didn't you tell me about this?"

"Well, at the time, you said you were too tired for any more stories, and then after we got home, we didn't really talk all that much until we met back up at the coffee shop."

"You could've texted."

"You said you were busy, so I didn't want to bother you."

"I would've had a minute to read a text."

"Okay, but...wait, why is this so important?"

"Forget it. Just fire it up. Everyone's waiting."

Feeling confused and flustered, Joel took a deeper breath than usual before he started up the standard routine for activating the Sight.

Step one: relax.

Step two: clear my mind.

Step three: think of a list of random details.

Let's see...let's go with...names of solid-body guitars produced by the Gibson Guitar Corporation, in alphabetical order: 335-S, Alpha Q-2000, Alpha Q-3000, Blueshawk, Corvus, Digital, Dark Fire...

The scene around him shifted and swirled. Then, after a few seconds, he caught a glimpse of a large, ghostly shape moving through the canyon some sixty-five feet away.

"Anything?" Felicity asked.

"Anything what?" Joel replied, his focus still squarely on the hazy apparition.

"Do you see anything."

"Oh—uh, yeah, it's like...like someone sitting on top of a giant slug, or something."

"That must be him," Redstem said. "He probably managed to subdue a fangworm and turn it into a mount somehow."

"I agree." Fireflower nodded. "Joel, do you see which way he was heading?"

"That way," Joel replied, pointing.

Everyone started walking in the direction that Joel had indicated. After he took up a position in the middle of the pack, everyone stopped.

"Um—is something wrong?" he asked.

"We're following you, dude," Felicity said. "Only you can see the image, remember?"

Fireflower smiled. "Yes, Joel, do not be afraid to take the lead."

"Oh—uh, okay." Joel nodded. Despite the improved sense of confidence that he had gained over the course of his previous adventure, he still felt a bit uncomfortable with the idea of being in charge of other people, whether it was a study group in school or a party of music-magicians walking through a colorful gully filled with oversized Popsicles. Reluctantly, he moved out in front of the others, keeping his gaze locked on the misty image of what was now clearly Darkeye riding what was apparently, based on what Redstem had said, a fangworm—a large gastropod-like creature that moved way too fast for its appearance.

"Everyone, get your wavebows ready," Fireflower said. "This may be a trap."

Joel stopped and turned around. "Me too?"

"Yes."

"Way ahead of ya," Felicity said, already brandishing her instrument. "I assume this place is filled with other creepy crawlies too, right?"

"Actually," Riverhand responded, "Chroma Canyon is one of the few places on the island that is not known to house any dangerous fauna. It is difficult to get in and out of, and there are no good sources of food."

"That's a first." Felicity sniffed.

Moving his wavebow into playing position, Joel turned back around and continued walking. He followed the Darkeye image through a particularly dense cluster of crystal formations, taking a moment to reflect upon how, up until now, he hadn't even really noticed just how amazing this whole area looked.

Guess this is all starting to become—what was the expression?—oh yeah: "old hat."

Finally, after another seven minutes of stalking across the canyon floor, Joel observed the Darkeye apparition stopping in front of a crystal pillar that was of a slightly darker hue than the others. The image of the pillar itself seemed to shift: one moment, it was perfectly smooth, like the rest of the formations around it, while the next moment, it had shallow circular indentations scattered all about its surface, like little pockmarks. Joel took another few steps closer before he came to a halt.

"What do you see?" Fireflower asked.

"He's...taking out a knife," Joel narrated as the action unfolded. "And now he's, like, I dunno, chipping at the crystal with it."

"Hmm," Fireflower said. "He must have harvested tiny pieces of the crystal—which is why it looks the way it does."

Her words made Joel realize why the image of the pillar was shifting: he was perceiving its past and present forms simultaneously.

"It must be an ingredient for some sort of potion," Riverhand said.

"Fireflower, what do you suppose he is up to?" Redstem asked.

"I am not sure," Fireflower replied. "I can only assume it is not good."

Joel kept watching as Darkeye's image patiently chipped away at the crystal pillar. A couple of minutes passed.

"Hey, man," Felicity said, "does this new power of yours have, like, fast-forward or something? This is starting to get kinda boring."

Joel squinted as he tried to speed up the image, but his attempt failed. "I think I can only fast-forward through stuff I've already seen," he responded without looking at her.

"Great."

Finally, after another minute or so, Joel saw Darkeye gather up all of the crystal chips and place them in a small sack.

"Okay, he's done," Joel announced as Darkeye remounted the fangworm. "And now he's leaving."

"Continue to follow him," Fireflower said.

Joel did so. Along the way, he observed Darkeye performing the regurgitation ritual that the old native used to produce his various concoctions.

"That's so gross," Felicity remarked after Joel had related that bit of information to everyone. "Glad I didn't have to see him doing it this time."

"Does anyone hear that sound?" Redstem asked.

"What sound?" Riverhand said.

Joel looked over his shoulder. Everyone had stopped.

"It is like a...a rumbling of some sort," Redstem said.

"Yes, I hear it as well," Fireflower said.

"Yeah, me too." Felicity frowned. She turned to Riverhand. "I thought you said there weren't any dangerous creatures down here."

"There should not be," Riverhand responded with a puzzled look.

"Maybe Darkeye prepared some sort of trap," Redstem theorized. "Perhaps the potion that Master Joel saw him creating is an explosive."

"That is possible," Fireflower said. "Everyone, be on guard."

"Isn't that what we were already doing?" Felicity muttered.

They followed the Darkeye and fangworm images to the far side of the canyon. As they approached the edge, Joel spotted a cave-like hole in the canyon wall, large enough for a mounted rider to fit through. "I think they're going in there," he said, pointing.

"That is odd," Riverhand said. "The last time I was here, I do not recall seeing a cavern."

Darkeye and his mount arrived at the wall. When they did so, Joel saw the cave entrance disappear, and then reappear, and then disappear again, switching back and forth with every blink of his eyes. Darkeye dismounted and appeared to feed something to the fangworm. Then, after a moment, the giant slug-like creature shuddered, turned a dark shade of red, and began to burrow its way directly into the canyon wall.

"Oh—they made the cave," Joel announced.

"What do you mean?" Fireflower asked.

"The fangworm dug it—just like it was a mole or something."

"How?" Redstem said. "Fangworms do not have that kind of strength."

"I think he gave it a potion first," Joel responded.

"Ah, of course," Riverhand said. "So now, they must be hiding in that cave, ready to fight."

Redstem snorted. "Augmented strength or not, I cannot believe he thinks he and his new pet would be able to hold us off for long."

"Do not get overconfident, Redstem," Fireflower gently scolded. "Remember, Darkeye can be a very cunning opponent. You and Felicity—prepare to perform stunning casts. Riverhand—you and I will have shield casts at the ready."

"Um, what about me?" Joel asked.

"A light cast, please. We will flank you as you follow where Darkeye's image leads."

A small chill ran down Joel's spine. *Remember*, he told himself, steeling his nerves, *be confident. You've done a lot of stuff like this already.* "Okay." He nodded.

Joel played a brief note, lighting up his instrument with a bright white glow. Then he entered the cave, staying a few paces behind the Darkeye apparition, who was following after the burrowing fangworm.

"I hear that rumbling sound again," Redstem whispered.

"Just stay alert," Fireflower responded under her breath.

About twenty feet in, it looked to Joel as if the cave was about to take on a gradual incline, although it was getting harder to tell the difference between his past-vision and what was presently in front of him. A gentle, warm breeze started to drift past his face, carrying little fragments of Aura with it, like translucent dandelion seeds.

"Is it just me, or is this thing starting to slope upward?" Felicity murmured, confirming to Joel what he had just seen.

"And where is that breeze coming from?" Redstem said.

"Joel, what can you see?" Fireflower asked.

Joel tried his best to focus. After a few seconds, he witnessed the fangworm burrowing upward, away from them, at about a twenty-five degree angle. He relayed this observation to the others.

"It sounds like the fangworm must have dug its way out of the canyon," Riverhand said. "This wind appears to be coming in from outside."

"So he escaped!" Redstem exclaimed, no longer keeping her voice down.

"Quiet," Fireflower hissed. "He could still be waiting for us somewhere."

"Yeah, and that rumbling noise is getting louder, fast," Felicity noted. "I'm beginning to think that maybe he—whoa!"

Joel blinked. Charging down the tunnel toward them was a pack of what looked like Komodo dragons with rainbow mohawks. Unsure if he was seeing the past or the present, Joel hesitated for a moment before a stream of red Aura streaked past him and struck one of the lead reptiles. Instinctively, he took aim with his wavebow and played a short riff, launching a stunning cast of his own. Unfortunately, this also had the effect of dousing his light cast, so now it was much harder to see the oncoming rush of creatures.

"Turn it back on!" Felicity shouted.

"Sorry!" Joel restarted his light cast as a dome of yellow shielding Aura sprang up around him and the others.

"Well, I guess that works too," Felicity said to Fireflower, who had just set up the Aura-shield with a single, swift chord.

"That was close," Redstem exhaled.

"What are these things?" Joel asked as a veritable flood of the strange creatures skittered over and around the protective energy dome.

"Colorheads," Riverhand answered. "They live outside the canyon, around the perimeter. Usually not dangerous unless startled or provoked, in which case they can be quite deadly."

"Naturally," Felicity remarked.

"Darkeye and his fangworm must have chased them down into this tunnel," Redstem grumbled. "Poor things. Hopefully they can find their way back out, otherwise they will starve to death down here."

"We can fly them out, if necessary," Fireflower said.

Felicity raised an eyebrow at the Wavemaker leader. "After we stun them, I assume."

"Of course." Fireflower nodded. "But first, we need to track down Darkeye before he is able to cause any further havoc."

The colorheads continued to swarm past the Aura-dome in a seemingly endless stream. Then, a few seconds later, a lilting chime rang out from Fireflower's wavebow as its strings lit up with a faint yellow glow.

"Hey, you changed your ringtone!" Felicity exclaimed. "This one is a lot better, I gotta say."

"Yes?" Fireflower spoke into her instrument as if it were a giant phone.

"We have arrived at the Pit of Ashes," Thornleaf's voice sounded. "And we have a problem."

"A problem? What is it?"

"Marshall and the Lightsnakes...they are gone."

Joel and Felicity exchanged wide-eyed glances.

"What do you mean, 'gone'?" Fireflower said.

"They escaped, apparently. When we got here, we found the attending guards unconscious, and the cages below are all empty."

"We will be right there."

CHAPTER 5: GROANING GEYSER

While Riverhand stayed behind to clean up the colorhead mess, Joel, Felicity, Fireflower, and Redstem flew at top speed to the Pit of Ashes, an enormous underground chasm where Spectraland's worst criminals were housed.

Worrying is a waste of time, Joel kept reminding himself along the way. *Marshall couldn't have gone far. I'm sure we'll be able to recapture him real soon.*

They landed near the hut that covered the entrance to the Pit. There, Thornleaf was standing around with a group of natives, a couple of whom Joel recognized: Whitenose, a friend of Thornleaf's who had served in the Silencer organization, and Amberweed, another one of the tall shaman's friends who, apparently, was still stuck doing guard duty at the Pit of Ashes. Auravine was also there, flanked by the armed guards who were at her trial. Joel avoided looking directly at her.

"Is everyone all right?" Fireflower asked as the remains of her flying cast dissipated.

"Yes, we are," Amberweed replied. "Fortunately, they left us unconscious but unharmed. Thornleaf was able to revive us."

"Thank the Aura," Fireflower exhaled.

"Unfortunately, however," Whitenose said, "It appears that they made off with all of the guards' weapons and supplies."

"Whatever little there were," Amberweed added.

Fireflower nodded in grim acknowledgment. "Thornleaf, did you warn Windblade at the temple?"

"I did."

"And were you able to find any clues as to where they might have gone?"

"I have not had the time yet—we just arrived not too long ago."

Joel raised his hand, as if volunteering to speak in class (something he had just started doing recently, after constant reminders by his teachers to do so). "I, uh, I can try my new Sight power again," he offered.

"My thoughts exactly," Fireflower said. "We need to find them before they attack any of the villages. Hopefully, we are not too late."

Taking a few steps closer to the prison hut, Joel cleared his mind and activated the Sight. After a few moments, he saw plumes of smoke billowing out of the hut's only door while someone opened it from the inside. Then, one dramatic pause later, a pair of man-sized creatures with gator heads and multiple limbs—the Lightsnakes—emerged from the smoke, followed closely by the deformed zombie-like person that was Marshall Byle and another, shorter humanoid: Darkeye.

"Darkeye helped them escape!" Joel exclaimed.

"Where did they go?" Thornleaf demanded.

"Um, hold on," Joel said, looking around. The fangworm was nowhere to be seen, but it became obvious a few seconds later that the escapees did not require its services as a mode of transport anymore; one Lightsnake picked up Marshall, the other picked up Darkeye, and together they launched themselves into the sky. "They flew away—in that direction," Joel said, pointing.

"So the Lightsnakes still possess that ability," Fireflower muttered, shaking her head. "This is worse than I had imagined."

"Do you know if this was before or after Darkeye was at Chroma Canyon?" Redstem asked.

"I'm not sure," Joel replied, "but I think it was after. The images I'm seeing now look more, I dunno, like, solid. In fact, it may have just happened a little while ago."

"Then maybe we are not too far behind," Fireflower said. "We need to follow them immediately."

"I will join you and the others while the guards take care of Auravine here," Thornleaf said.

Fireflower nodded. "Very well." She turned to Joel. "Can you lead the way, please?"

"Um, sure." Joel played the flying cast melody and took off after the images of the two airborne creatures and their passengers. Occasionally glancing over his shoulder to make sure the other Wavemakers were still behind him, he followed the Lightsnakes until they began to descend over a flat, circular section of land that was filled with many—Joel counted fifty-nine in all—round holes in the ground, each of them about five feet in diameter and about two to three feet away from its closest neighbors. From his vantage point, the area looked like the top of a gigantic saltshaker cap, or perhaps a showerhead, surrounded by spots of marshland densely populated with tall, glowing cattail-like plants. "They went down there!" he shouted to the others.

Fireflower shouted something back that sounded like "watch out" followed by some other words, but Joel couldn't hear her with the wind rushing past his face.

Just as he was about to ask her to repeat what she had said, he heard a loud moaning noise, and then a second later, streams of water came shooting out of the holes in the ground, tall enough that one of them smacked him right in the stomach. Startled, he lost focus, and his flying Aura cocoon disintegrated.

"Joel!" someone yelled.

Frantic, Joel grabbed his wavebow and tried to play the flying cast melody, but, unable to properly concentrate as he fell, the only thing that came out of his instrument were little bursts of green sparks. He was about thirty feet above the ground when Fireflower swooped overhead and caught him with her flying Aura, extending its reach like it was a giant net. Descending quickly, she swerved between several tall columns of water and then landed on the outside edge of the showerhead-like area and gently set Joel down on the ground.

"Thanks," he exhaled.

Fireflower leaned toward him and cupped her ear. "Could you repeat that, please?" she said with a raised voice. The loud moaning noise was still going strong, along with the spouts of water that now reached up nearly seventy feet into the sky. The other Wavemakers all touched down a couple of yards away.

"Um, I said, thanks," Joel repeated, louder this time. "You know, for catching me."

"Oh—you are welcome." Fireflower nodded. "Are you all right?"

"Yeah, just a little wet."

"What is this place?" Felicity said. "It's like a giant upside-down showerhead."

"Hey, that's what I thought too!" Joel exclaimed.

"This is the Groaning Geyser," Redstem answered.

"I shoulda guessed," Felicity said.

"When I was very young," Redstem continued, "my father brought me here once to play in the water. After I joined the Wavemaker Order, Fireflower was generous enough to allow me to return every so often."

"How long does it keep doing this?" Joel asked.

"It should stop in a few seconds."

Sure enough, after four more seconds, the columns of water fell back down and the moaning noise faded away.

"Do you think they came here to get another potion ingredient?" Felicity asked.

"Quite possibly," Redstem replied. "The geyser's water has some unique properties that I am sure Darkeye knows how to exploit."

"Joel," Fireflower said, "can you see where they may have gone?"

Joel started up the Sight again and scanned the area. He was startled when the water spouts suddenly reappeared, but then he realized that he was seeing them in the recent past. He walked around for a minute before he spotted Darkeye kneeling next to one of the spouts with his arm extended toward it. Marshall and the Lightsnakes stood nearby, watching the wizened old native.

"I see them—over there," Joel told the others. He hustled over to the images, where he observed Darkeye withdrawing his arm; the native held a gourd-like jug in his hand that he then sniffed at for a second before sealing it with a stopper. "He was collecting some of the water."

"Where did they go after that?" Fireflower asked after she had caught up.

Joel continued watching the scene. "Looks like...that way." He pointed to where he saw the four fugitives heading into the adjoining marshland.

"Not flying? Just walking?"

Joel took a moment to process the double question. "Um—yes, and yes."

"The Lightsnakes must have run out of Aura energy," Thornleaf suggested. "This might be the perfect opportunity to catch them."

Just then, out of the corner of his eye, Joel spotted a small round object rolling on the ground toward him like a putted golf ball. It appeared to be a bit more solid and vivid than the images of the giant water spouts, and it was leaving a barely visible trail of smoke in its wake, so in the three seconds or so that he had before it arrived, he deduced that this event was (a) happening now, in the present time, and (b) probably dangerous.

"Look out!" he yelled, pointing at the rolling object.

In one smooth motion, Fireflower spun around, aimed her wavebow, and fired out a stream of Aura energy that engulfed the object a moment before it exploded, successfully containing its grenade-like effect.

"It must be them!" Thornleaf said. "Which way did that come from?"

Joel blinked. The images of the past and present were starting to blur together, giving him an awful headache, so he disengaged the Sight and simply started to run toward where he assumed the object had emerged from. "Follow me!" he said, raising his wavebow as he went.

"Wait!" Fireflower shouted.

Joel pulled up, confused. "But...I thought you said not to be afraid to take the lead."

"Under certain circumstances, yes." Fireflower said. "In this case, however, it would be wiser not to rush in. We should all go in together, slowly. I think they are trying to ambush us in order to obtain a wavebow for Byle."

"Um, okay."

Flanked on either side by Fireflower and Thornleaf, Joel walked into the marsh, following the line in the dirt created by the rolled explosive. Felicity, Riverhand and Redstem made up their rearguard. With all of them holding their wavebows like small-scale rifles, Joel suddenly felt like he was in one of those old war movies that his dad used to watch after Joel had gone to bed (or so his father thought). He reengaged the Sight, trying to keep his focus on events happening in the present. The sounds of the geyser erupting once more could be heard in the background.

"No matter what," Fireflower whispered to everyone as they made their way through the glowing cattails, "make sure that Byle does not gain possession of a wavebow."

"Yeah, I think that goes without saying," Felicity responded in a hushed tone.

With their heads on swivels, the six Wavemakers stalked through the marsh for what seemed like a very long time (but was, in reality, only forty-seven seconds) before Joel spotted a flicker of movement some thirty feet away.

"I saw something," he whispered.

"Where?" Fireflower asked.

"Over there—I think it's hiding in that bunch of plants."

"Approach it with caution," Fireflower instructed. "I will follow alongside you. The rest of you, keep an eye out for projectiles."

"Why don't we just blanket the whole area with stunning waves?" Joel asked.

"No," Thornleaf replied. "If it is not them, then that would give away our position."

"Oh—right."

"Dude," Felicity said, "no wonder you're so bad at first-person shooter games."

"What? I'm not that bad. It was just that one time you were watching me play *Battlefront* with Trevor on the tour bus, and I got distracted because—"

"We should continue moving," Fireflower said.

Step by careful step, Joel walked over toward the patch of cattails. Whatever he had seen, if it was still there, was being completely still and silent. When he arrived a few feet in front of the plants, he gave Fireflower a questioning glance, wondering what they should do next. She responded with a series of hand gestures that seemed to say something like *you go around that way, and I will go around this way, on three*. He nodded. She placed both hands back on her wavebow and began silently mouthing the countdown.

One.

Two.

Three—

Joel jumped around the right side of the patch, wavebow raised. Something was there, all right, cowering with its hands over its head. For a split second, he thought that it was a hunkered-down Darkeye, but then he realized it was a two-foot-tall bipedal creature that resembled an oversized rat with an armadillo shell.

Fireflower turned. "It is just a hardback," she announced to the others. She lowered her instrument, so Joel did the same. Sensing its opportunity, the hardback swiftly turned and skittered away.

"Odd," Redstem said. "The hardbacks should not be awake during this time of the night."

"Obviously, it was startled by Byle and the others." Thornleaf sniffed.

Redstem shook her head. "No—it is not that easily awoken. They must have roused it on purpose."

"To create a distraction," Felicity said.

"Is that what you do when you play first-person shooters?" Joel asked.

She smirked. "I'm not telling you my secrets."

Joel replied with a smirk of his own. Or, at least, with what he hoped was a smirk. He'd been practicing that expression in the mirror the last few days on Earth, and he thought he was getting pretty good at it.

Felicity shot him a curious look. "What is that you're doing with your face? Are you okay?"

"If that was meant as a distraction," Fireflower said seemingly to herself, her eyes darting around, "then—"

"Another one!" Redstem cried. She played a quick note on her wavebow, but it was a little too late; a sound like a firecracker went off, and she was suddenly engulfed by a cloud of purple smoke.

"Everyone, hold your breath!" Fireflower shouted as Redstem crumpled to the ground. The Wavemaker leader played a short progression of chords, and the smoke began to dissipate. As it did, Joel noticed a couple of large shapes hiding amongst the plants a little over eighteen feet away.

The Lightsnakes.

He looked over at Fireflower, who was kneeling and tending to Redstem. He considered what she had told him about not rushing in and how taking the lead should only apply under certain circumstances. He decided that this was one of those circumstances.

"I'm going after them!" he exclaimed.

"What?" Felicity said, waving away remnants of purple smoke that were drifting past her face.

Without pausing to respond, Joel took off running. The Lightsnakes apparently saw him coming and dashed out of the cattails. As they did so, he noticed that each of them was carrying another being on their backs: one short, and one about as tall as the Lightsnakes themselves.

They're piggybacking Darkeye and Marshall, he realized. *Ha—they'll never get far that way.*

Still charging, Joel took aim with his wavebow and prepared to play a stunning cast.

You're all going back to jail! he yelled in his mind.

He chased them around and through several thick patches of cattails. Then, when he finally had a clean shot, the Lightsnakes launched straight up, as if they were being yanked out of the scene by stunt wires.

"Dangit!" Joel yelled out loud. He reformed the fingers of his left hand and ignited a flying cast. During the few seconds that it took for the dark-green Aura energy of the wavecast to completely envelop him, Thornleaf and Felicity caught up.

"That was them!" Thornleaf exclaimed.

"No, it wasn't," Joel replied as he started to float up off the ground, "I'm flying after a couple of hardbacks."

Felicity grinned, apparently out of appreciation for Joel's attempt at sarcasm. "Not bad, dude," she said, starting up a flying wavecast of her own.

Despite the serious nature of the situation, Joel returned her grin before he rose up over the cattails and into the sky above.

CHAPTER 6: THE CHASE

While Joel soared through the air in hot pursuit of the four fugitives, he took a few moments to wonder how the Lightsnakes had developed the ability to fly in the first place. As far as he knew, nothing in Spectraland had been able to do so until he himself had introduced the concept of flying to the island some nineteen Spectraland years earlier, when he, Felicity, and Fireflower had used that particular cast to catch up to Marshall at Crownrock before the Biledriver singer could steal all of the island's Aura.

But then, just recently, the very same Lightsnakes that Joel was now chasing had flown up into the Moonfire portal while carrying kidnapped Wavemakers. At the time, he'd thought that maybe it was a temporary ability, some kind of levitation power that was dependent upon the Moonfire wavecast. Obviously, that assumption was incorrect. Maybe Auravine had taught them the flying cast? If so, that would be another mark against her...

He noticed his own flying Aura starting to fade just a little, probably because of his wandering thoughts. So, after glancing around to make sure Felicity and Thornleaf were still flying beside him, Joel refocused his attention on their targets, who were heading in a northeasterly direction over a long stretch of mountainous terrain.

Thornleaf flew over closer to Joel. "Speed up!" the tall shaman shouted.

Joel nodded and increased his speed. For a moment, he became concerned that doing so would sap their Aura energy more quickly, but since the Lightsnakes weren't going very fast, he figured they could catch them and put an end to this soon.

"What are we gonna do once we get close?" Felicity yelled through the wind.

Good question, Joel realized. *We can't perform stunning casts while maintaining our flying casts. Hmm...unless one or two of us takes over flying for everybody, then someone would be freed up. But that would mean we'd have to switch in midair, and since we're using more energy by going faster, that would mean—*

Joel's train of thought was interrupted by the sight of Thornleaf pulling a blowgun out of one of his belt pouches and holding it aloft.

Ah, right—sleepdarts. That should work.

"After I knock them out," Thornleaf shouted, "land quickly and then catch their bodies as they near the ground!"

Catch their bodies? Joel wondered. *Oh, right—with a levitation cast. Duh.*

"Got it!" Felicity shouted back.

They started to close in. Marshall and Darkeye were no longer being carried by the Lightsnakes, but were instead cruising right below them, apparently supported by the Lightsnakes' flying Auras. Marshall turned his head and gave his pursuers a grisly sneer, the bones of his lower jaw still exposed as a result of his interrupted regeneration process.

Jerk, Joel thought, narrowing his eyes. *We're gonna get you.*

The Lightsnakes attempted to perform what apparently were some evasive maneuvers, but they didn't amount to much more than minor shifts from left to right, so the three Wavemakers were able to stay tight on their tails.

So close...

They got to within ten feet. Thornleaf put the blowgun to his lips.

Seven feet.

Four feet.

Thornleaf fired the dart. Just as he did so, however, the Lightsnake he was aiming at veered sharply upward. The dart missed Darkeye by a couple of feet and fell down toward the mountains below.

Dangit!

While Thornleaf reloaded, the other Lightsnake made a ninety-degree turn.

"Ha-*ha*!" Marshall exulted. "Woo!"

Unsure of exactly what to do, Joel swerved to follow.

"Out of the way!" Thornleaf shouted.

Joel turned to see Thornleaf aiming the blowgun right in his direction. He dove out of the way just as the tall shaman fired a dart at Marshall's Lightsnake, who dodged the projectile by doing an acrobatic loop.

"They are toying with us!" Thornleaf exclaimed.

The two Lightsnakes circled around for a few seconds like a couple of crazed vultures, and then they formed up next to each other and zoomed away at a much faster rate of speed than before.

"How are they doing that?" Joel shouted, stopping and hovering in place.

"Never mind, just follow them!" Thornleaf responded.

"But our energy might—" Joel started to say before Thornleaf extended his arms and took off. Felicity shrugged and followed after the tall shaman.

—run out.

Joel exhaled and took off as well. He strained to push himself forward at a velocity equal to that of the Lightsnakes. After another minute or so, the mountain range below gave way to grassy fields populated by sporadic herds of squid-goats, and Joel saw that the Lightsnakes were heading toward the Flaming Fields, the large canyon where he had originally learned about his Sight power. At first he thought they were just going to fly over it, but then they suddenly swooped down, as if pursuing some sort of prey. He, Felicity, and Thornleaf followed. After entering the canyon, he saw that Darkeye's Lightsnake was skimming a few feet above the white-flame-covered surface, while Marshall and his Lightsnake maintained a slightly higher altitude. Darkeye appeared to be holding out a flask or container of some sort, like he was trying to scoop up some of the flames as they went along.

That must be another potion ingredient, Joel surmised.

Then, out from behind several of the many tall stone obelisks that dotted the canyon floor, packs of flame-feeders—the spider-wolf creatures that inhabited the area—emerged. Growling and barking, they chased after Darkeye and his Lightsnake. Just as they got close enough to leap, though, the reptilian creature and its passenger rose up out of their reach. Joel could've sworn he heard Darkeye cackling.

Yeah, you're laughing now, but just wait until—

"WHAT IS THE MEANING OF THIS DISTURB-ANCE?" a booming yet distant voice sounded.

—the Heatwraith shows up! Joel finished his thought. The Heatwraith was the guardian of this area, whom Joel had befriended (sort of) during his first adventure, and he was hoping that the powerful entity would be able to assist them now. "Hi, uh, Heatwraith?" he shouted as he swerved around an obelisk, still in pursuit. "Can you help us catch these Lightsnakes?"

"YOU ARE THE CHILD WITH THE SIGHT," the Heatwraith intoned.

Joel could almost hear Felicity saying *yeah, no kidding.* He decided to go with something a little more tactful. "Yeah, um, it's me. So, can you help? They're up to no good!"

No response. Joel frowned, thinking that the Heatwraith had chosen not to get involved.

I guess I can't blame it—after all, its main purpose in life was just to prevent passage by the wrong people into the Caves of Wrath, where the Songshell was hidden.

But then a gigantic flamefeeder—the Heatwraith—appeared directly ahead, perched on a web made up of thin red beams of light that stretched from one canyon wall to the other. "ANCIENT INTRUDERS—STOP AT ONCE," it ordered.

The Lightsnakes veered away from the large spider-wolf and circled back around, weaving their way through a series of obelisks as they did. Joel, Felicity and Thornleaf turned to follow. Large pieces of rock dislodged themselves from the canyon wall and hurtled through the air at the Lightsnakes, who barely managed to avoid getting struck. The yellow and red Aura fields within the canyon started to swirl faster and faster, like the beginning stages of a tornado. Thornleaf fired more sleep-darts, but none of them hit their intended targets.

"Keep following the one with Byle!" Thornleaf shouted after he missed with the last of his darts. "I will cut it off from the front!"

Joel and Felicity did so as Thornleaf split off from them. Following Marshall's Lightsnake around more obelisks and dodging the occasional errant flying rock, Joel noticed Darkeye's Lightsnake skimming the surface once again while it was being chased by hordes of angry flamefeeders.

He probably needs more white fire, Joel thought.

Thornleaf flew in front of Marshall's Lightsnake and came to an abrupt stop, apparently preparing himself to grab the creature and possibly wrestle it to the ground. The Lightsnake was ready for that maneuver, however, and it simply dove underneath the tall shaman at the last moment, forcing Joel and Felicity to skid to a halt before they crashed into Thornleaf.

"Any other bright ideas?" Felicity said, hovering in place.

Before anyone could answer, Joel saw Darkeye's Lightsnake starting to ascend. Marshall's Lightsnake fell in behind it, and together they began to fly straight up and out of the canyon.

"They got what they needed!" Joel exclaimed. "They're leaving!"

"I can see that!" Felicity shouted before she took off after the fleeing Lightsnakes.

Joel followed after her, casting a quick glance at the Heatwraith. "Thanks anyway!" he called to the giant wolf-spider.

They chased the Lightsnakes over the Colorbridge (the Aura-wave tunnel that led to the Caves of Wrath), past the nearby cove, and beyond the edge of the island itself. As they flew farther and farther out above the rolling green ocean, Joel began to wonder exactly where the Lightsnakes thought they were going. He had previously learned that the Aura was confined mostly to Spectraland proper; the farther you got away from the island, the more the Aura seemed to dissipate. So they and the Lightsnakes would all eventually run out of the energy needed to maintain their flying casts if they continued on this current course.

"We should turn back!" he shouted to his companions.

"No! Just keep going," Thornleaf responded. "It will be fine!"

"What's the plan?" Felicity yelled.

"Once they run out of energy, they will fall into the ocean, and then we can subdue them!"

"But I don't know how to swim!" Joel said, painfully aware that *he* would be falling into the ocean as well.

"It will be fine!" Thornleaf repeated. "Trust me!"

Easy for you to say, Joel grumbled silently, but he decided to do what the tall shaman said.

They continued to fly away from the island. In his head, Joel could feel his Aura energy starting to run out. Everyone, including the Lightsnakes, was slowing down as their flying casts began to fade.

Soon after, an unwelcome landmark—or wouldn't it technically be considered a watermark? Joel wondered— came into view: a dark strip of water in the ocean known as the Far Edge. If anyone or anything tried to pass beyond it, the Forbidden Tides, a gigantic tsunami-like wall of waves, would be triggered. And, obviously, one could not just simply fly over the waves, as there would be no more Aura energy to draw upon once they got that far. Joel had survived his previous encounter with the Forbidden Tides, but he'd had a canoe to hang onto that time.

The Lightsnakes pulled up about ten feet in front of the Far Edge. Thornleaf came to a stop about six feet away from them, so Joel and Felicity did the same. Everyone's flying Auras were now almost completely gone; it would be just a matter of seconds before they all fell into the sea below.

"Nowhere left to run, Byle," Thornleaf growled.

"Ah yes, so it would seem," Marshall said. "But how, pray tell, do you intend to capture all four of us once we are swimming around like a school of slippery fish? You know that at least one of you will be occupied with saving Joel there from drowning."

"You will find out in a moment," Thornleaf shot back.

Joel glanced at Thornleaf, wondering what the tall shaman was planning. *Shouldn't he have filled us in earlier?*

"Sorry to disappoint you," Marshall said with a hideous grin, "but I'm afraid I don't have that kind of time."

The ex-Biledriver singer pulled something small out of his tattered tunic. Joel couldn't quite see exactly what it was—a lifepod, perhaps, or maybe even an internal organ—but a second later it didn't really matter, as Marshall tossed it over his shoulder into the dark waters of the Far Edge.

"What are you doing?" Thornleaf exclaimed.

"What does it look like he's doing?" Felicity shrieked as a rumbling noise started up. "Let's get out of here!"

Thornleaf shouted something in response, but the rumbling had grown so loud so quickly that it completely drowned him out. The three Wavemakers turned to flee, but at that moment, whatever was left of their flying Auras blinked out of existence. As they fell, the Forbidden Tides rose up, much faster than Joel had remembered them rising up before; it was like a geyser eruption, if the geyser spout in question was about a hundred feet wide.

Joel hit the water and squeezed his eyes shut. Submerged, he flapped his arms and kicked his legs in a desperate attempt to get back to the surface. To his surprise, these motions actually worked, and a few moments later his head reached air. Gasping, he glanced up and saw something he was not expecting: Marshall, Darkeye and the two Lightsnakes were now *flying over* the enormous wave.

What the heck? he thought while he scrambled to stay afloat. Thornleaf swam over to him, holding out a glowing yellow rock in his fingers. The native said something that Joel couldn't make out before he pressed the rock against Joel's temple. After feeling the same electric-shock sensation that he had when Felicity had pressed her yellow rock to his head in a similar manner, Joel knew what he had to do. He grabbed his wavebow and, even as he sank back down again, managed to play the notes of the flying cast underwater. Green Aura energy poured out of the instrument's headstock and surrounded him, and then he rocketed out of the ocean just as the tsunami-like wave started to crash down.

♪♪♪

"Great plan, by the way," Felicity remarked once she, Joel and Thornleaf had made landfall on a long stretch of beach dotted by yellow and orange seaweed-palm trees.

"What they did was completely unexpected," Thornleaf retorted, apparently picking up on her sarcasm.

The three of them trudged up to the tree line and sat down, soaked and exhausted. The jolt of energy from Thornleaf's yellow rock had given them just enough strength to fly back to the island, but the long chase had taken its toll, and Joel knew that they would need to rest for at least a few minutes before they could fly anywhere else.

"I, uh, I think we probably should've seen that coming, though," he said.

Thornleaf narrowed his eyes. "What do you mean?"

"Darkeye knows how to make an Aura-boosting potion—he had one when we were going after Marshall way back when. I figure that's what gave them the extra power-up to get over the Tides."

Thornleaf made a sound that Joel assumed was the Spectraland equivalent of clicking one's tongue. "Ah, of course," the tall shaman said.

"So now what?" Felicity asked in the tone that she used whenever she already knew the answer to that question.

"I guess we have no choice but to tell Fireflower and request her approval," Thornleaf replied.

"Her approval of what?" Joel said.

"The loudstones."

"The what?"

"Loudstones, dude," Felicity said, pulling out her own yellow rock. "These things."

"Oh—is that what they're called?"

"Yeah, I just told you that."

"So, um, what are they?"

"Loudstones are small mineral fragments that can store and transport Aura energy, similar to what the Songshell was able to do," Thornleaf answered. "They are the culmination of many years of work and research on my part."

"Oh yeah!" Joel said, a light bulb going on in his head. "I remember you mentioning something about that when we were at Spiral Landing. But didn't Fireflower say that she was against using them?"

"She did."

"Then why..."

"Fireflower's main objection was that the Silencers would view them as a threat," Thornleaf said. "But now that our groups are finally on the way to resolving our differences, I figured that it would not hurt to revisit my research."

"Look, this whole deal was kind of on the down low, okay?" Felicity said. "That's why I wasn't telling you about it."

"Does anyone else know you're using them?" Joel said. "What about the other Wavemakers?"

"None of them know," Thornleaf replied.

"So...it's only the two of you?"

"Yes."

Joel looked at Felicity but avoided making direct eye contact. "So you already had a loudstone during the three days we were back on Earth?"

"Duh, obviously."

"But why?"

Felicity exchanged a furtive glance with Thornleaf. Finally, she sighed and said: "We just wanted to keep in touch while I was gone, that's all. So, before we left, he gave me one, and I used it to power up my wavebow at home. You know, so we could do that whole phone-thing with it."

"How did you guys work around the time differences?"

"It's like talking to someone in a foreign country. Just a little more extreme."

"What did you guys talk about?"

"Dude, seriously?"

"I'm just curious."

"Just some random stuff, all right?"

"The details of those conversations are not important," Thornleaf stepped in. "What is important right now is that we inform Fireflower of what has transpired and ask for her permission to use the loudstones to their fullest potential. That is the only way we will be able to fly over the Tides and continue our pursuit."

"Okay," Joel grudgingly agreed.

Thornleaf played a short lick on his wavebow, causing its strings to light up. A few seconds later, Fireflower's voice sounded from the instrument: "Thornleaf? What happened? Did you capture them?"

"I am afraid they got away. How is Redstem?"

"She was badly injured, but I was able to heal her. How did they manage to escape?"

"They used an Aura-boosting potion and flew over the Forbidden Tides."

There was a pause that seemed to last for a very long time. Finally, Fireflower said: "That is...unfortunate."

"Agreed. However, I know how we can follow after them."

"I know what you are going to suggest."

"And you approve?"

Another pause. Then: "Meet me at the temple. We will discuss it there."

CHAPTER 7: THE DEBATE

Joel, Felicity, and Thornleaf flew to the Wavemaker Temple, where they found Fireflower in a large, pyramid-shaped hut that stood in the center of a lily-pad-like platform. Riverhand, Windblade, and Redstem (who showed no outward signs of having been hurt at all) were also there, sitting on wooden stools around a flat cylindrical rock resembling an oversized hockey puck.

"So, the Lightsnakes actually *flew over* the Tides?" Windblade said, sounding more impressed than concerned.

"That they did," Thornleaf responded as he took a seat. Felicity sat to the left of the tall shaman, leaving Joel to occupy the remaining open stool between Thornleaf and Redstem.

"It is too bad that they are the first Spectraland inhabitants to do so." Riverhand shook his head. "It spoils what would otherwise have been quite a historic event."

"*We* could have made that history ourselves quite a while ago," Thornleaf muttered under his breath.

"All right, now that we are all here," Fireflower said (Joel couldn't tell whether she hadn't heard Thornleaf's remark or she was just choosing to ignore it), "we need to decide on what course of action to take with regards to the escaped prisoners."

"Should we not consult the Chieftain Council?" Redstem asked.

Fireflower nodded. "We should, but I wanted to achieve a consensus amongst ourselves before I approached them. As you are all aware, we do possess a means by which to continue our pursuit of Byle and the others: namely, the loudstones. The question is, do we actually want to use them?"

"You already know my opinion," Thornleaf said.

"I say we use them," Redstem declared. "I must admit, I have been waiting for an opportunity like this. I realize you disapprove, Fireflower, but really, I see no harm. With Stoneroot and the Silencers out of the picture, there will be no one to—"

"They are *not* out of the picture, Redstem," Fireflower interrupted. "Even with Stoneroot in prison, the opinions of his former followers and supporters have not changed. We are still in the middle of resolving our differences with them. Employing the loudstones now could have an adverse effect on our discussions, which were already fragile to begin with."

"I am sure the Silencers will understand," Thornleaf argued. "During my talks with them, they all expressed tremendous gratitude toward the Wavemaker Order—"

Felicity interrupted by clearing her throat in an exaggerated fashion.

"—the offworlders, especially," Thornleaf continued, hardly missing a beat, "for capturing Byle and putting an end to his plans once again. If we tell them that the loudstones are required to find him and put him back in prison, I am confident that they will not object."

"But that is not really the main issue," Riverhand said. "The concern for everyone, ourselves included, is that this could lead us down the same path as before, when Graymold first discovered the Songshell all those years ago."

Thornleaf gave an exasperated sigh. "I have said this many times already: since each of us will have a loudstone, there will be no opportunity for abuse. It will be just like having a wavebow."

"Except that a single shaman cannot combine wavebows to create additional power," Windblade pointed out. "If one user were to have some or all of the loudstones at once..."

"Are you suggesting that we are not trustworthy?" Redstem said.

"Well, we did trust Auravine, did we not?" Riverhand noted.

A hush fell over the group. Joel noticed everyone giving each other side-eyed glances.

"While I believe that everyone here is of the highest moral character," Fireflower broke the silence by saying, "I agree that the use of the loudstones still carries with it much risk. That is why I never approved of them before. But what are our alternatives? Any ideas?"

"Byle and the others will have to come back to the island at some point," Riverhand said. "Darkeye cannot keep producing his potion forever. We can simply wait until we observe the Tides rising up once more, which will be the sign that they have returned. Then we can catch them."

"Or we could set up an Aura shield around the entire island," Windblade suggested. "They will be stuck out there, never to bother us again."

"But we do not know what, exactly, is out there," Redstem said. "It is dangerous to allow them to be roaming free."

"I'm with her on that," Felicity said, pointing a thumb at Redstem. "Like I've said before, leaving bad guys unaccounted for is never a good idea."

"And," Thornleaf said, "I think it is entirely possible that *they* have some idea of what is out there."

"How would they?" Riverhand said. "No one has ever crossed the Tides before."

"That we know of," Redstem retorted. "Maybe someone has. Or maybe Byle was able to gain some insight during his time as a wraith."

"That's a good point," Felicity added. "Otherwise, why would they take the chance of going out there in the first place? It wouldn't make any sense."

Riverhand shook his head. "I still do not like it. I have always agreed with Fireflower on this matter; using the loudstones will inevitably lead to more harm than good."

"You are just afraid," Thornleaf scoffed. "Ever since I have known you, you have shied away from taking chances."

"That is untrue," Riverhand shot back, standing up. "I can think of many instances where I—"

"Enough," Fireflower said sternly. "I invited discussion, not petty arguments. Now, I think we know where each of us stands on this. Except for you, Joel—you have been very quiet. What are your thoughts?"

Joel glanced around the room. All of the other Wavemakers, including Felicity, were looking at him expectantly. "Um, well, I..."

"C'mon, man, just say what you think," Felicity said, her tone a strange cross between encouraging and exasperated. "Confidence, remember?"

Joel nodded. Despite his prior successes at speaking his mind, he was still uncomfortable in situations like this one, when it was more like a classroom discussion than an urgent life-threatening crisis that demanded immediate action. He took a moment to gather his thoughts.

Okay, what is my opinion on this, really? I mean, everyone has some good points...like Riverhand said, even though all the Wavemakers seem trustworthy now, the temptation of the loudstones might be too strong to resist...Thornleaf, especially, seems like a good candidate to turn bad. Then again, Redstem and Felicity are right—what if Marshall knows about some other kind of power that lies past the Tides, and they manage to get it, come back, and destroy everyone? Both scenarios seem equally likely, and the worst case for each of them is pretty bad. I think I'm gonna go with...

"Um, I say we do it. We use the loudstones."

"Good choice," Felicity said.

Fireflower folded her arms and cocked her head, making Joel feel a bit nervous—he had learned from experience that that particular example of body language usually indicated displeasure of some sort. "May I ask what your rationale is?" she said.

"Well, uh, I think both choices are risky, but the risk of not going after Marshall is probably greater than the risk that one of us will abuse the power of the loudstones. With us, we'd all be together, so we can kind of, I dunno, like, keep tabs on each other, or whatever. But with Marshall, he's really good at planning evil schemes and stuff, and if he's out of sight, who knows what he could come up with? And as for the Silencers, if there were any good time for us to do this, it would probably be now, when we still have some amount of—what's the word?" He turned to Felicity.

"Goodwill?" she said.

"Yeah, that. So, there you go—that's my, um, what did you say again? Oh yeah, my rationale."

Fireflower looked down at the table in front of her. Then, after a long pause, she nodded and said, "Thank you for that. I still harbor my concerns about the loud-stones' use, but I agree that this situation may, in fact, be serious enough to warrant it. And since the majority of us are in favor, then that is the course we shall take. Any final comments or questions?"

Joel didn't look at any of the Wavemakers directly, but in his peripheral vision he could see that Riverhand appeared disappointed, concerned, or both, while Redstem was having trouble containing a victorious grin. Everyone else remained mostly expressionless, and no one said anything.

Fireflower got to her feet. "Very well. I will contact the Chieftain Council and obtain their blessing," she announced.

Just as Joel was about to ask her how she was going to do that, she picked up her wavebow and played a complex arpeggio that sounded an awful lot like the beginning to the guitar solo from Metallica's "Leper Messiah." A few moments later, four hazy clouds of Aura energy materialized next to the stone table, eventually coalescing into what looked like portals into another world, or perhaps Snow White-style magic mirrors. In one of the clouds, Joel saw an image of a familiar heavyset native sitting on a tall-legged chair made out of pieces of carved wood that were lashed together with rope and vines.

"Greetings, Fireflower," the image of the native said.

"Hello, Chief Raintree."

"I take it this is not a social call?" Raintree said.

"I am afraid not." Fireflower smiled.

"That is too bad," the Spearwind chief craned his neck, apparently trying to get a view of Joel and Felicity, "as I did not get a chance to speak to the offworlders at Auravine's trial."

"I promise we will make time for that later," Fireflower said. "But for now, I must inform you of a rather unfortunate turn of events."

"Oh? Have you contacted the other chiefs as well?"

"Yes, but they have not joined us yet."

Raintree chuckled. "They are still getting used to this wonderful Aura-communication system that you set up for us. I, on the other hand, am obviously quite proficient with it already."

"I agree," Fireflower said. "Please pardon me a moment while we wait for them."

"Of course."

The cloud with Raintree's image dimmed slightly; Joel assumed that was the equivalent of him being put on hold or mute. Fireflower turned to Thornleaf. "In the meantime," she said, "go ahead and start readying the loudstones, one for each of us. You may use as much energy as we have available in the Main Hall basin."

Thornleaf stood and nodded. "Right away."

"Windblade and Redstem," Fireflower continued as Thornleaf turned and exited the hut, "make travel preparations and inform my mother of what is happening. Be warned—she may not be very happy about it."

"Understood," Windblade said.

"I can handle your mother." Redstem smirked as she turned to leave.

After the pair departed, Felicity aimed a thumb over her shoulder. "I like her," she said.

"Fireflower? Hello?" a voice said. It was Chief Twotrunk—or, half of him, at least, in one of the Aura clouds. "Are you there?"

Fireflower played a short note on her instrument, and Twotrunk's entire image came into view, as if someone had adjusted the camera angle on the burly native. "Yes, hello, Chief Twotrunk. I have important news for the council; we are just waiting for Chief Silverfern and Chief Scarskin to join us."

"Very well." Twotrunk nodded, still looking a bit unsure as to where he should be facing. His cloud dimmed.

"Why won't your mother be happy?" Joel asked Fireflower.

The Wavemaker leader sighed. "Starpollen has been rather...difficult, shall we say, without Auravine around. With the rest of us available to help, it has been manageable, but now my mother will have to be alone with the boy for possibly an extended period of time, depending on how fast we can find Byle and the others."

"I will stay back and assist her," Riverhand said with an air of defeated grumpiness. "I do not want to take part in the use of Thornleaf's creation."

"I know you are not happy with this turn of events, Riverhand," Fireflower said, "but we need all of us to—"

"Fireflower," two voices said at nearly the same time. "I am here," one voice continued; it was Chief Silverfern, her image coming into focus in the third Aura cloud. "What is the reason for this contact?"

"It had better be a good one," Chief Scarskin rasped from the fourth cloud. "I was sound asleep when one of my guards said that she heard your signal."

"Forgive the intrusion, my chiefs," Fireflower said, "but this is rather urgent. I am afraid to report that Byle and the Lightsnakes have escaped from the Pit of Ashes."

All four chiefs reacted with similar expressions that seemed to combine alarm with surprise.

"How did they manage that?" Twotrunk was the first to demand.

"Darkeye broke them out," Fireflower answered. "With the help of Joel's Sight power, we tracked them to the Groaning Geyser, where they attacked us before fleeing."

"Fleeing?" Silverfern echoed, looking both concerned and confused. "To where? Why did you stop pursuing them?"

Fireflower turned. "Joel, can you explain to them, please, since I was not there."

Joel glanced at Felicity; his initial impulse was to ask her to do it, but he decided that this would be a good opportunity for him to show some confidence and initiative. "Okay, uh, well," he started, forcing himself to look at the assembled images of the chiefs and not at the ground, "after Darkeye threw a bomb or something at us near the Groaning Geyser, Redstem got hurt, and then Fireflower stopped to help her, but then they ran away, so I figured that I should—"

"Dude," Felicity interrupted, "remember: summarize."

"Oh—yeah, right. Um, so...they flew away, we chased them, they flew over the Forbidden Tides, and now we're back here. The end."

Somehow, the chiefs all managed to look even more alarmed and surprised than before. Felicity snickered. Everyone turned to look at her.

"Sorry," she said, half covering her mouth with a fist. "That little summary was kinda funny, that's all."

"The Lightsnakes have retained their new ability to fly," Fireflower said hastily, "and we believe that Darkeye used a powerful Aura-augmenting potion to fuel them past the Tides and on to an unknown destination."

"I *knew* that your creation of flying would eventually lead to dire consequences," Twotrunk grumbled.

"Let us not get into that debate again, Twotrunk," Silverfern said, like an adult daughter admonishing her grouchy father. She turned back to Fireflower. "This is a very unfortunate development. Do you have a plan?"

"I do," Fireflower replied. She proceeded to outline the Wavemakers' intended course of action, explaining, after all of the chiefs voiced concern, that the loudstones would be used only for the purpose of recapturing the fugitives and nothing more. She informed them that all seven available Wavemakers had to go, as they would need numbers to give them the best chance of countering any possible attacks from Byle and his gang. The four members of the Chieftain Council then held a brief discussion before they unanimously approved of the plan, with one caveat.

"Thornleaf will have to remain on the island," Twotrunk said. "As the Wavemakers' representative in the mediation talks between your order and the Silencers, he will need to assuage any fears or objections that they may have about your use of these so-called 'loudstones'."

"That may be problematic, my chief," Fireflower respectfully objected, "as he is the one most familiar with the loudstones and how they work."

Joel glanced at Felicity. "I thought that you—" he started to say, before she silenced him with a don't-say-anything-about-how-I-already-used-a-loudstone grimace plus a subtle shake of the head.

"Then you, Fireflower, must be the one to remain," Silverfern said. "As the leader of the Wavemaker Order, I am sure the Silencers will accept your reassurances."

"I will stay," Riverhand offered. "The search party will need a strong healer, in case of an emergency. Besides the fugitives, who knows what other dangers could be lurking out there?"

"No offense, Riverhand," Scarskin grunted, "but Roundbark and the other Silencers will not take you quite as seriously as your more experienced colleagues. Either Fireflower or Thornleaf must be the one to stay."

Riverhand looked down at the table. "Understood, my chief."

No one spoke. Then, after a few moments, a puzzle piece fell into place in Joel's mind.

"I have an idea," he declared. "Since we need a healer—what about Auravine?"

CHAPTER 8: NEW DISCOVERIES

Just so you know," Felicity said out of the side of her mouth, "I still don't think this is a good idea."

"What?" Joel said. "I thought you were in favor of using the loudstones." Dressed in their traveling cloaks, they were standing in the clearing in front of the Wavemaker Temple along with the other shamans, including Auravine but sans Fireflower, who had left earlier to meet with the Silencers. They were all lined up in a loose semicircle around Thornleaf, who was holding a small cloth pouch, with Windblade and Redstem on one end, Felicity and Joel in the middle, and Riverhand and Auravine on the other end.

"Not them, her," Felicity said, motioning with her head toward Auravine. "And this whole temporary work release deal."

An array of potential responses popped into Joel's head, ranging from *Why, are you jealous?* to *Then maybe you should have admitted you already knew how to use a loudstone and was using one to talk to Thornleaf behind everybody's back,* but despite his nascent proclivity for speaking his mind, he filtered out those replies as being a bit too much, and instead went with: "Don't worry, I'll keep an eye on her."

"I bet you will," Felicity muttered, barely audible.

"And so remember," Thornleaf said, finishing up an instructional speech that seemed to Joel to be about ten minutes too long, "you must continuously monitor the level of energy in your loudstone. I cannot stress this enough. As long as it still has some energy left, it can be recharged by your personal Aura. However, once it has been completely drained, it can only be recharged back here, at the temple."

"Yes, yes, we know," Redstem sighed. "You have told us that three times already. Can you just give us the loudstones now?"

"Man, I was gonna say that." Felicity smirked and gave Redstem an approving nod.

Ignoring them, Thornleaf pulled a small yellow rock out of the pouch and dropped it into Windblade's open palm. The slender shaman reacted by widening his eyes and hastily transferring the rock to his other hand, as if it were a hot piece of coal. "You were not joking earlier." He grinned. "It feels like it contains enough energy for a thousand wavecasts."

"Not quite, but almost," Thornleaf said with a haughty air. He proceeded down the line, handing out loudstones to the rest of the group. Joel had braced himself for it, but he was still surprised by the amount of power that he could sense within the little fragment. He held it up closer to his face and noticed some aspects that seemed familiar—its rounded edges and frosty surface were reminiscent of the pieces of sea glass his mother used to collect from the beaches in Hawaiʻi, and the Aura energy inside the stone seemed to swirl and pulse in a pattern that he was sure he had witnessed before.

"Um, where did you find these, anyway?" he asked Thornleaf.

"On the beach near Crownrock," the tall shaman replied. "Years ago, I was looking for something else down there when I happened to detect their presence, scattered and buried beneath the sand."

Felicity turned to Joel. "You're thinking what I'm thinking, right?"

"I think so," he said. "That these are..."

"Pieces of the Songshell," they said together.

"Jinx," Felicity said.

"What?"

"Never mind." She turned to Thornleaf. "I'm assuming you knew that."

"Of course," Thornleaf said as he stopped in front of Auravine, who was intently inspecting the tops of her Spectraland footwear. "From the very moment I discovered them."

"Another reason Fireflower and I were opposed to their use," Riverhand said. "I was hoping this subject would not come up. I believe that even talking about it invites negative energy into our sphere. Some of the stories of what that shell was used for are"—he paused to shudder—"simply abhorrent."

"Then stop talking about it," Redstem said.

"You are stealing *all* of my lines." Felicity chuckled with mock indignation.

"As you know, Riverhand, I performed blessing incantations on them more than a few times already," Thornleaf said wearily. "There is nothing to worry about." He glared at Auravine as the latter held her hand out. "Almost nothing, anyway."

"I promise I will not betray any of you again," the young healer said, still looking at the ground.

"If you do," Thornleaf growled, "I will make you wish you were still back in the Pit of Ashes."

"Understood."

Thornleaf dropped the last loudstone into Auravine's open palm and turned away. "So," he said, addressing everyone, "the plan is to follow the offworlder, who will use his Sight ability to trace the fugitives' path from the point where they flew over the Forbidden Tides. From there, we will continue searching until either we recapture them or we become in danger of fully depleting our energy. And remember: we will need to conserve as much of the loudstones' energy as possible, so do not use them until we are close to the Far Edge and I give the signal. Is all of that clear?"

"It already was the first three times you said it," Felicity quipped. She elbowed Redstem in the arm. "Beat ya there."

Thornleaf smirked in response. "Then here we go."

The seven Wavemakers raised their wavebows like rifles at a salute and played the flying cast melody in unison, creating a divine chorus that sounded larger than anything Joel had heard from Joe Satriani's G3 project or latter-day Iron Maiden. Clouds of green Aura energy burst forth from their instruments and enveloped all of them at once. They took off into the air and headed for the beach, arranged in a classic *V* formation with Joel at the front.

It wasn't long before they were out over the ocean. The sun was rising, creating a beautiful pattern of colors along the horizon. As they got closer to the Far Edge, Joel could feel his Aura energy starting to wane. He shot a glance at Thornleaf, who responded by shaking his head, as if to say *not yet*.

How did he know what I was thinking? Joel thought. *I still don't know how people do stuff like that.*

Eventually, they began to slow down involuntarily. It was the same sensation that Joel had felt when they were chasing the Lightsnakes earlier.

"Now?" Felicity shouted through the wind.

"Not yet!" was Thornleaf's response.

A few more seconds passed. The Far Edge was now just thirty feet or so in front of them.

"Now?" Redstem shouted.

"Not yet!"

They all continued slowing down until they basically drifted over the Far Edge, like air-hockey pucks running out of momentum. The telltale rumbling of the Forbidden Tides started to crank up as everyone's flying Auras faded and flickered.

"Now!" Thornleaf yelled.

Joel pulled out his loudstone and pressed it to his temple (which was much less painful than when Felicity and Thornleaf had basically jabbed theirs into his head). Energy surged through him—much stronger than it had the previous two times he had received a loudstone's boost—and he suddenly felt wide awake and hyperalert, kind of like the time Art let him sample one of his double espressos. Without even having to play another note on his wavebow, Joel's flying Aura suddenly sprang back to life, brighter than ever before, just as the massive water wall that was the Forbidden Tides surged up out of the ocean in front of him.

Wow was all he could think.

He and the rest of the Wavemakers pressed their arms to their sides and rocketed up and over the wave, which at its crest was nearly thirty stories tall. Then, once they were a safe distance away, they all came to a stop in midair and turned around. There, Joel and the others watched as the wave churned in place for a few more seconds before it started its watery rampage toward the island.

"Well, that's that, I guess," Felicity said once she could be heard. "Lead the way, Mister Sight Guy."

"Um, right." Joel started to engage the Sight, but he paused when he saw the looks on the faces of the native Wavemakers. All of them except for Thornleaf appeared to be breathlessly awestruck, as if they were astronauts from Earth that had just landed on the moon (or Joel himself, when he first arrived in Spectraland). As for the tall shaman, he wore a proud, smug expression that seemed to say something along the lines of *see, I told you we should have used the loudstones a lot sooner.*

"I...I cannot believe we are actually here," Windblade said, eyes wide. "To finally travel past the Tides...simply amazing."

"You know that Fireflower already traveled to a completely different world, or dimension, or whatever the Earth is, right?" Felicity said. "I would think that that would be just a *little* more amazing."

"You do not understand," Thornleaf said. "Access to your world is something that has been available to Wavemakers ever since the time that Byle was first brought over. This, however"—he gestured at the wide-open ocean surrounding them—"has been cloaked in mystery as far back as anyone can remember. There are no historical records or evidence of anyone from Spectraland ever having crossed the Forbidden Tides—not even the ancient indigenous beings."

"You mean like Nineteen?" Joel asked. "And the Lightsnakes?"

"Correct."

"Okay, well, yippee and all that." Felicity shrugged. "But shouldn't we be soaking it all in later? Right now, we've got some bad guys to catch."

"She is right," Redstem said, seeming to snap out of her trance. "Please, lead the way, Master Joel."

Joel was tempted to ask her to stop calling him "master," but he knew that she was using that title as a sign of respect for his accomplishments and abilities as a Wavemaker, not as an indication of their relationship to one another, so he let it go. Besides, it did sound kind of cool. "Uh, sure," he said, starting up the Sight.

Almost immediately, an image of the fugitives flying away to the north appeared before his eyes. It was so vivid that for a brief moment he thought that they were actually there, trying to flee after having been in hiding nearby.

Must be the effects of the loudstone, he figured.

He took off after the image, and the other Wavemakers followed. At first he was excited to be venturing into a new, unknown territory, especially since he had now visited most of the significant areas of Spectraland, but after an hour of flying over miles and miles of nothing but pure green ocean, the excitement started to wear off. To help stave off boredom, Windblade suggested that they sing some traditional Spectraland folk songs, which they did (Joel tried his best to join in, while Felicity abstained). After the fifteenth such song, Joel spotted, in his peripheral vision, a tiny island far off to the east. He announced his discovery just as Windblade was starting up the next song.

"Island?" Redstem said. "I do not see anything."

"Trust me," Felicity said, "if he sees it, it's there."

"Is that where they went?" Thornleaf asked.

Joel looked back at the now-not-as-vivid image of Marshall and company, which was still headed in a northerly direction. "Um...no, I don't think so."

"Then it is not important," Thornleaf said.

"I disagree," Riverhand said. "The long flight has drained much of the energy from my loudstone. That island could be a good place to stop and rest."

"Tired already?" Thornleaf scoffed. "You need to become more efficient with your wavecasts, Riverhand."

"My loudstone is running low as well," Auravine said.

"Yeah, uh, mine too," Joel said. It wasn't *that* low, but he was afraid that someone was going to suggest leaving Riverhand and Auravine behind.

"Very well," Thornleaf sighed, giving Joel an exasperated glance. "I suppose we have no choice. Will you be able to pick their image back up once we return to this spot?"

"Um, sure," Joel guessed.

"Then lead the way."

Joel changed course and headed toward the island. As they approached it, he saw that it was an atoll, roughly shaped like a star and densely covered in vegetation. He led the party down to a relatively clear section of beach near one of the atoll's points. Upon landing, he noticed that the sand was white and grainy, similar to what he was used to back on Earth, and the nearby flora—trees, bushes, grass—all looked remarkably Earth-like as well; all of it was green or brown, and nothing swayed on its own or gave off any kind of sound or luminescence.

"We can set up camp here," Thornleaf said. He started to play the wavecast that would create a shelter of Aura energy. "Whoever needs to recharge can rest first. I will keep watch."

"Keep watch for what?" Windblade asked, sounding genuinely curious.

"Wild creatures," Thornleaf replied. He glanced at Auravine. "Or other potential threats."

"I'll join you," Felicity said to Thornleaf.

"I will too," Redstem said.

"All right," Thornleaf agreed. "The rest of you can sleep. We will wake you when it is your turn."

Not feeling particularly tired, Joel considered protesting, but since he had already seconded Riverhand and Auravine's desire to take a break, he realized that he didn't have much of a choice. So, feigning a yawn, he lay down on the sand underneath the large Aura canopy that Thornleaf had set up and curled into a fetal position. Riverhand, Auravine, and Windblade took up spots around him. After about a minute, he realized that he felt more worn out that he had originally thought, so he closed his eyes and tried to relax.

Then he heard a scream.

He bolted back up and found that everything around him had changed. The atoll and the other Wavemakers were gone, replaced by thick clouds of red smoke, and, although he couldn't see a fire anywhere, it smelled strongly like something was burning.

He got to his feet and took a few cautious steps forward. Still, there was nothing but red smoke. After another couple of steps, he could hear someone shouting in anger off in the distance: no words, just the tortured wail of a person who sounded like they were really, *really* mad about something.

Okay, he thought, *I've been through this enough times to know that I'm sleeping and that this is a vision. Of what, I don't know, but just to be safe, I'll wait right here until I wake up.*

He sat down, crisscross applesauce. The shouting and the burning smell continued, both of them growing stronger as the seconds ticked by.

I hope I wake up soon, 'cause I'm starting to get really uncomfortable.

Five more seconds passed. The temperature started to increase. Joel could feel beads of sweat forming on his forehead.

C'mon, he urged himself. *Wake up, wake up, wake up...*

Finally, just as he felt like he couldn't take it anymore, the shouting ended with a *whoosh*, and he found himself back under the Aura canopy, still lying on the ground.

Whew.

"—that will be so much fun," Redstem was saying.

"No it won't," Felicity's voice responded. "It'll be terrible. Horrible, even."

Redstem chuckled. "That is...the sarcasm, correct?"

"See? You're catching on."

Joel kept his eyes open, not wanting to drift back off into the red-smoke vision.

Maybe if I just lie here and stay awake, I can still recover some energy, he thought. *Sort of like a catnap.*

"Are you sure you were able to settle all of your matters back home?" Thornleaf asked.

"I told you already, it'll be fine," Felicity said. "Are *you* sure Fireflower will be cool with this?"

"She will, trust me. After all, we do have a vacant room in the temple now."

"Man, I was hoping you guys would just build me a new one."

"In time, perhaps."

"I am so glad you decided to move to Spectraland," Redstem said. "After this mission is over and Auravine goes back to prison, I will need another female in the order besides Fireflower. The boys can be quite insufferable at times."

Joel's already-open eyes widened even further.

Wait, what?

Joel stood up and stepped out from under the Aura canopy. Felicity, Redstem and Thornleaf were sitting on the sand, facing each other over a small bonfire.

"Oh—hey," Felicity said, turning to look at him. "That was a pretty short nap."

Joel gulped as he worked up enough courage to say what he wanted to say. "Yeah, I, uh, I thought I heard Redstem mention something about you moving to Spectraland?"

The three Wavemakers around the bonfire exchanged glances. None of them spoke.

"So," Joel went on, his lips tight, "what's that all about?"

"It is not something that needs to be discussed right now," Thornleaf replied.

"No, no, it's okay," Felicity said, shaking her head. She got to her feet and looked in Joel's general direction. "Look, dude, I was gonna tell you after this whole deal with catching Marshall was over, but...yeah, I'm moving here."

"To this atoll?"

"No, to Spectraland."

"When were you going to move?"

"Like, now, pretty much. I wasn't planning on going back."

Joel could feel his stomach knotting up, just like it did on the day his parents told him they were getting divorced. "Why? Why are you moving? Why aren't you going back?"

"I dunno," Felicity sighed. "It's...it's complicated."

"Is it because of him?" Joel pointed at Thornleaf. "Is that why?"

"There's a whole bunch of reasons, all right?"

"But...but what about your sister? And the band? And your car?" *And me*, he added silently.

"I got most of that worked out already. I just told Vicky that I'm going off the grid for a while. Believe me, after a year or so she won't even remember that I'm gone. And I have some papers to give you for the band stuff."

Joel clenched his fists to keep his hands from trembling. "You—you can't do this."

"What? Of course I can," Felicity said, her brow furrowing. "It's my life, dude."

"Yeah, I know, but...I mean, we have that arena show next month, and we're supposed to start writing for the album pretty soon, and..."

"Oh, c'mon, you'll have no problem finding a new guitar player."

But where am I gonna find a new Felicity? is what Joel wanted to say. Instead he blurted out, "I can't believe you're throwing everything away just so you can be with this...this *guy*!"

Felicity's mouth dropped open. "I told you, it's not just about that! What do you think, I'm some kind of flighty rom-com chick who drops her whole life the minute she falls for someone?"

"That's what it sounds like!"

"Well, I guess you really don't know me, then!"

Redstem stood up. "I hate to break up this entertaining discussion, but I think someone is watching us."

CHAPTER 9: A MYSTERIOUS FIGURE

Joel looked around. Even in his agitated state, he was able to spot the short, cloaked figure lurking amongst a group of trees some forty-two feet away.

"I do not see anything," Thornleaf said, craning his neck. "Is it one of the fugitives?"

"It kinda looks like Darkeye," Joel replied.

"So they did come here after all," Redstem said.

"No one make any sudden movements," Thornleaf said, slowly reaching for his wavebow. "Just act natural. In fact, offworlders—resume your argument. Then, while he still thinks we are unaware, Redstem—fire a stunning cast, broadwave, in his direction. The others might be with him."

Just as Thornleaf finished his sentence, the figure retreated, partially to Joel's relief; he didn't really feel like resuming his argument with Felicity.

"Um, he left. I think he might have heard us."

"After him!" Thornleaf exclaimed, jumping up.

Redstem took off, with Thornleaf and Felicity right behind. Joel was about to follow as well when he remembered that Riverhand, Auravine, and Windblade

89

were all still sleeping. Not wanting to leave them behind, he ducked back into the tent.

"Hey—uh, guys, wake up," he said. When none of them did, he knelt down and shook Riverhand's shoulder. "Riverhand?"

"Joel?" Riverhand said, snapping awake. "What is it?"

"We think we saw Darkeye."

Riverhand got up and helped Joel rouse the others. Then each of them picked up their wavebows and followed Joel over to the spot where he had seen the cloaked figure. No one was there.

"I, uh, I can use my Sight to find out where they went," Joel offered.

"No need," Riverhand said, examining the ground in front of him. "They left tracks."

The tracks led them deeper into the trees, where, after a couple of minutes, Joel spotted Felicity, Thornleaf, and Redstem standing in the middle of a small clearing, looking befuddled. He jogged over to them. "What happened?" he asked. "Where did he go?"

"We lost him," Thornleaf growled.

"We were right on his heels when suddenly he was gone," Redstem said. "No trail, nothing. It was like a ratworm vanishing back into its hole."

"What about a tracking cast?" Windblade asked.

"Tried already," Felicity said. "Nada."

"You should have come with us," Thornleaf said to Joel. "We could have used your ability."

"But—I didn't want to leave the others," Joel protested.

"That was actually pretty smart," Felicity said. "It could've been a trap. Maybe Darkeye wanted to lead us away so Marshall could grab their wavebows or something."

Joel glanced at Felicity. He was still a bit upset with her, but he appreciated her support in this moment. "Um, thanks."

She shrugged. "Hey, it's just basic shooter-game strategy."

"Perhaps you can use your power now," Auravine suggested to Joel.

"Oh—yeah, good idea."

Joel activated the Sight. It took a little longer than usual, but finally, after he reached *Minnesota* in an alphabetical list of National Football League cities, an image of the cloaked figure appeared. It dashed through the clearing and swiftly scooted up one of the nearby trees. Then, after it got near the top, it began to jump from tree to tree as if it were a monkey (or perhaps an oversized squirrel).

"That sounds rather nimble for Darkeye," Redstem commented after Joel related what he had seen.

"Well, he did manage to escape from the Pit of Ashes," Windblade said.

Joel led the others into the trees as he followed after the image, which took a rather twisty path through the foliage. Eventually, it climbed down and looked around, as if checking for pursuers, before it walked directly into a large, seven-foot-high mound of dense bushes and tall grass.

"He went through there," Joel said softly, pointing at the mound.

"Probably trying to throw you off his trail," Thornleaf said. "We should go around."

They walked around the mound, but after they got to the other side, Joel couldn't see any sign of the image.

"I...I think he might still be in there," he said, keeping his voice down.

"We have him, then," Thornleaf said. He raised his wavebow and strummed a loud chord, creating a wave of red Aura energy that surrounded the entire mound for nearly four seconds. "That should take care of it. I will go in and retrieve him." He walked up and reached into the mound to push aside some of the vegetation. "Hmm— there is a solid surface behind these plants."

Redstem yanked away a fistful of grass, exposing a wall made out of what looked to be red mud or clay. "This is a hut," she declared. "Disguised very well, I must say."

"Would they have had time to construct such a thing?" Windblade said.

"Unlikely, but possible," Thornleaf answered. He turned to Joel. "Show me where he entered."

Joel walked back around and pointed out the spot where the image entered the mound. Thornleaf cleared out all the bushes and grass there, revealing a round wooden door that reminded Joel of the entrance to a hobbit hole. It looked a bit wobbly, and there didn't seem to be any kind of lock on it.

"All right," Thornleaf said. "On three, I will kick down the door. Then everyone charge in and spray the interior with stunning casts, using as much power as you can afford. Ready?"

Everyone nodded and raised their wavebows.

"One."

Joel's fingers formed the proper chord for a maximum-strength stunning cast.

"Two."

I hope Marshall is in there, Joel thought, setting his jaw.

"Three."

Thornleaf kicked the door open.

"Wait!" someone from inside the hut cried. It was the cloaked figure. He didn't sound like Darkeye or anyone else familiar. "Please!"

Thornleaf played his instrument, but instead of firing out a stunning cast, he created a yellow energy shield that filled up the doorway. "Who are you?" he called out.

"Someone you may remember," the figure said, taking a few steps forward. He pulled back his hood, revealing the face of a middle-aged Spectraland native with long salt-and-pepper hair and a leathery dark-green complexion. "Or perhaps not. When we last met, you were still just a toddler."

"Blackspore...?" Thornleaf gaped.

"Yes. Hello, Thornleaf. You look so much like your father."

"How—I—we thought—" Thornleaf stammered, uncharacteristically rattled.

"That I was dead?" Blackspore chuckled. "Ah, well, do not blame yourself for being wrong. I did an excellent job of covering my tracks, if I do say so myself."

"Wait," Redstem said. She pushed her way up in between Joel and Thornleaf like a young child anxious to see a zoo animal. "This is Blackspore? The Wavemaker who brought Byle over from the other world during the Fourfoot War?"

"It is," Thornleaf replied through clenched teeth.

"Do you have anyone else in there with you?" Redstem asked, peering through the Aura-shield at the interior of the hut.

"Of course not," Blackspore replied. "Why would I?"

"No reason," Redstem said. She turned to Thornleaf. "What should we do with him?"

"Stun him and tie him up," Thornleaf spat. "We can come back for him later."

"No, wait!" Blackspore protested. "I beg you, please, do not take me back to Spectraland. I...wait, did you say, 'come back for him later'?"

No one answered.

"So you have not come on a mission to find and arrest me?" Blackspore continued. "Then what has brought you out here?"

"We're trying to catch Marshall Byle and Darkeye," Joel said. "Oh, and, uh, two Lightsnakes."

"How...interesting," Blackspore said, looking at Joel like he was not only fascinated by what Joel had just said but by the offworlder himself. "So, they are fugitives now?"

"Um, yeah. Pretty much."

"Enough talk," Thornleaf grunted. "Redstem—stun him."

"With pleasure."

"Wait!" Blackspore exclaimed. "What if...what if I make you a deal?"

"A deal?" Thornleaf snorted. "You are a war criminal, Blackspore. We do not make deals with people like you. And what could you possibly have to offer, anyway?"

"I can help you...with your mission."

Thornleaf raised an eyebrow. "How?"

"I believe that I know where Byle is headed. I can tell you. Show you, even. Just, please...do not take me back."

"How do you know where Byle is headed?" Redstem demanded. "Are you in league with him again?"

"No, of course not. I know because of the discussions that I had with him before..."

"Before he killed off the Wavemakers," Thornleaf said.

"I was going to say 'before the end of the war,' but yes, that too."

"I, uh, I don't think we need your help," Joel said, feeling a desire to advocate for his usefulness. "I can see stuff that shows us where they're going."

"Ah, because you have the power of the Sight, correct?"

How does he know about that? Joel wondered.

"Well, are you sure that the Sight is completely reliable?" Blackspore went on. "That you can call upon it anytime you wish, and it will reveal to you exactly what you need to see? Are you sure you want to take that chance?"

"Um..." Joel glanced at Thornleaf. "I dunno, uh, maybe we should take his deal."

"I agree," Riverhand said. "The more information we have, the better."

Thornleaf's face twisted into a scowl, as if he had just bit into a rotten lifepod. Then, after a pause that seemed to last forever, he looked at the others and sighed. "What do the rest of you think?"

"I think that we should take it," Windblade said.

"Yeah, I don't see why not." Felicity shrugged. "I mean, out here, it's like he's basically in prison already, right?"

"I also agree," Redstem said, "but on the condition that we place him under a truth cast."

Blackspore nodded. "I consent to that."

"All right, very well," Thornleaf said, not waiting to hear what, if anything, Auravine had to say about the matter. "Blackspore, we accept your deal."

A little over three minutes and one truth wavecast later, Joel found himself sitting on the ground in the middle of the hut, bunched up with the others. Black-spore stood nearby, scooping liquid out of a stone pot and into a pair of wooden bowls.

"So," the ex-Spectraland resident said, "Thornleaf is the only one of you that I know by name. What do the rest of you go by?"

"Riverhand."

"Windblade."

"Redstem. Thornleaf already introduced me when he asked me to stun you."

Felicity chuckled. "I'm Felicity."

"Auravine."

"Um...Joel. Joel Suzuki."

"Joel Suzuki...very interesting," Blackspore said absently, carrying the bowls over and sitting down next to everyone. "Oh—and I apologize, we will have to share these amongst ourselves. I am not prepared to entertain guests, as you might imagine." He offered one bowl to Felicity and one to Joel. "The two of you can go first, as honored offworlders."

"No thanks," Felicity said. "I'm not hungry."

Joel looked into the bowl. The thin brown liquid inside it resembled muddy water, and it smelled vaguely like paint thinner. He wrinkled his nose. "Um, me neither."

"Suit yourselves," Blackspore said, setting one bowl down and taking a long sip from the other. "Anyone else?"

"We are not interested in your food," Thornleaf said. "Just tell us what you know, and quickly."

"Spoken just like your father!" Blackspore laughed. "Yes, well, you see, I believe that Byle has fled to a place called...the Six States beneath the Shroud," he said with a dramatic wave of his hand, as if he were telling a campfire story. He paused and gave everyone an expectant look.

"Where is this place?" Windblade asked, taking the bait.

"Far away from here, yet still part of this world," Blackspore responded. "It is big—much bigger than Spectraland. In fact, you could probably fit a hundred or more Spectralands inside of its borders." He paused to take another long sip from his bowl.

"Go on," Thornleaf said.

"Hold on, my boy, I am eating. You really should as well. Twig soup—delicious." Blackspore licked his lips. "All right, where was I? Ah, yes, the Six States...very big, all of it covered in perpetual shadow, and inhabited by beings similar to us yet still very different. They live in huge, sprawling villages filled with bizarre huts and other strange structures...it reminds me, somewhat, of the Bluerock," he said, casting a glance in Joel's direction.

"What's the Bluerock?" Joel asked.

"Your homeworld. Where I found Byle."

"Um, actually, it's called Earth."

"That is what I just said."

Joel was about to argue the point when he remembered that the translation cast that allowed him and Felicity to speak with the people of Spectraland usually conveyed the figurative, rather than literal, meaning of what the other person was trying to say. So, in effect, when Joel said "Earth," Blackspore was probably hearing it as "Bluerock." Or something like that—Joel had never really figured out exactly how the cast worked, and the one time he'd asked about it, the explanation was so confusing that he'd decided to just stop thinking about it.

"How did you learn about this...Six States, as you call it?" Redstem asked. "I thought no one knew what lay beyond the Forbidden Tides."

"Ah, well, you see, when I first started scanning the great beyond for someone to help my village during the war, I did not start with the Bluerock. No, I started with our own world. Much closer. Much easier. Right? So, during my search I discovered the Six States. I even made contact with one of their inhabitants, who told me all about their people. At first I was very excited—he told me that they had a great appreciation for music, and that they were also skilled in combat. It sounded perfect.

"But as I learned more, I realized that none of them had the special abilities that I was looking for. They had no one with enough power to compete with even a single fully trained Wavemaker. So, reluctantly, I gave up on them and turned my search elsewhere. And that is when I discovered Marshall Byle."

"And so now he is going there to hide," Riverhand theorized.

"Well, it does sound like his kind of place," Felicity noted, "being—what did you say again?—'covered in perpetual shadow,' or whatever. Like, all dark and creepy."

"It is somewhat dark, but it is actually quite beautiful as well," Blackspore said. "In fact, I was trying to go there myself when I fled Spectraland. Unfortunately, I was not able to make it that far, and I ended up being stranded here."

"How did you manage to cross the Forbidden Tides, anyway?" Windblade asked.

"A short-range teleportation wavecast that I figured out from observing swordcats," Blackspore responded. "I was not sure that it was going to work, to be honest, but I was quite desperate. It got me past the Tides, but no further. I only wish I had the kinds of new skills that you young ones seem to have developed."

"All right," Thornleaf said, sounding impatient, "so tell us how to find these so-called 'Six States'."

"Are you sure you do not want some soup first?" Blackspore asked, holding out his bowl.

"Very sure."

"Trust me, you do not know what you are missing," Blackspore said before he took yet another sip. He let out a loud burp before continuing. "Yes, well, if one of you will allow me to borrow your wavebow and some Aura energy, I can show you how to get there. It will be easier that way."

"What happened to *your* wavebow?" Redstem asked.

"It ran into some...unfortunate consequences, shall we say," Blackspore replied, somewhat sheepishly. "Trust me, I will not use yours for any other purpose but to give you the information that you want."

Redstem turned to Thornleaf. "What do you think?"

"He is still under the truth cast, so I believe him," Thornleaf said. "Auravine—lend him what he needs."

"Me? But..."

"Just do it."

With one hand Auravine handed over her wavebow, its formerly bright white finish still tarnished from her battle with Joel and Felicity when she was under Marshall's influence. With her other hand she grasped Blackspore's wrist, and he grasped hers. Both of them closed their eyes, and in the moment that followed, Joel could see a wisp of Aura energy make its way down Auravine's arm and up Blackspore's.

"Interesting..." Blackspore said after the wisp faded away. "You are the healer who restored Byle's physical form."

"How did you—?"

"When energy is transferred, memories can be passed along as well," Blackspore answered with a sudden air of authority. "I take it none of you ever learned that?"

Everyone either remained silent or shook their heads.

Blackspore chuckled. "Well, that is a fairly advanced trick, I will admit. I *was* a rather powerful master back in my day, you know. Anyway, before Thornleaf loses his temper..." he trailed off and began to play a soft melody on Auravine's instrument. A cloud of Aura flowed out of its headstock and formed a large sphere, like a giant crystal ball, that hung over everyone's heads. Joel looked up at it. A few seconds later, an image appeared within the sphere: a bird's-eye view of the atoll that they were currently on.

"So from here," Blackspore said, "you must travel in a northerly direction"—the view zoomed away, as if it had been filmed in super-fast motion—"until you see this particular set of islands." The view paused on an archipelago that looked almost unsettlingly like an angry face. "Then, turn east. Eventually, you should be able to spot—especially with the Sight—a set of dark clouds that appear to never move. It is under those clouds that your destination lies."

"Why can't we just scan the whole place remotely to find out where Marshall and his goons might be hiding?" Felicity asked.

"Unfortunately, that would take much more energy than I sense all of us have here combined," Blackspore replied.

"I shoulda guessed," Felicity muttered.

"I can, however, show you an image of an inhabitant of the Six States."

Blackspore played a different melody, and the image in the sphere swirled and shifted before it reformed into something that Joel found even more unsettling than the Angry Face Archipelago: his own dad.

"Whoa, wait, hold on," Joel stammered, transfixed. "That's not a—that's—that's my—"

"Wow, that is one creepy-lookin' dude," Felicity said.

"What?" Joel said, glancing at her. "You think so?"

"Of course, man. I mean, just look at him."

Joel looked back at the sphere. To his surprise, the image had changed; it was still a male humanoid figure with short black hair who resembled his father in stature, but now it looked a bit more like the kind of alien you might see in a documentary about UFOs. It had big, dark eyes, pale gray skin, and a pair of long, pointy antennae. It was wearing something that looked like a plain white bathrobe, and it had vertical red streaks on its forehead and cheeks.

"This is a typical representation of one of their citizens," Blackspore said. "Before you depart, I will tell you how to adjust the translation cast so that you may converse with them, if necessary."

"Perhaps you should come along with us," Windblade suggested.

"No," Thornleaf grunted before Blackspore had a chance to respond. "He is to remain here, in exile. It is bad enough that we already have one former ally of Byle's in our party. I certainly will not welcome a second."

"Who are you...oh," Joel said, noticing that Thornleaf was giving Auravine what, back in Hawai'i, was commonly known as the "stink eye."

"Then at least allow me to teach you some other casts. Though they require a large amount of energy, they may prove to be quite useful to your mission," Blackspore said. "For example, the muting cast, to silence the air around you, and the invisibility cast, to hide yourself when necessary."

"But those are forbidden casts, thought to be lost long ago," Riverhand said. "How do you know them?"

Blackspore smiled. "When I was searching for the cast to bring someone over, I happened to stumble upon some...additional records, shall we say."

The Wavemakers all looked at each other.

"So, Thornleaf," Blackspore continued, "you seem to be the leader here. What do you think?"

Thornleaf folded his arms and paused for five full seconds before responding. "Very well."

CHAPTER 10: KEEPER OF THE LIGHT

Not long after, the Wavemakers left the atoll and headed north. Joel was relieved that he didn't have to try to pick up the image of the fugitives again, as he was still distracted by thoughts about Felicity moving to Spectraland. He didn't broach the subject—and neither did she—as they flew for several more hours over the ocean, with Windblade leading another songfest along the way. Eventually, they spotted the Angry Face Archipelago, made a right turn, and then, after another hour and forty-seven minutes of being airborne, the dark, unmoving cloud bank came into view.

As it turned out, locating the cloud bank was rather unnecessary, as the large land mass underneath it was probably just as obvious, if not more so; specks of light scattered across its surface made it look like a big Earth city as you approached it by airplane during the night. Per the plan that they had settled upon before leaving Blackspore's atoll, they lowered their altitude until they were just about skimming the surface of the water, so as not to attract too much attention. They headed for a stretch of land that seemed to be the least populated, if you went by the amount of lights, and once they got close enough, Joel saw that the shore was lined with tall stone columns shaped like giant bowling pins. Scattered among the columns were a few house-sized structures that defied easy description; the closest thing that Joel could think of was that they resembled giant brains wrapped in coiled wire. Thornleaf led the way to a spot about two hundred yards away from the nearest brain-building, and there they landed on a surface made up of tiny red crystals that gave off a constant hissing, crackling noise.

"Hey, this stuff is like Pop Rocks," Felicity said as she crunched them underfoot. "You know, the candy?"

"Oh—uh, yeah," Joel said, pulling his cloak tighter. It was warmer here than he had expected, maybe around fifty-five degrees or so, but for some reason, he felt rather chilly.

"Dude, did you ever try eating them and drinking soda?"

"No. "

"That's supposed to make your stomach explode."

"Um, okay."

Felicity let out an exasperated sigh. "Don't tell me you're still thinking about me moving here."

"Okay, I won't."

"You know that's not what I meant."

Joel didn't respond. He really didn't want to talk about that particular subject right now, even though it was just about the only thing on his mind. Fortunately, Thornleaf came to his rescue.

"All right," the tall shaman said, redirecting the situation to the matter at hand, "let us move on to the next step in our plan."

"I still think there should be another way to do this," Riverhand objected. "If Fireflower found out that we were planning on using this wavecast—"

"She would completely understand, given the circumstances," Thornleaf interrupted.

"Besides, it is only forbidden in Spectraland," Redstem added. "And obviously, we are no longer there, so..."

Riverhand shook his head. "You are defying the spirit of the law."

"Enough," Thornleaf said. "No more discussion. Windblade, if you will."

Windblade played a series of chords on his wavebow. As he did so, the air around everyone appeared to blur and shimmer. Then, a few moments later, they all vanished from sight.

"Nice," Felicity's voice said. "I've always wanted to be invisible."

"Now," Thornleaf's voice said, "use your ability to see if you can pick up the fugitives' trail."

"Who, me?" Joel said.

"Yes."

Joel took a deep breath. *All right, forget about Felicity moving...try to think of something else. What about...band names that start with the letter C...no, because that reminds me of playing in my band, which she's quitting. Maybe...enemies from* Xenoblade Chronicles, *listed in reverse alphabetical order...ugh, no, because that makes me think about video games, which reminds me about how she's good at first-person shooters and how she'll never be able to show me her strategies for them...*

"Anything?" Thornleaf's voice asked.

"Huh?"

"Do you see anything yet?"

"Oh—uh, no, not yet. Hold on."

Eventually, Joel settled on Major League Baseball pitchers who threw perfect games, listed in chronological order.

Lee Richmond, John Montgomery Ward, Cy Young...

"Perhaps we should have had Master Joel do this *before* we arrived here," Riverhand's voice said. "That way, maybe we could have found the precise location where Byle and the others landed."

Addie Joss, Charlie Robertson, Don Larsen...

"Not every plan can be perfect," Thornleaf's voice said. "If he cannot pick up their trail from here, we will just keep searching around until he does."

Jim Bunning, Sandy Koufax, Catfish Hunter...

"But that could take days," Riverhand said. "Weeks, perhaps. I think we underestimated just how large this land really is."

"Well," Redstem said, "then you should have made that suggestion earlier."

Len Barker, Mike Witt, Tom Browning...

"Hey, be quiet, you guys," Felicity said. "I think he's trying to concentrate."

At that moment, Joel spotted something—but it wasn't Marshall, Darkeye, or either of the Lightsnakes.

"Um, I saw one of those people," he said, his voice lowered. "You know, with the big eyes and the antennae and stuff."

"You did?" Thornleaf said. "Where?"

"It's behind one of those bowling pins. I mean, columns. I think it's hiding or something."

"Is it there now, or in the past?" Felicity asked.

"Now."

"How far away is it?" Riverhand asked.

"Thirty-six feet."

"Perhaps we should talk to it," Auravine said. "Maybe it can help us."

"You are not here to make suggestions," Thornleaf said. "And no, we need to try to stay incognito until we have a better grasp of the situation."

The being emerged from behind the column and took a few cautious steps forward.

"I, uh, I think it's coming toward us now," Joel whispered.

"Should we flee?" Windblade asked.

"No," Thornleaf replied. "It will see our tracks in the sand. Just remain perfectly still."

The being continued its careful approach, its antennae twitching. It looked similar to the image that Blackspore had shown the party, except that it had long neon-green hair and, underneath its bathrobe-like garment, a more feminine body shape. In one of its hands it held a device that resembled a TV remote, which it was pointing straight at the Wavemakers.

Looking around at his fellow shamans, Joel found that if he squinted, he could just about make out their outlines. He wondered if the alien being could see the same thing, or if it was a result of his Sight ability. Either way, all of them except for Auravine were raising their wavebows, so he did the same.

Then the being spoke. Or, at least, Joel thought it did. Its mouth was moving, but the sounds coming out of it were more like the tones of a wind chime. None of the Wavemakers responded, but Joel could see Thornleaf slowly aiming his wavebow in the being's direction.

Hmm, he thought. *I'm not sure if that's a good idea—*

The being pressed a button on its remote, and Joel heard a high, squealing noise that he assumed was coming from the device. A moment later, he felt a strange sensation in the muscles of his body, as if someone had just stuck a million needles under his skin. He tried to play his wavebow, but he found that his arms and hands were frozen in place. The being pressed a few more buttons, and Joel's legs began to move forward on their own.

What the heck?

He glanced at the outlines of the others. Apparently, the same thing was happening to them, as they all lined up in a single file behind the being and began to march. Joel tried to break formation, but he had no control over any part of his body below his neck.

Should I say something? he wondered. *But no one else is talking...and I'm not sure what I would say, anyway.*

The being led them past a few bowling-pin columns and toward the nearest brain-shaped building, glancing around and apparently talking to itself along the way. Once they reached the building, a door slid open automatically and they all went inside. The interior was dimly lit and small, about the size of a studio apartment. The walls had a honeycomb pattern to them, and plain white bathrobes were scattered on the floor around large objects that seemed to be made up of a combination of organic and mechanical material. Some of those objects had moving parts that made Joel wonder whether they were alive and sentient or just fancy pieces of furniture.

Joel's legs walked him over to the far end of the space, where he stopped with his back up against one of the honeycomb walls. Glancing around, he noticed that the being had lined everyone up, shoulder to shoulder, according to height: Felicity, Riverhand, and Thornleaf were to his right, while Redstem, Auravine, and Windblade were to his left.

"What should we do?" Redstem whispered. Joel wasn't sure who she was talking to.

"Give me a minute to think," Thornleaf replied.

"You could have been thinking while we were being forced to walk over here," Riverhand muttered.

At the other end of the space, the being was pacing back and forth, holding both hands to its head and letting out a continuous stream of soft wind-chime sounds.

"That thing looks pretty stressed out," Felicity noted.

"Odd," Windblade said, "since we are the ones who have been captured."

"I think it's not sure what to do with us," Felicity went on. "Maybe we just need to reassure it that we're not harmful. You know, we come in peace, and all that."

"How do you know this?" Auravine asked.

"I've been studying body language."

The being paused, put its hands on its hips, and then resumed pacing.

"So what do you propose?" Riverhand asked. "Obviously, we cannot communicate with it, nor can we play our wavebows to adjust the translation cast."

"Yeah, I haven't gotten that far yet," Felicity replied.

As soon as she finished speaking, a puzzle piece fell into place in Joel's head. "Oh—I, uh, I have an idea: we could sing."

"Seriously?" Felicity said.

"Yeah, 'cause, you know, Blackspore said that these people have a great appreciation for music. So maybe if we sing, it'll...I dunno, it'll like us more, or something."

"Sounds like you're reaching a little bit there."

"And since it seems to speak in tones," Redstem said, "what if we accidentally say something that offends it?"

The being stopped next to an object that looked like a hutch constructed out of steel rods and layers of ground beef. It pressed a button on it, and a panel slid open, revealing an array of intricate and very sharp-looking knives.

"Unless anyone has any better ideas, I say we try it," Riverhand said.

"Very well," Thornleaf said. "Windblade, start us off."

Windblade cleared his throat. "All right. Which...which song should we sing?"

The being picked a knife out of the hutch.

"Anything," Thornleaf said. "Something simple."

Windblade launched into "Down the Landvein River," a jaunty, upbeat tune that ironically was about fleeing a pack of drone Lightsnakes after the singer's brother had been kidnapped by them. Joel joined in right away—they'd sung the song three times on their way to Blackspore's atoll, so he knew it by heart. He only paused after the second verse when he noticed that Felicity's voice was missing from the choir.

"Hey, uh, Felicity," he said, "aren't you gonna sing, too?"

"Ugh," she sighed. "All right, fine."

She joined in for the third verse, and then, as they worked their way through the chorus, the being put the knife back in the hutch and started to slowly walk over to them, tilting its head in a quizzical manner. It was about six feet in front of them when the song came to an end.

"Let's do it again," Joel said.

And so they did. When they hit the chorus, the being opened its mouth and started to make tones that nearly matched the pitches of the notes they were singing, even though it didn't enunciate any of the words.

"We should just keep repeating the chorus," Joel suggested.

They sang the chorus again, and again. By the fifth time, the being was singing along perfectly in tune and in time, and it sounded like it even got some of the words right (how it did that when, technically, the Spectraland natives and the offworlders were singing in two different languages, Joel had no idea). After one more go-around, the being took out its remote-control device and pressed a few buttons on it. Instantly, Joel regained control over the rest of his body. At the same time, the invisibility cast wore off and everyone stopped singing.

"Um...we mean you no harm," he said to the being.

The being made a few wind-chime sounds in response.

"I'm, uh, I'm going to play some music on this instrument," he said, pointing to his wavebow. "It'll allow us to understand each other better. Okay?"

The being made a single high-pitched noise, like the *ding* of a triangle.

I hope that means okay, Joel thought. He played one of the wavecasts that Blackspore had taught them, the one to adjust the translation cast for denizens of the Six States.

"All right," he said after he was done, "can...can you understand me now?"

"Yes, I c-can," the being responded in a lilting female voice that sounded like it was being run through an Auto-Tune. For some reason, it had an English accent. "Can you understand m-me?"

"Um, yeah, pretty much." Joel nodded. He turned to the others. "Can you guys understand it—uh, her?"

All the shamans responded in the affirmative.

"Okay, so, uh," Joel said, turning back to the being, "I'm Joel. Joel Suzuki."

"I am c-called Keeper of the Light."

Interesting name, Joel thought. "Um, nice to meet you."

"Are you f-from the Land under the Rainbow?"

"Huh? The what?"

"I think she means Spectraland, dude," Felicity said. "You know, 'cause of how the Aura surrounds the island, and stuff."

"Oh—uh, then yeah. Yes, we are. Sort of. I mean, five of us are, and the other two are from another world, but we went to Spectraland before we got here, so technically, we—"

"I thought so," Keeper of the Light said. The Auto-Tune effect seemed to have worn off; Joel reasoned that the translation cast probably just needed some time to calibrate properly. "Are you looking for your friends?"

"Friends?" Joel echoed.

"The ones who arrived here earlier. I have been hearing all the rumors...but I was not sure if they were true."

"I think she's talking about Marshall and company," Felicity said.

"Oh—right," Joel said. "They're, uh, they're not our friends. They're actually escaped criminals. We're trying to catch them and take them back to Spectraland."

"So you are...officers of law enforcement?" Keeper of the Light asked, leaning into Joel's personal space. That alone was off-putting, but the combination of her human female form and her alien facial features coming in close like that made for a very uncomfortable overall experience.

"Um, yeah," Joel said, pressing his back against the wall. "More or less."

Keeper of the Light nodded and backed away, much to Joel's relief. "That is good to know," she said. "I had heard that your friends—I mean, your fugitives—were potentially dangerous, so I thought that you were as well. I apologize for my actions, but I was not sure what else to do."

"Well, if hostile aliens landed in *my* backyard, I probably would've just called 911," Felicity said.

"I would have contacted our own law enforcement officers, but..."

"But what?" Thornleaf said.

"Our government is trying to cover it up—the arrival of the rainbow folk. They are denying everything, and anyone who is even suspected of spreading the rumors is subject to arrest and possible disciplinary action."

"Then how did you hear about it in the first place?" Redstem asked.

"Come, I will show you." Keeper of the Light walked over to a nearby object that was either a medium-sized desk or a skinned, headless, flat-backed creature standing perfectly still on all fours; it was hard to tell exactly which. On top of it was something that looked like an empty fish tank, and in front of it was a relatively normal-looking cubic stool. Sitting down on the stool, Keeper of the Light touched her finger to a spot on the tank, and a blurry 3-D image appeared inside of it, along with scrolling lines of strange characters that Joel assumed made up the written language of this land.

"Whoa," he said, examining the image. It looked like a holographic version of a security camera snapshot. "That's...that's Marshall. And the others too."

"This is a recent feed from our underground information exchange network," Keeper of the Light explained as everyone gathered around. "Users from around the Mono Realm have been anonymously posting these accounts ever since the sightings began. The administrator of this particular bulletin system knows the most, however. He has been writing articles about you—the rainbow folk, I mean—for many years. He seems absolutely obsessed with the subject. But no one has ever really taken him seriously until now."

"Ah, so it's like a conspiracy theory blog on the Internet," Felicity said.

"If I understand what you just said correctly, then yes, it is sort of like that," Keeper of the Light replied.

"Are you sure the translation cast is still working?" Redstem asked. "Because you are all starting to speak gibberish."

Felicity chuckled. "I'll explain it to you later."

"Um, what's the Mono Realm?" Joel asked.

"That is the name of our country," Keeper of the Light replied.

"Oh...I thought it was the Six States beneath the Shroud."

Keeper of the Light made a sound that, translated, came out as a cross between a sigh and a wheeze. "It *was* called that," she said, "until the Unification War. The leader of one of our states gathered an army, conquered the other states, and then declared himself the Uniter, the grand ruler of it all."

"Just like what Fourfoot attempted to do," Windblade said.

Thornleaf let out a little grunting noise, a sign that the tall shaman was growing impatient. "All right, well, before we start exchanging history lessons, I think that we should resume our search. So if you will find out for us—"

He was interrupted by a banging sound coming from outside, followed by a gruff male voice that shouted, "Keeper of the Light! Open up at once!"

CHAPTER 11: SOULSHIFTER

Based on years of watching similar scenes unfold in movies and on TV, where an unwanted guest unexpectedly busts in on the main characters, Joel's immediate instinct was to find a closet, or a cellar, or anything in which to hide. Glancing around, however, he saw nothing of the sort; Keeper of the Light's domicile was a single open room with no obvious doors except the main one, and none of the organic-mechanical objects, such as the knife-hutch, looked large enough to contain one person, let alone seven.

No wonder she keeps all of her clothes on the floor, Joel thought. *No place to store them. I wonder where she sleeps?*

"What is happening?" Redstem asked.

"The authorities are here!" Keeper of the Light hissed, sounding frantic. "Someone must have seen us on the beach...if they discover you, we will all be in very big trouble!"

"Keeper of the Light!" the voice outside repeated. Oddly, it too had an English accent. "Open up now, by order of the town leader!"

"I can replay the invisibility cast," Windblade offered.

"But will that work?" Riverhand said. He gestured toward Keeper of the Light. "If *she* could still see us, then—"

"You have three seconds," the voice called out. "After which, I will have no choice but to force your door open!"

"I—I have my hands full at the moment!" Keeper of the Light shouted, moving over to a basin-like object that resembled a giant metal oyster perched on an elephant-leg pedestal. "Just give me a little longer—thirty seconds!" She touched the side of the pedestal, and the metal oyster sprang open.

"Very well, thirty seconds. But no more!"

"What should we do?" Auravine said, looking at Joel.

"Let him in," Thornleaf scoffed, raising his wavebow. "We can just stun him once he enters."

"No, that will only make matters worse," Keeper of the Light said as she rummaged through the metal oyster's mouth. "I have an idea." She pulled out what looked like a small, clear jar full of strawberry jam—or possibly some other, less edible red-colored substance—and unscrewed its lid. "All of you—stand close and face me, please."

While the Wavemakers did what she asked, Keeper of the Light dipped her finger in the jar and stepped in front of Joel, invading his personal space once more. Before he could protest or back away, she painted vertical lines on his forehead and cheeks with her finger, as if she were applying eye black to his face, only in the wrong direction.

"This will make you look like us," she said, moving on to the others.

Yeah, well, maybe a little, but what about the big eyes? Joel wondered. *And the antennae? And the—*

"Ten seconds!" the voice outside shouted.

Joel was about to vocalize his question when suddenly he felt a warm, tingly sensation that started in his head and neck and then spread to all the other parts of his body.

Whoa...now, that's weird.

Keeper of the Light continued down the line, quickly applying the red substance to everyone's faces.

"So, what is this," Felicity said, "magic makeup?"

"Five seconds!"

Keeper of the Light finished up and dashed over to the door, which slid open in response to her approach. A Mono Realmer wearing a plain white jumpsuit was standing there, holding something that looked like a space-age bayonet.

"Hello, Officer," Keeper of the Light said. "Pardon the delay. What can I do for you?"

The officer pushed past her and entered the room. "We have reports that you may be harboring some...undesirable individuals."

"What sort of individuals might those be?"

Joel felt his face flush. He wasn't sure if it was due to nervousness, the effect of the red substance, or a combination of both.

"Who are these people?" the officer demanded, glaring at each of the Wavemakers in turn.

"My relatives," Keeper of the Light responded, "visiting from the Town below the Mountain. They just arrived tonight."

The officer moved up close to Joel. Apparently, personal space was not a thing here in the Mono Realm.

Joel tried his best to stand his ground, even as the officer stared at him with those large, unblinking eyes.

"As you can see," Keeper of the Light said, "their energy signatures are quite similar to mine."

"I will need to see some identification," the officer said in a skeptical tone, one that was probably used by law enforcement officials all over the universe.

Joel gulped. "Um—"

"Unfortunately, their identification discs were lost on the way here," Keeper of the Light said. "They were all packed into one bag, which ended up being misplaced— very careless, if I do so say myself. My relatives will apply for replacements as soon as they return home in a few days."

The officer tilted his head and lingered in front of Joel for five more unsettling seconds before he moved on to the others, looking each of them over as he went. When he was finally done, he turned to Keeper of the Light and said, "For your sake, I hope that you are telling the truth. The penalties for forging an energy signature can be quite severe."

"Yes, yes, I know," Keeper of the Light said.

"I will need to run a scan of the interior."

"Be my guest."

The officer pushed a button on his bayonet, and it started to hum. He waved it around and pointed it at various objects for what seemed like a very long time (but was, in fact, only twenty-two seconds) before he pushed the button once more and the humming sound ceased.

"Clean," the officer said, as if to himself.

"Naturally," Keeper of the Light said. "So now, if your business is concluded, I would appreciate it if you took your leave. After a very long day, we are all quite ready to retire for the evening."

The officer walked slowly toward the door, glancing back at the Wavemakers after every other step. "Just be aware," he said, "that I will return if any follow-up reports are filed."

"Of course," Keeper of the Light said, seeing the officer out. "Have a good night."

"Sorry for the interruption," the officer said, although he didn't sound particularly sorry.

The door slid closed and Keeper of the Light exhaled in relief. "That was close."

"So, um...what just happened?" Joel asked, glancing down at himself and then at the rest of his party. Aside from the red marks on their faces, they all still looked like themselves. "Why did he think that...you know, why did he believe you?"

"Because of the soulshifter," Keeper of the Light replied.

"The what?"

"The salve that I applied to your faces. It changes your internal energy signal. Can you not tell?"

"Oh—okay, I think I get it," Felicity said. "We see stuff because light reflects off of it, but you guys see stuff because of the energy inside of it, or whatever. Kinda like in *Predator*. Remember that, Joel?"

"I haven't seen that movie yet."

"What? Seriously? I thought we...dude, we'll rent it when we get...er, I mean...just watch it."

"I still do not understand, though," Windblade said. "Why do you need such a salve?"

Keeper of the Light made a noise that sounded vaguely like a snort of disgust. "Normally, each individual's energy signature is highly unique. After the war, however, the Uniter decreed that everyone in the Mono Realm must look..."

"Identical?" Riverhand said.

"No, but we must conform to one particular standard of appearance," Keeper of the Light replied, dumping the jar back into the metal oyster. "So now, by law, all citizens are forced to wear this abhorrent, disfiguring slime."

"What happens if you do not comply?" Redstem asked.

"If you are caught, you are put to death."

"That is terrible," Auravine said. "Why does your ruler—the Uniter—demand this?"

"Simply put, he believes that diversity leads to conflict. That the only way to have a truly peaceful society is through uniformity."

Thornleaf glared at Auravine. "Sounds similar to what you were trying to accomplish with Byle."

"I admitted that I was wrong," Auravine said, obviously seething; her voice was soft, but her teeth were clenched.

"Well, um," Joel said, anxious to quell the budding tension in the room, "at least with this soulshifter stuff we can go around undetected now, right?"

"True," Keeper of the Light replied. "Although it does wear off over time, so you will need to reapply it."

"Can you give us an additional supply?" Riverhand asked.

"I suppose I could."

"Good," Thornleaf said. "So, as I was about to say before we were interrupted by that guard, I would like you to ask these so-called 'users' from your information feed where we can find our fugitives."

Keeper of the Light's antennae twitched. "Well, I would, but..."

"But what?"

"This particular bulletin system was frozen several days ago. I believe that the authorities became aware of it and shut it down."

"Boy, we always have such great timing, don't we?" Felicity said, rolling her eyes.

"Um...do any of the older posts say where Marshall and the others were seen?" Joel asked.

"They were sighted in a number of different locations," Keeper of the Light replied. "They definitely were not sitting still."

"We could go to their most recent known location," Windblade suggested.

"No, that would be a waste of time." Thornleaf shook his head. "I am sure they are long gone from there by now. It sounds like they know we are on their trail."

"If this bulletin system, as you say, is shut down," Redstem said to Keeper of the Light, "could we just go to see these users in person?"

"Especially the one that you said knows the most," Riverhand added. "The administrator."

"Uh, hello," Felicity said, "she said that they were all posting anonymously, remember? So unless Joel here can hack into this alien Internet and trace his IP address or whatever..."

Joel shrugged. "I guess I could try."

"Dude, I was kidding."

Keeper of the Light moved back over to her fish tank and began to swipe her finger across one of its sides, as if it were a touch screen. "I do recall some postings a while back, long before the sightings, where people were hypothesizing about the possible identity of the administrator. I did not pay much attention at the time, but...ah, here we go."

Joel looked over her shoulder at the fish tank. He saw a 3-D image of a male Mono Realm citizen who had wild, scraggly white hair and a garment that looked less like a bathrobe and more like a suit of tin foil.

"According to this," Keeper of the Light said, reading the scrolling type next to the image, "he used to work for the government, until something traumatic happened to him and he was forced into isolation."

"What happened?" Joel asked.

Keeper of the Light continued swiping. "Hmm...it does not say. It does, however, pose some theories about where he may be living now. Apparently, he was last sighted in the City by the Lake."

"Then that is where you must take us," Thornleaf said.

"I...I am not sure I can do that," Keeper of the Light demurred. "The City by the Lake is rather far from here, and I have no private means of transportation."

"We could fly," Windblade said.

"Are you referring to that action whereby you travel unassisted through the sky?" Keeper of the Light asked.

"Yes," several Wavemakers answered at the same time.

Keeper of the Light shook her head. "That would be highly risky. Nothing in the Mono Realm is capable of such a feat. The government would become immediately aware of your presence."

"Ugh, of course," Felicity said. "Is there another way to get there? Like, a bus, or a train, or something?"

"We do have a public transit system..."

"Then that is what we shall use," Thornleaf declared. "Now, let us be off. We do not have much time."

"I still do not think I should do this," Keeper of the Light protested. "I have become way too involved as it is."

"But you must help us," Thornleaf said. "You *will* help us!"

"I beg your pardon?" Keeper of the Light exclaimed, standing and getting right up into Thornleaf's face. The tall shaman played a chord on his wavebow in response, creating a blue cloud of energy that instantly filled up half the room.

"Thornleaf!" Riverhand hissed. "Mind control casts are expressly prohibited by the—"

"Quiet, Riverhand," Thornleaf growled before he turned back to Keeper of the Light. "I said, you *will* help us," he repeated slowly, as if trying to perform a Jedi Mind Trick.

"I am under no obligation to do such a thing!" Keeper of the Light replied, apparently unaffected. "How dare you demand that of me?"

"You will help us, or I will—"

"All right, all right, everybody just chill," Felicity said, separating the two like a boxing referee. "Look, can you at least give us a map or something?"

After a tense pause, Keeper of the Light sighed. "Very well." She went back to the fish tank and swiped it again. Then, out of a narrow aperture on the side of the desk (around where the rib cage would be, if it were, in fact, a creature), a sheet of paper emerged. About ten by twelve inches, it displayed a veritable maze of lines and characters, all of it printed in vibrant gold and silver ink.

Redstem picked up the sheet. "I cannot make any sense of this," she said, turning it over and around. "Master Joel, can you?"

Joel took the sheet from her and inspected it. It reminded him of a subway map, only more complex and obscure, with routes that seemed to lead absolutely nowhere. Maps were one of his favorite things, but he had to admit that even he would be hard-pressed to follow this one. "Um, no, not really."

"Great," Felicity muttered. "So now what?"

That was a good question. Joel racked his brain in an effort to come up with an idea, but nothing came to mind. It didn't help that he still felt flushed and light-headed from the soulshifter salve. Everyone stood around and looked at each other, as if they were having some kind of unarmed standoff. Finally, Auravine broke the silence.

"Please," the healer implored, turning to face Keeper of the Light, "I beg you, come with us. We need to capture these fugitives as quickly as possible. They are dangerous not only to our people, but to yours as well. They are duplicitous and capable of great destruction."

"As you would well know," Thornleaf muttered under his breath.

"I...I am not sure," Keeper of the Light said, folding her arms. "I have never done anything like this before."

"I too was once faced with a very difficult choice," Auravine said. "But in the end, thanks to the wisdom of a brave young man, I found the courage to do what was right."

Wait, Joel thought, *is she talking about me?*

"If you helped us," Auravine continued, "you would be doing your land a great service. You would be a hero."

For the next twelve seconds, Keeper of the Light stood in near-complete silence with her lips pursed. The only sound was a soft clicking noise that seemed to be coming from her antennae, which were twitching back and forth. Then, taking a step closer to Auravine, she said: "All right. I will guide you to the City by the Lake and help you locate the administrator. After that, however, you will be on your own. Agreed?"

Auravine nodded. "Agreed."

CHAPTER 12: THE TRIPLETS

They set off soon afterward. Keeper of the Light—who agreed to be called just Keeper, at Felicity's insistence—informed them that she had been sleeping all day and, therefore, was not tired. Joel, on the other hand, was starting to feel a bit fatigued, but he didn't want to be the one to slow down their mission, and besides, the only place to lie down in Keeper's residence was the cold, hard floor (according to Keeper, all Mono Realmers slept standing up).

They hiked through a long field of bowling-pin columns until they arrived at what Joel figured was the Mono Realm equivalent of a sleepy coastal town. There was very little to be seen in the way of buildings and structures, and the few they encountered looked like slightly larger, more run-down versions of Keeper's brain-house. There were no sidewalks, roads, or paved areas—the ground was just a continuation of the red sand from the beach—and, as far as Joel could tell, the eight of them were the only living beings who were up and about.

"There," Keeper said, pointing at a nearby brain-like building. "That is the public transit terminal."

"I'll take your word for it," Felicity said.

"Remember to keep your musical instruments hidden within your cloaks," Keeper told the group as she glanced around warily. The coast seemed clear, so she led everyone into the terminal, which looked even shabbier on the inside than it did on the outside. The walls appeared to have been vandalized, a stale odor hung in the air, and there were pieces of what Joel assumed to be litter scattered about. A circular platform, about eight inches high and ten feet in diameter, took up the space in the middle of the floor, and a sign hanging over it by a wire displayed rows of glowing, handwritten Mono Realm words, as if someone had jotted down a menu using fluorescent ink.

"Everyone stand on the platform," Keeper said. "I will make payment and then join you."

"This isn't some kind of disintegration chamber, is it?" Felicity said. "Like, we stand there, you press a button, and then—poof!—we're toast."

"If I truly wanted to kill you, I would have done it while you all were singing," Keeper said.

"Good point."

Joel stepped up onto the platform, which had twelve glowing circles lined up along its perimeter. It reminded him a little of the transporter from *Star Trek*. He took up a spot on one of the circles, excited that he was about to experience "beaming" in real life. As everyone else did the same, Keeper inserted a disc into a slot in the wall that Joel originally thought was part of a piece of graffiti.

"I do not suppose any of you have a transit system like this where you are from," she said.

"No," Thornleaf grunted. "We do not."

"We have it in a TV show," Joel said. "But it's fake."

"I see. Well, just be prepared. It can be a bit disorienting, especially on your first time." The disc popped back out of the slot. Keeper retrieved it and stepped up onto the platform.

Joel took a deep breath as a whining noise started to crank up from somewhere underneath the floor. For a moment he thought about making some kind of *Trek*-related reference, knowing that Felicity would probably get it, but that thought only made him sad, so he squashed it.

Who else will I be able to talk to about this kind of stuff after I get home? he lamented privately.

"Please keep your legs together and your arms pressed against your sides at all times," a recorded Englishwoman's voice said over some hidden loudspeaker.

Huh, Joel thought. *They never had to do* that *in* Star Trek. *I wonder if—*

A buzzer sounded. In a flash, the circle beneath Joel's feet slid aside like a trap door. He fell, but before he even had a chance to scream, he realized that he was now in a narrow tube and some kind of vacuum-like force was propelling him along at a high rate of speed. After about eight seconds of dizzying twists and turns, he came to an abrupt stop, his feet hitting a solid surface. He was pretty sure he was standing upright. A section of the tube in front of him slid open, and he stepped out, trying not to stumble as he did so.

Whew...okay, that was more like Futurama *than* Star Trek.

Regaining his bearings, he saw that he was in a large room surrounded by a number of other tubes, all of them painted green, that stretched from ceiling to floor; it was like standing in a small forest of very thick bamboo trees. The rest of his party had all just emerged as well.

"That certainly was...disorienting," Windblade said, shaking his head as if to clear it.

"Let's go again," Felicity remarked.

"We will," Keeper said. "We still have to make thirteen more transfers before we reach our destination."

"What? Aw, man, I was just kidding."

They walked into an adjoining room that was similar to the one they had just left, with a circular platform in the middle of the floor. This one was a little nicer, but not by much. From there, they repeated the tube-traveling process, sometimes going through terminals that were significantly bigger and cleaner, until finally, they arrived at a terminal that was the largest of them all so far. There were even other travelers present, none of whom seemed to take any interest in Joel and his party.

"We are here," Keeper announced.

"Thank goodness," Felicity sighed.

Exiting the terminal building, they emerged into a cityscape that was quite a bit different from Keeper's small, quiet town. Large cathedral-like buildings were interspersed with metal and mechanical structures of all shapes and sizes, and tall stone pillars adorned with glowing lights cast a pallid glow over the entire scene. Intersecting cobblestone roadways ran in between the structures, and Joel was sure that he saw what looked like the taillights of a moving vehicle fading off into the distance. A constant mix of buzzing and hissing sounds could be heard, and the air smelled like burning meat.

"Amazing," Redstem breathed.

"Eh, sorta reminds me of downtown Camas," Felicity quipped.

"So, how do we plan on locating the administrator?" Thornleaf said.

"We will just have to ask around," Keeper replied. "Ah, excuse me," she said, stopping a passerby, "are you familiar with this person?" She held out her remote control, pressed a button on it, and a small 3-D holographic image of the wild-haired Mono Realmer popped up.

"No." The passerby shook his head and resumed walking.

"Well, this seems like a friendly neighborhood," Felicity remarked.

"We will keep trying," Keeper said. "Eventually, we should be able to find someone who has some information."

They approached a few more locals on the street, but the responses they received were more or less the same. After that, they tried a couple of establishments; one seemed like the Mono Realm version of a convenience store, while the other resembled an art gallery. No one knew anything about the wild-haired man.

"We should split up," Keeper suggested. "I have a spare countercom that one of you can use."

"A what?" Windblade asked.

Keeper held up her remote control. "This device."

"Ooh, okay, I'll take it," Felicity said. "That thing looks like fun."

"Be very careful with it, now. They are quite difficult to procure."

"What, like, there's a long permit process or something?"

"Actually, they are...black market goods." Keeper confessed. "Not even the government has them."

"Whoa, look at you." Felicity grinned. "A little outlaw streak, huh?"

"A girl has to protect herself."

"And it's okay to flash them around?"

"Just not to a law enforcement officer."

"Gotcha."

Keeper gave Felicity a crash course in how to use the countercom, which, based on the Mono Realmer's explanation, was like a smartphone/self-defense weapon; in addition to the energy-lock function, it could also be used to talk to someone else who had a similar device, as long as you were both within a certain range. Apparently, despite the presence of an Internet-like network, live long-distance communication was still a relatively new thing here.

The lesson over, the party decided to break up into two groups of four people each.

"All right," Keeper said. "Each group should have one person who can use the countercom."

"I will accompany the female offworlder," Thornleaf said.

"I will too," Redstem volunteered.

"Windblade, you should come with us," Thornleaf said.

"What? Oh—very well."

Joel looked around at everyone. This whole process reminded him a little of grade school dodgeball, where each of the teams just sort of came together before he even knew what was going on.

"My group will head down this road," Keeper said, gesturing over her shoulder, "while your group goes in that direction. Whoever discovers something first will contact the other group."

"Sounds like a plan," Felicity said.

Keeper's group—Joel, Keeper, Riverhand, and Auravine—walked down the cobblestone road and visited several more establishments, including something that was kind of like a bowling alley (Joel wanted to linger there for a while, but he knew that now was not the time), until they ended up at a restaurant-like place that was filled with a strong, fishy odor.

"I am not familiar with that person," the maître d' said after inspecting the hologram, "but you should talk to the Triplets, at the bar near the end of the road. If anyone knows anything, it would be them."

"Thank you," Keeper said.

They headed to the end of the road. Joel couldn't see anything that looked like a bar, but he did hear faint strains of music coming from somewhere nearby. He scanned the area until he spotted a downward flight of stairs, next to one of the buildings, which seemed to be where the music was originating from.

"I think it might be down there," he told the others.

Sure enough, the stairs led to a venue that reminded Joel of a particularly divey spot in Seattle that his band had played when they were first getting started. He and the others walked right in—apparently, checking IDs to make sure patrons were of a legal drinking age was not a thing here in the Mono Realm—and started glancing around for people that would fit the description of "the Triplets." The place was relatively busy; Joel figured that there were thirty-eight patrons present, most of whom were sitting at tables around a small stage area. The rest were lined up at the bar, absently watching a video monitor showing footage of a blond Mono Realm woman (it seemed sort of like a newscast, but there was no sound, so Joel couldn't tell for sure) while they waited. Standing atop the stage was a male local holding what was probably a microphone, warbling an exceptionally off-key melody into it. Accompanying music blared through several nearby speakers, but there were no live musicians to be seen.

"Is this...karaoke?" Joel asked.

"If by that, you mean singing along to a prerecorded piece of music, then yes," Keeper replied.

The song ended. Loud cheers and applause ensued.

"Either those are his relatives, or your people do not understand what good music really is," Riverhand remarked.

"Neither," Keeper said. "Our citizens are simply starved for music of any sort."

"Why?" Auravine said. "Was it outlawed?"

"No, but it may as well have been. For us, music comes from joy, of which there is not much anymore."

Joel was about to ask exactly how much joy this particular singer needed to put on such a horrid performance when he noticed that the bar was being tended by three female Mono Realmers who bore a strong physical resemblance to each other: they all had bushy orange hair, extra-long antennae, and professional wrestler-size arms.

"I, uh, I think I see them—the Triplets."

"Where?" Keeper asked.

"Behind the bar."

Keeper tilted her head. "Ah, yes, they do have very similar energy signatures."

They got in line. The karaoke singer bludgeoned his way through another tune before he was replaced by someone from one of the tables who, amazingly, managed to sound even worse. Joel felt like plugging his ears with his fingers, but he didn't want to appear rude, so he just started humming the verse melody of "Down the Landvein River" to himself in an effort to drown out the offending noises. Finally, after three more songs, they reached the front.

"What will you have?" one of the Triplets said in a gravelly, English-accented voice.

"A cloudrunner six with extra crystal," Keeper said.

"And you?" the second Triplet said, nodding her head at Joel.

"Um...do you have any soda?"

"Just water for my three companions, please," Keeper intervened.

"Twenty-seven currents," the third Triplet said.

Keeper handed over her payment disc. "May I ask a question?"

"Make it quick," the second Triplet said as she filled a small, clear glass with a jet-black liquid that Joel hoped was Keeper's drink and not this bar's idea of water.

"Do you know this man?" Keeper said, producing the holographic image.

All three bartenders stopped what they were doing and looked.

"He has been in here once or twice, perhaps," the first Triplet said.

"What is his name?" Keeper asked. "Do you know where we can find him?"

"Are you officers of law enforcement?" the second Triplet said. "Show us your credentials."

"Would a law enforcement officer have a device like this?" Keeper replied. "No, we are merely...friends of his."

"Information like that costs currents," the third Triplet said as the first one handed out glasses of water to Joel, Riverhand, and Auravine. "You barely had enough to pay for this round."

"Please," Keeper said, "this is very important. Is there anything else we can do?"

"You could give us that device," the second Triplet said.

"I am sorry, but that is not an option," Keeper said. "What else?"

The Triplets glanced at each other.

"You handle this," the first one said to the third one.

Just then, someone tapped Joel on his shoulder, nearly causing him to spill his water.

"Yo."

Joel turned to see Felicity, along with the rest of her group. "Oh—hey," he said. "You found us."

"Duh, obviously," Felicity said. "We got a tip about this place. Apparently this is, like, the central gossip hole or something."

"Oh—were you at that fish restaurant too?"

"What? No, we ended up at this...er...I don't even wanna talk about it."

"She wants us to follow her," Keeper said. The third Triplet had moved out from behind the bar counter over to a nearby door.

"Why?" Thornleaf asked, sounding suspicious.

"I am not sure. Apparently, this is the only chance we have to learn more about the administrator."

The Triplet grabbed the door handle, which was shaped like a giant lizard, and pulled the door open. "Do you want your information or not?" she snapped.

"Yeah, I don't like the looks of this," Felicity muttered.

"Just stay alert," Thornleaf grunted.

"You know, I'm glad you said that, 'cause I was planning on sleepwalking," Felicity quipped.

They went through the doorway and into a long, dimly lit hall.

"What will we need to do?" Keeper asked as they walked.

"You will see," the Triplet responded.

After several turns, the hall led to a flight of stairs that ended in a landing on the ground level of the building next to another door. The Triplet inserted a disc into a slot in the door, which then opened inward. Beeping and humming sounds could be heard.

"This is our other business," the Triplet said, leading everyone into a large room filled with strange machines of various shapes and sizes. A few locals were either standing in front of or sitting in some of the machines. Flashing lights were everywhere.

Whoa, Joel thought, taking in his surroundings. *This looks like...a video game arcade!*

"Those over there pay out in currents if you win," the Triplet said, pointing at a row of machines along the far wall. "Win one hundred currents, and I will tell you where you can find your friend."

"How much is it to play?" Keeper asked.

"One current per attempt."

"But...I only have five currents left."

"I know. Good luck." With that, the Triplet turned and headed toward what looked like an enclosed office nearby.

Joel inspected the machines. They were all the same: each of their monitors displayed a ten-by-ten grid, and within every little square there was a character of the Mono Realm's written language. The control panel consisted of just a single round red button.

"I am afraid we may be out of luck," Keeper said. "I am no good at these kinds of games."

"Well, fortunately for us," Felicity said, grinning, "we have a ringer in our little group."

"We do?" Joel asked. "Who?"

"You're kidding, right?"

"Yeah."

Felicity chuckled. "Nice one."

Joel walked up to one of the game machines, and everyone fell in around him. "Okay, so how do you play this?"

"I thought she said you were a ringer." Keeper frowned.

"Well, um...I'm pretty good at games, in general. I just need to know the details."

"Each of these characters is a number," Keeper explained. "Most of them are zeroes. Some are ones, a few are tens, and this one here"—she pointed at a square near the middle of the grid—"is one hundred. The squares will light up randomly, one at a time. You have to try to press the button when a square with something greater than zero lights up. If you do, you win that number of currents."

Joel nodded. "Sounds simple enough."

Keeper inserted her current disc into the machine. A little electronic fanfare sounded, and the squares began to light up. At first, they started slowly, with each square lighting up for nearly two seconds at a time, but, as one might expect, the only ones to do so were the "zero" squares.

Okay, I see how this is gonna go, Joel thought. *They'll start flashing faster and faster, and then after a while they'll start lighting up the "ones," and then the "tens," and then finally the "one hundred." So I'll just wait for a little bit until—*

The "one hundred" square lit up. Surprised, Joel slapped the red button like he was trying to beat the buzzer on a TV game show. Unfortunately, it was too late; the game had already moved on to another "zero" square, and a set of words scrolled across the screen.

"That means 'game over,'" Keeper said.

"Dangit," Joel said. "I wasn't expecting that. I'll try again."

"I only have four more currents, you know."

"Wait," Felicity said, "you mean to tell us you're almost broke?"

"I am afraid so. Transporting eight people all the way over here was not cheap."

"Then how were you planning on getting back home?"

Keeper paused before replying. "To be honest, the administrator had offered a five-hundred-current reward for any tangible evidence of the rainbow folk's existence. I figured that delivering you to him in person might be even more lucrative."

"Oh, so this wasn't about being a hero, it was all about the money."

"I am still helping you apprehend these fugitives, am I not?" Keeper said, sounding defensive.

"Um, I'll get it this time," Joel said, wanting to stave off an argument.

Grumbling under her breath, Keeper reinserted her payment disc. The game started up once more.

All right, just stay patient, Joel told himself. *Focus...concentrate...and...there!* He hit the button. Just missed.

"Are you sure you can do this?" Keeper asked.

"Don't ask him stuff like that," Felicity said. "You have to be positive and encouraging. Like, 'c'mon, Joel, you can do this.'"

Keeper sighed and inserted her current disc again. Joel waited a little longer this time, trying to see if there was any rhyme or reason to the order in which the squares lit up. Keeper was right, however; it was totally random, with no discernable pattern to it at all. He took a shot. Another near miss.

"I think this machine might be rigged," he said. "Or it's on a super hard setting or something."

"You're using the Sight, right?" Felicity asked.

"Well, I dunno if that would work, necessarily. I mean, the Sight's more for spotting tiny details, not anticipating timing stuff like this, and—"

"Just try it."

"Okay."

Joel engaged the Sight. Unfortunately, it had the effect of showing him the last game that he played on top of the one he was playing now, so he ended up missing badly.

"I only have one current left," Keeper reminded Joel unnecessarily. "You might want to try for the ten instead."

"No, no, I got it."

Okay, Suzuki, relax. You can do this. You can do this.

"You can do this, Joel," Auravine said, echoing his thoughts.

Joel took a deep breath. He stared at the screen as the squares took turns lighting up. Blocking out all other external stimuli, he let it continue for what felt like a very long time and, as he expected earlier, they started to flash at a much faster rate, with the "one hundred" square lighting up at more frequent intervals. He focused his gaze on it, ready to pounce.

You can do this.

The "one hundred" square lit up.

Now!

He pressed the button, feeling triumphant.

And there it is…wait, what?

The same words as before scrolled across the screen: *game over.*

CHAPTER 13: THINKER OF DEEP THOUGHTS

Joel stared at the game in disbelief.

What the...how did I miss it?

"So...you were unsuccessful?" Windblade said, sounding amazed.

"He was," Keeper sighed.

"Now what are we going to do?" Redstem said.

"We could keep asking around," Auravine suggested.

"I told you before," Thornleaf said, wagging a finger at her, "you are not here for your ideas. You are here for one purpose and one purpose only: to heal someone if they are injured."

"But I—"

"*And no protests.* Understood?"

Joel glanced at Auravine. Her mouth was twisted into a grimace. For a moment, he thought that she was going to explode with anger, but instead she simply said, after a lengthy pause: "Understood."

"But what other alternatives do we have?" Riverhand said.

Thornleaf took out his wavebow, like a mafioso pulling a tommy gun out of his trench coat. "We will try a more direct approach."

"No! What are you doing?" Keeper hissed. "If anyone sees you—"

"Okay, okay, everybody relax," Felicity said, pushing Thornleaf's wavebow back under his cloak. "I'll take care of this." She turned and headed for the enclosed office.

"What are you going to do?" Keeper asked as everyone followed.

"You'll see."

Felicity knocked on the door. A moment later, a panel in the door slid open like an automatic car window, revealing the face of the third Triplet.

"Yes?"

"Hey," Felicity said, "we didn't win your little game over there, but we do have a deal for you."

"Oh? What kind of deal?"

"If you tell us how to find this guy, we'll come back later and pay you double. Two hundred currents."

The Triplet scratched her orange hair. "Hmm..."

"C'mon, whaddya say?"

"How do I know that you will come back with the money?"

"How do we know you're giving us accurate info?"

The Triplet chuckled. "Fair enough...but I want triple. Three hundred currents. Plus collateral."

"Two-twenty-five."

"Two-fifty."

"All right, done."

"I will still need some collateral, though."

"Yeah, yeah, hold on," Felicity said, rummaging through her supply pack. "How about...this?" She held up a lifepod. "Rare, exotic fruit. I'll bet you've never seen anything like it before."

"Ha," the Triplet scoffed. "Nice try. I am sure that is something you can afford to part with. What about your identification discs?"

"We don't have 'em."

"They will be applying for replacements in the morning," Keeper added.

"Come back then," the Triplet said. The door window-panel started to slide shut.

"Wait," Felicity said. "There must be something else we can use."

"Hmm," the Triplet mused as the window-panel slid open again. Her tone suggested that she would be narrowing her eyes, if only she were physically capable of doing so. "Actually, there might be," she finally said. "I noticed something in your pack...something small, but with a very strong energy signature. What is it?"

"Oh, it's a...a piece of jewelry. Yeah, pretty valuable."

The Triplet's antennae twitched furiously. "I will accept that, if you are willing to offer it."

"Okay, sure."

♪♪♪

The party exited the arcade through the front door and headed down the street, following the directions that the Triplet had given them.

"So, you traded your loudstone for the information?" Redstem asked Felicity, incredulous. In Spectraland, concepts like money and collateral were foreign, as their culture ran on a basic barter system economy.

"No, no, she's just gonna hold it for now. We'll get it back later," Felicity reassured her fellow Wavemaker. She turned to Keeper. "You're sure this guy is gonna give us the currents, right?"

"That was his offer." Keeper shrugged. "But now, after your deal, I will end up with only half of the original amount."

"Hey, half of something is better than all of nothing."

"I suppose."

Felicity explained the details of the bargain she had just struck to the other shamans as they walked through the city. Joel remained quiet, feeling upset and guilty that she'd had to make that deal in the first place—if only he had been able to win that game! He knew that he shouldn't beat himself up for it, but repressing those feelings wasn't an easy thing to do, especially when it involved the risk of possibly losing a loudstone.

After about twenty-seven minutes, they reached a fenced-off area near the city limits that was filled with large square bins and piles of what looked like scrap metal.

"He lives in the junkyard." Felicity snorted. "Classic."

They entered through one of many holes in the fence and made their way through the yard, carefully stepping over and around metal fragments, glass shards, and other assorted pieces of debris. They searched around for about five minutes before it started to rain, causing the ground to turn muddy.

"So, where is he?" Redstem asked.

"She did not say, specifically," Keeper replied.

"Um...why don't we try a tracking cast?" Joel suggested, his first words since they left the arcade.

"That would only be effective if we had had prior contact with who we are looking for," Riverhand said.

"Oh—I didn't know that."

"Keep your voices down," Thornleaf said, not following his own instruction. "We do not want to frighten the—"

There was a sound like an eagle's screech, and the tall shaman fell, face-first, to the ground.

"Thornleaf!" Redstem cried.

The sound rang out again.

"We are being shot at!" Keeper shouted, ducking behind a nearby bin.

Joel whirled around, looking for shelter. As he did so, he caught a fleeting glimpse of a small red light within a makeshift shed-like structure some thirty-nine yards away.

"He is hurt!" Redstem yelled, crouching over Thornleaf's prone figure. "Auravine!"

"Coming!"

Everyone else, including Joel, took up defensive positions behind various bins and piles. As Auravine knelt down next to Thornleaf, Redstem played a short note on her wavebow; instead of the expected shield of Aura energy, however, only a faint cloud of yellow sparks emerged from her instrument's headstock.

"Something is wrong!" she exclaimed, a shocked look on her face.

Another shot was fired. Fortunately, it didn't seem to hit anyone.

"Someone," Redstem said, "help me get Thornleaf to cover!"

Joel was about to jump up, but Felicity beat him to it. She and Redstem dragged Thornleaf behind a nearby stack of debris. Auravine followed them, playing her wavebow along the way, but she appeared to be encountering the same lack of success as her fellow shaman.

"It must be the administrator," Keeper said as another shot rang out. "He probably thinks we are government officials."

"If we show him that we are—what did you call us?—rainbow folk," Windblade said, "would he stop attacking?"

Keeper nodded. "Perhaps."

"Can we use the rainwater to wash off the salve?" Riverhand asked.

"No," Keeper replied. "The salve is waterproof. I—I do have a freecloth, however." She pulled what looked like a small white handkerchief out of a pocket in her garment.

"Are you gonna wave that, like, to surrender?" Joel asked.

"What? No, this is a piece of fabric that can wipe off the soulshifter. At least, I think it can—I have never actually used it before."

"I'm, uh, I'm not sure we want to do that anyway, though—he's kind of far away," Joel said. "He might not see us and just keep shooting."

"You know where he is?" Keeper said, sounding surprised.

"I think so. I saw a red light over that way." Joel pointed over his shoulder. "It was inside this thing that looked sort of like a shed."

"How far?"

"Like, thirty-nine yards, give or take a few inches."

Keeper peeked out from behind her trash bin. After another shot was fired, she aimed her countercom in the direction that Joel had indicated and pressed a few buttons.

"That should do it," she said. "I hope."

"What did you do?" Joel asked.

"The same thing I did to all of you—put him under energy lock. Since I cannot see him, I am unable to force him out here, but he should stop shooting at us at the very least. We should just wait a few minutes to be sure."

"How is Thornleaf?" Riverhand called out.

"Not good!" Redstem replied. "He is critically injured, and our wavebows are not working properly!"

Joel set his jaw and got to his feet.

"What are you doing?" Keeper said. "It is not safe yet!"

"We don't have a few minutes," Joel responded. "That administrator guy must have something that's interfering with our wavecasts. We need to get him to turn it off, so Auravine can save Thornleaf."

"But—"

Joel knew that he was risking his life, but he was determined to make up for his failure at the arcade. He stepped out from behind his hiding spot and raised his arms, offering himself up as a target.

"Dude!" Felicity exclaimed.

Joel looked at the shed. The red light was still there. He held his breath and braced himself for the worst. Eight nerve-racking seconds ticked by, and no shots were fired.

"Okay, I think we're good," he said, exhaling. "Let's go."

Joel started for the shed, and everyone else followed. As they approached, Thornleaf coughed a couple of times.

"What is...what is wrong with your healing, Auravine?" the tall shaman rasped as Felicity and Redstem carried him along, his arms draped around their shoulders. "You should have more than enough energy in your loudstone!"

"I—I do not know," Auravine replied.

"You cannot even perform the one task that—*cough*—made us bring you here! You are worthless!"

"Thornleaf, please," Redstem said, "I could not perform any wavecasts either. Now stop talking."

"That was very brave of you, what you just did," Windblade said to Joel.

"Oh—uh, thanks."

"Or foolish," Keeper said, shaking her head.

They arrived in front of the shed, which was made up mostly of metal panels leaning against one another, like a giant house of cards.

"Stay back!" a shrill, frantic male voice with a vaguely Scottish accent shouted from inside the shed. "I will not warn you again!"

Joel peered through one of the gaps between the panels. Amidst a surprisingly well-organized interior—it was neater than Blackspore's hut, at least—stood a Mono Realmer who looked almost exactly like the hologram image of the administrator, tin foil suit and all. He was carrying a rifle-like firearm that was aimed at one of the other gaps.

"Um, hello," Joel said with a little wave.

"I know nothing, I tell you!" the Mono Realmer snapped. His head was turned toward Joel, but his body was facing to the side—more evidence that Keeper's device had done its job.

"We are not with the government," Keeper said, moving up next to Joel.

"Then who are you? Why are you here?"

Keeper beckoned Windblade, the Spectraland native closest to her, to come forward. "Hold still for a moment." She took out her freecloth and wiped his forehead and cheeks with it. At first, the salve refused to go away, but after a few more seconds (and a bit of elbow grease), it finally started to come off.

"Very interesting," Keeper said under her breath. "It really does work."

Once the last of the salve was gone, Windblade blinked rapidly, as if he had just been broken out of a trance. "Well, that certainly is a relief," he said. "That substance was beginning to give me an awful headache."

The administrator's jaw dropped. "My word," he breathed. "Are you from...?"

"The Land under the Rainbow," Keeper said. "Yes, he is. And he has others with him as well. May we come in?"

"Well, uh, yes, certainly," the administrator stammered. "The door is right over there." He motioned with his head.

Cautiously, Joel slid aside one of the panels, which seemed to be the closest thing to a door, hoping the whole structure wouldn't come falling down as he did so. Fortunately, it didn't, and everyone went inside. Felicity and Redstem laid Thornleaf down on a spread of tattered cushions next to a desk covered with sophisticated technological equipment that looked highly out of place in a junkyard like this.

"Oh—your friend...I fear his life energy is rapidly fading," the administrator said, looking over at them. "I apologize—those were just supposed to be warning shots."

"Yeah, uh, so," Joel said, "can you turn it off now?"

"Are you talking to me?" the administrator said.

"Yes."

"Turn what off?"

"Whatever you have that's keeping us from wavecasting."

"I have no idea what you are talking about."

"Wavecasting? It's, like, we play music on these instruments, and then the sound waves combine with our brain waves to create—"

"No, no, I know what you people can do. I meant, I do not have anything that would be interfering with your abilities. At least, not that I know of."

"You don't?" Felicity said. "Then where's the nearest hospital?"

"I am afraid you will not make it in time," the administrator replied. "Again, I am truly sorry, but there is nothing that can be done for your companion. Is he from the rainbow land as well?"

"Wait," Joel said as a puzzle piece fell into place in his mind. "Hey—uh, Windblade?"

"Yes?"

"Can you try playing a wavecast? Something simple, like, um, a light cast."

Windblade took out his wavebow and plucked a note. The instrument's headstock instantly lit up with a bright white glow.

"It's the soulshifter," Joel declared. "It's affecting our brain waves." He turned to Keeper. "Quick—wipe it off of Auravine."

Using her freecloth, Keeper removed the soulshifter salve from Auravine's face. The young healer blinked and winced, as if someone had just stuck her with a needle.

"Try it now," Joel said.

Auravine proceeded to play a progression of lush, complex chords on her instrument. After a few moments, a shimmering golden blanket of Aura energy appeared over Thornleaf's body.

"Is it working?" the administrator asked.

"Better hope so," Felicity said. "Now shut up—she's concentrating."

A full forty-five seconds went by as Auravine continued to play. Joel started to feel nervous. In his experience, healing casts usually didn't take this long unless the problem was quite serious. Finally, after another thirty-two seconds, Auravine stopped playing and the energy blanket faded away.

"Were you successful?" Redstem asked.

"I believe so," Auravine said in between gasps. "Thornleaf? How...how do you feel?"

The tall shaman's eyes remained closed, and he didn't appear to be breathing.

"Thornleaf?" Redstem said.

Felicity placed two fingers on Thornleaf's neck. "Well, he still has a—"

Thornleaf abruptly grabbed Felicity's wrist—like in those movies where the supposedly dead person is still alive—and she let out a little yelp.

"I am fine," he said, his eyes still closed.

"Jerk." Felicity chuckled.

"That was amazing!" the administrator marveled. "Then again, I suppose that I should not be surprised by anything that your people can do. Wavemakers, you are called, correct? I cannot tell you how pleased I am to finally meet some of you in the flesh!"

"Which raises the question," Riverhand said, "of how you know so much about us in the first place."

"Well, I have been studying your land from afar for years now! Ever since that fateful day when we first made contact."

"First made contact?" Windblade echoed. "With who?"

"Why, Master Blackspore, of course. Is he not here with you?"

"Oh," Joel said. "So you're the one Blackspore talked to when he was looking for someone to help him."

"Indeed. I was rather disappointed when he decided to move on, I must say. Back in my prime, I would have been quite an asset to his war effort. Anyway, after our meeting, all I wanted to do was learn more about this incredible island of yours, where music is magic and...and how did that whole war business turn out, anyway?"

"Master Blackspore found someone else to help him," Windblade answered. "An offworlder named Marshall Byle. He helped Master Blackspore's village win the war, but then he turned around and killed off all the remaining Wavemakers before taking over Spectraland completely."

"Oh...I see. That sounds rather unfortunate."

Joel glanced over at Felicity, expecting her to say something along the lines of "yeah, just a little," but she was too busy tending to Thornleaf.

"Fortunately," Windblade continued, "two other offworlders, Joel and Felicity"—he nodded in their direction—"along with our leader, Fireflower, were able to vanquish Byle and restore the island's Aura after he had attempted to steal it."

"Ah, yes, I do recall observing a momentary reduction in your surrounding rainbow."

"But now," Riverhand said, "Byle has returned. And he is here, in your land, along with three of his cohorts."

"Oh, so *that* is who has been spotted! How very interesting..."

"Um, yeah, and we're here to catch them," Joel said. "So we need your help."

"In what way?"

"In one of your last posts before the bulletin system was shut down, you said that you knew where they would have gone," Keeper replied. "But you did not give any specifics."

The administrator chuckled. "Ah, yes, well, I did not want to reveal that kind of information in a public forum, you understand."

"Well, since we are now in a *private* forum," Keeper said, "you can tell us."

"Perhaps you could release me from your energy lock first?"

Keeper took the firearm out of the administrator's hands and set it on the ground before she pressed a couple of buttons on her device.

"Ah, much better," the administrator sighed, stretching his arms. "Now, since we got off on the wrong foot, how about we start over in a more proper fashion and begin with some introductions? I am known as Thinker of Deep Thoughts."

Everyone introduced themselves briefly, with Felicity adding a request (or demand, depending on how you interpreted her tone) that she be allowed to call Thinker of Deep Thoughts, simply, Thinker.

"All right," Thinker said, "now, I can tell you that the ones you are looking for have been taken to a secret government facility where I was once employed. There they will be examined, and possibly experimented on."

"Oh—kinda like Area 51," Joel said.

"Or Project Cadmus," Felicity said.

"Your translation magic is so wonderful that I almost got the basic gist of what the two of you just said!" Thinker grinned. Joel wasn't sure if he was being sarcastic or not.

"Where is this facility?" Keeper asked.

"Within the confines of Outpost Eight."

"I have heard of that place." Keeper nodded. "That is the most secure government base outside of Sector One, is it not?"

"Indeed it is. Now, I can take all of you there, but I just have one request."

"Hold on," Keeper said, "I am not going with you. I told these rainbow folk that once I collected the reward for introducing you to them, I would be returning home. I have no desire to get entangled in this situation any further."

"Reward?"

"Yes—the five-hundred-current reward you offered for tangible evidence of the rainbow folk's existence."

"Oh, ah, well, about that...you see, that is an old offer. I am afraid I no longer have that much money."

"How much *do* you have?" Keeper demanded, aghast.

"Perhaps...twenty currents?" Thinker replied with a sheepish tilt of his head.

Felicity clicked her tongue. "I should've known this was gonna happen," she muttered.

CHAPTER 14: FIRELIGHT HIGHWAY

Though Thinker didn't have much money, he did have an old, beat-up vehicle that he had been planning to sell. The currents that he could have gotten for it wouldn't have been enough for the whole party to take the public transit system all the way to Outpost Eight, so it was decided that they would, instead, use it as their primary means of transportation. Keeper's reward and Felicity's loudstone would just have to wait.

"So, getting back to my request," Thinker said as he dug out the vehicle, which was hidden under piles of junk, where it was very well camouflaged, "after I help you catch your fugitives, I would like to ask if you could take me back with you as well."

"Back to Spectraland?" Riverhand said.

"Yes. There is nothing for me here anymore. You see, after I met Master Blackspore, the government relieved me of my duties and destroyed my reputation. They said I was mad. No one would employ me. My spouse left, taking our children with her. I lost my home, my friends, my family...everything. Now I am a wanted criminal, simply for spreading the word about your existence. But on your island, I could begin a new life."

"You see, this is why I did not want to get involved," Keeper grumbled to no one in particular.

"What do you think, Thornleaf?" Windblade said.

"That is an acceptable request." The tall shaman, fully back to strength, nodded. "He may be able to teach us some things about his technology."

"Yes, yes, of course!" Thinker exclaimed. "We could learn so much from each other. Oh, I am so excited."

Thinker finished uncovering his vehicle. It had an open top, a pair of rocket-booster-like appendages, and some kind of antigravity feature that allowed it to hover a couple of feet off the ground. The interior had only two rows of three seats each, which meant that they would have to squeeze in together; fortunately, all of the Spectraland natives besides Thornleaf were of smaller stature than the average Mono Realm citizen.

"This was our family vehicle," Thinker said with a wistful sigh.

"You can drop me off at home first," Keeper said. "Send me my share of the reward later, after you sell off all your possessions. Do not go back with them until you do, understand?"

"Oh...I cannot do that, I am afraid."

"What? But I fulfilled the conditions of your offer! Exceeded them, even!"

"No, no, not the reward—taking you home. I only have enough fuel to make it to Outpost Eight, or maybe just a little further."

"Then how were you planning on..."

Thinker turned to the assembled Wavemakers. "I was hoping my new friends would be able to carry me along with them in the sky." He smiled. "Perhaps they can carry you as well."

"We can do that," Thornleaf agreed. "After we capture the fugitives, it will not matter if we are seen anyway."

"My thoughts exactly," Thinker said.

"But then *I* will be seen with you!" Keeper protested.

"Oh, I have several different varieties of soulshifter salve that you can use," Thinker reassured his fellow Mono Realmer. "How do you think I have been managing to get around these past few years?"

Keeper groaned. "It is as if the forces are conspiring against me."

"Hey, it's called destiny, hon." Felicity smirked, placing a hand on Keeper's shoulder. "I know how you feel—I got swept up in it too. Just go with it."

Muttering to herself, Keeper reapplied some soulshifter salve to Windblade and Auravine's faces. Then they piled into the vehicle, breaking up into the same groups that they used in the city: Thornleaf, Felicity, Redstem, and Windblade sat in the back, while Keeper, Joel, Auravine, and Riverhand crammed into the front row alongside Thinker.

"How long will it take to get to this facility?" Thornleaf asked.

"About three hours," Thinker replied, starting up the vehicle. It sounded similar to a computer's optical drive after you inserted a disc into it, only louder.

"Like going from Seattle to Portland down the I-5," Felicity remarked. "Well, in that case, I'm gonna take a nap. Wake me up when we get there." She folded her arms and closed her eyes.

"That is a good idea," Redstem said. "We should all take this opportunity to recharge our energies."

Thinker pushed a few buttons on the vehicle's dash-board and then steered it through the junkyard at about five miles per hour, weaving around piles of debris along the way. Feeling completely exhausted at this point, Joel considered taking a nap as well, but he really didn't want to experience another occurrence of the red-smoke vision that he had back on Blackspore's atoll.

"Hey, uh, Keeper," he said. "If I fall asleep, can you wake me up?"

"Yes," she replied, still sounding a little grouchy.

"Why do you want to stay awake?" Auravine asked.

"Oh, uh...you know, I just want to see as much of the Mono Realm as I can while I'm here." It wasn't a com-plete falsehood; he really did want to take in the alien landscape, as the public transit system hadn't quite af-forded him that opportunity. "I can do an antifatigue cast later or something."

"Are you sure that is a good idea?" Riverhand said. "As you know, an antifatigue cast is a poor substitute for actual rest."

"I'll be fine," Joel replied.

Exiting the junkyard, Thinker sped the vehicle up to about twenty-two miles an hour. He drove it along some of the city's side streets until they reached an upward-sloping ramp leading away from the city and toward a set of roadways that resembled intersecting roller coasters.

"Really, you are taking the Firelight Highway?" Keeper scoffed. "In this thing?"

"Of course," Thinker replied with what sounded like mock offense. "I used to drive it on the highway all the time."

Keeper shook her head. "If you say so." She tied her neon-green mane into a ponytail and tucked it under her collar.

"Well, here we go," Thinker said, flipping a switch on the dashboard.

Suddenly, Joel felt very heavy, as if some invisible force was pressing down on him. "Whoa," he said, "what is that?" He glanced around at his fellow shamans to gauge their reactions; all of them were already sound asleep.

"What is what?" Thinker asked.

"That...I dunno, like, um," Joel stammered, struggling to find the right words to describe the sensation. He made a downward pushing motion with his hands.

"Oh—that is the vehicle's safety restraint feature," Thinker said.

"What? You mean...like a seat belt?"

Thinker tilted his head. "I am not quite sure what you just said, but if you are referring to something that prevents you from falling out of the vehicle, then yes."

Before Joel could ask any more questions, Thinker flipped another switch and the vehicle took off, accelerating to nearly ninety miles an hour in less than a second. As it rocketed up the ramp, Joel's immediate instinct was to grab ahold of something, but since there was nothing to grab, he just clenched his fists and squeezed his eyes shut.

"Not bad for an old bucket of bolts," Keeper said impassively, her voice somehow cutting through the din of the whooshing air.

"I am glad you think so," Thinker replied.

Joel kept his eyes closed as the vehicle made a couple of sharp turns. It was actually a rather smooth ride, not like the herky-jerky sensations of a roller coaster, but he was still unnerved by the whole process of riding in an open vehicle without any seat belts or safety bars—especially one that was going this fast.

"Are you all right, there?" Thinker asked.

Joel wasn't sure if the old Mono Realmer was talking to him, but he decided to answer anyway. "Um, sure."

"This is all perfectly safe, I assure you," Keeper said. "If you could handle the public transit tubes, then this is nothing."

Emboldened by her words, Joel decided to open his eyes. He did so just in time to see that the vehicle was about to go into a loop-the-loop that curled around a couple of dividing straightaways. Evidently, Mono Realmers didn't believe in boring methods of travel. He closed his eyes again.

"The gravitational pull between the vehicle and the rail ensures that we stay on track," Thinker casually explained as they flipped over. "And, as I mentioned before, the vehicle's safety restraint feature—another form of gravitational pull—keeps you securely in your seat at all times."

He continued talking, but Joel tuned him out, choosing instead to focus on a random list in an effort to calm down.

Phineas and Ferb *season two episode titles: "The Lake Nose Monster," "Interview with a Platypus," "Tip of the Day," "Attack of the 50-Foot Sister," "Backyard Aquarium," "Day of the Living Gelatin," "Elementary My Dear Stacy"...*

Feeling a bit more settled, Joel opened his eyes once again. This time, instead of another terrifying twist in the highway's path, he saw a huge crowd of Mono Realmers—five hundred and twenty-three of them, to be exact—gathered together at the base of a tower that resembled a cross between a medieval castle and a modern skyscraper. The highway itself had disappeared, along with the vehicle and all of Joel's companions; he was floating in the air about fifty yards away from the scene, surrounded by white mist.

Hmm, he thought after a brief moment of adjustment. *I must've fallen asleep, and now I'm having another vision. Well, at least it's not the one with the red smoke. Guess I'll go take a closer look.*

He pushed himself forward. As he did so, a hooded figure emerged from an opening near the top of the tower. It paused and waved before it walked out onto a small landing platform that jutted out from the side of the structure.

Wait a minute. Is that...Marshall?

The figure threw back its hood. "Greetings, citizens of the Mono Realm!" it said in an amplified voice, raising its arms theatrically. At the same time, large holographic versions of the figure appeared in the air all around the tower, like a horrible set of Bat-Signals.

Yup, that's him, all right.

"I would like to thank all of you, my loyal subjects, for coming out here today," Marshall continued.

Loyal subjects? What is he talking about?

"As you know, I have a very important announcement to make. One that will change the course of history in this great land forever."

Whoa. I need to hear this. If I'm seeing a vision of the future, then this could be information that I'll really need later on.

"Starting tomorrow, you will all—"

At that moment, something stung Joel on his arm. He flinched, and then, abruptly, the mist and the tower were replaced by his previous surroundings in Thinkers' speeding vehicle, as if someone had changed the channel on a TV.

"What the—"

"You wanted me to wake you up if you fell asleep," Keeper said, holding her countercom. "You were not responding to your name, so I gave you a little energy shock."

"Oh—uh, thanks," Joel said, rubbing his arm.

"You seem troubled. Rest assured, that shock was completely harmless."

"No, no, it's not that, it's...I was having this, um, this dream. A pretty important one."

"A dream can be important?"

"In my case, yeah." Joel went on to explain about how he had the ability, in this world, to see visions of the future, and that he had seen Marshall as the ruler of the Mono Realm.

"Is this ability of yours always accurate?" Keeper asked, sounding skeptical.

"Well, mostly. I mean, it's usually kind of vague, and sometimes it can be messed with, but—"

"Then I think someone is messing with it, as you say." Keeper chuckled. "Believe me, the Uniter would never allow someone to usurp his position. Especially not a fugitive stranger from the rainbow land. No offense."

"But...what if he didn't have a choice?" Joel asked, unsure as to why Keeper thought she had said something offensive. "Marshall could've done a...what was the word? Oh yeah, um, a coup. You know, like, overthrow him."

"That seems highly unlikely to me," Thinker said. "At the Outpost Eight facility, your fugitive and his companions will be under heavy guard at all times."

"You guys don't know Marshall, though. He's pretty tricky."

"And you do not know the Uniter," Keeper retorted. "He may be despicable, but he is also very astute. He would not be in his current position otherwise."

The vehicle zipped around the first of what looked to be a dizzying series of hairpin corners. Joel decided to drop the subject and go back to sleep, hoping that the vision would pick up where it left off. "I, uh, I'm just gonna rest for a bit," he said. "You don't have to wake me up this time." He closed his eyes.

The next thing he knew, he was still in the vehicle, coasting along on a seemingly endless stretch of straight track that had been built high up off the ground, surrounded by huge mountain ranges on all sides. There was something—someone's head—leaning on his shoulder. He looked to the right, keeping his body completely motionless. It was Auravine, fast asleep. Butterflies erupted in his stomach.

Is this...is this a vision?

He looked to the left. Keeper and Thinker had both apparently dozed off as well. Even though Joel wasn't sure if this vehicle had an autopilot function, Thinker's neglect of the road was, for some reason, much less frightening than what was happening on his right side.

"Hey, uh...Auravine?" Joel whispered.

She stirred but did not wake.

"Auravine?" he tried again, a little louder, wiggling his shoulder just a bit.

"Mmm...what?" Auravine said drowsily, her eyes fluttering open. "Oh—I am sorry, Joel." She lifted her head off his shoulder, although it didn't seem like she was in any real hurry to do so.

"No, uh, no problem."

"Are you all right? You seem a bit flustered."

"I was...I was just wondering if this was a vision. Or not."

"You mean, the events that are happening right now?"

"Yeah."

"If it is, then we must be having the same vision." She smiled. "Then again, I do not believe I have developed the precognitive ability yet, so this must be reality."

"Um, okay."

"Thinker looks to be asleep. Is that something we should be concerned about?"

"I don't think so," Joel replied, pulling himself together. "It seems like this vehicle can drive itself. On straight roads, anyway."

"Ah, like a slimeback."

"Sort of."

"Oh—look at that." She pointed to an approaching area down below that was filled with tiny twinkling lights.

"Must be another Mono Realm city," Joel noted.

"It is like the stars fell from the sky and made a home in this valley," Auravine said. "This is truly an amazing place. Master Blackspore was right when he said that it is actually quite beautiful."

Isn't this the time when another guy would say something like "but not as beautiful as you?" Joel wondered. *I dunno, though, that sounds kinda cheesy, and I really don't understand how you can compare a place with a person anyway...is there another way to put it? Eh, forget it.* "You could move here," he suggested out loud.

"What?"

"You know, so you don't have to go back to jail and stuff."

"Oh, no...I could not do that."

Joel glanced over his shoulder. Everyone in the back seat was still asleep. Redstem was even snoring a little. And...Thornleaf and Felicity were *holding hands.* "Then, uh, I know," he said, whirling back around, "you can move to Earth. With me. It's pretty similar to the Mono Realm."

Auravine smiled. "That is nice of you to offer, but I cannot do that either."

"Why not? We'll just have Fireflower do a minor shapeshift cast on you, so you can blend in, and no one will—"

She placed a hand on his arm. "I must serve out my sentence, Joel. If I did not return to Spectraland, I would be a fugitive—no better than Marshall or Darkeye. I accept that what I did was wrong, and I accept my punishment. I appreciate your concern for my welfare, but that is what I have to do. You understand, do you not?"

"Well, yeah, but, I dunno, I just feel like there should be some way for you to redeem yourself, you know? Like, how you helped us beat Marshall in the end, and now you're helping us catch him...that should count for something. Maybe the chiefs could grant you parole, or whatever, after, say, six months. Or five. Four-and-a-half."

"That is a very kind thought, but I am not so sure the rest of the island's villagers would be quite as forgiving. It is strange to consider this, but the Pit of Ashes might actually be the safest place for me."

"Hmm. That's what Chief Silverfern said."

"A wise woman."

They sat in silence for a minute as the vehicle continued to speed along. Joel's heart and mind both raced as he tried to think of something else to say. Before he could come up with anything, however, Auravine spoke again.

"It appears that your fellow offworlder and Thornleaf have taken a liking to each other," she noted.

Not really what I wanted to talk about, but whatever, Joel thought. "Yeah, I guess," he said.

"They seem well-suited. Thornleaf and I have never really gotten along. He has always been rather..."

"Jerkish?"

Auravine chuckled. "If I understand what you are saying correctly, then yes, I suppose that is an apt description. Felicity seems not to mind, however. It is almost as if she enjoys it. And given the way that she herself speaks...I believe it makes them a good match."

"What do you mean?" Joel said, a bit more defensively than he had intended.

"Well, like you said to me once before, she can be quite intimidating. To be honest, it bothers me somewhat when I hear the way she speaks to you sometimes."

"Oh...um, I'm kinda used to it now, actually."

"Even so, I think you might be happier if you found a companion whose nature was more in tune with yours—someone sensitive, reserved, and thoughtful. Do you agree?"

Joel gulped. Did he? "Um, sure. Maybe. I dunno."

"Just something to consider." She leaned over and kissed him lightly on the cheek. "In the meantime, you should get some rest."

"Yes. Rest. Okay."

Auravine returned her head to Joel's shoulder. He remained wide awake, barely blinking, until they arrived at their destination.

CHAPTER 15: OUTPOST EIGHT

Thinker parked the vehicle at the top of a ridge overlooking Outpost Eight. The outpost itself was nothing like its namesakes from the *Star Wars* and *Star Trek* universes; instead, it resembled a typical remote military installation back on Earth. Set in the middle of a dry, dusty plain and surrounded by a tall chain-link fence, it consisted of a dozen different nondescript buildings spread out over an area nearly two miles square. One of the buildings, located near the far end of the outpost, resembled a giant airplane hangar, or possibly an enclosed sports stadium. That building was, according to Thinker, where Marshall and his cronies were being held.

"So, what are we gonna do," Felicity said around a yawn, "just walk in the front door and say 'hi, we're here for your aliens'?"

"I thought that was basically the plan," Redstem said.

"Yes," Thornleaf agreed. "Stealth should no longer be an issue. We can just remove this salve now and charge in with our wavebows."

"It is not quite that simple," Thinker said as he rummaged through the vehicle's equivalent of a glove compartment. "This facility is connected to a private set of transport tubes. If the authorities are alerted to our presence, they may very well move your fugitives to another, unknown location."

"Of course," Felicity muttered, rubbing her eyes.

"Also, this outpost is home to hundreds of troops," Thinker went on. "Even with my rifle, Keeper of the Light's countercoms, and your instruments, we would still be hopelessly outnumbered. You would be captured and experimented on, right along with the ones you are hoping to find."

"What if we tell the Chieftain Council that Byle and the others are safely in custody, here in the Mono Realm?" Windblade suggested.

"That is a good idea," Riverhand concurred. "If they are under such heavy guard, they should not pose any further threat to us."

"Nuh-uh." Felicity shook her head. "Remember what I said about leaving bad guys unaccounted for?"

"Yeah, um, I think we need to find them," Joel said, recalling his vision about Marshall taking over the Mono Realm. "I'd feel a lot better if we did."

"What is all this debating about?" Keeper said, returning with Auravine; the two of them had adjourned to a nearby cluster of boulders to answer the call of nature. "Thinker of Deep Thoughts, I thought we already came up with the plan on the way here, while everyone else was asleep. Did you not tell them?"

"I was busy looking for this," Thinker replied, pulling out a small, clear jar filled with a purple-colored substance. "I was worried I had forgotten it."

"That would have been rather inconvenient," Keeper said with what Joel could have sworn was a smirk, although with her alien facial features, it was hard to be completely sure.

♪♪♪

Joel went over the plan again as he, Thinker, Felicity, and Thornleaf walked up to the outpost's main entrance: while Keeper and the others stayed with the vehicle, the four of them, disguised as Outpost Eight troops (the purple-colored substance was the appropriate soulshifter salve for such a disguise; Thinker had stolen it after he was fired), would enter the facility, find Marshall and his cronies, and then sneak them out via one of the transit tubes to Dwelling of the Lights, a nearby town where Thinker used to live. There they would meet up with Keeper and the others—whom Felicity would have notified via the countercom about when they were on their way—before selling the vehicle. Then, with those funds in hand, they would fly back to the City by the Lake, pay the fee to retrieve Felicity's loudstone, send Keeper on her way, and then begin the long trek home to Spectraland.

Simple enough, Joel thought.

The four members of the "strike team," as Felicity dubbed them, had been selected via a thought process that went something like this: Thinker, of course, would lead the party, as he was the one with inside knowledge of the facility; Joel would go, since the Sight could come in handy with tracking down Marshall; Thornleaf would go as well, because his proficiency with the loudstones might be needed in case of an emergency where a lot of wavecasts had to be performed at the same time, and Felicity would round out the group, due to her familiarity with the countercom device. Joel felt as if that last reason was rather flimsy. Why couldn't she or Keeper just teach *him* how to use it? But it quickly became apparent—Joel inferred this from his mom's relationship with Art—that Thornleaf and Felicity were now in that annoying stage of coupledom where they basically had to do everything together, so he decided that it wasn't going to be worth it to argue the point.

The main entrance was a hinged gate in the fence, secured by a heavy lock and guarded by two tall Mono Realmers in full metal suits, each of them wielding what looked like futuristic flamethrowers.

"Squadron Eight-Six-Four-A, reporting in," Thinker said.

"Eight-Six-Four-A? That is part of a discontinued regiment," one of the guards responded. He sounded almost exactly like David St. Hubbins from *This Is Spinal Tap*, one of a spate of R-rated movies that Joel binge-watched after his seventeenth birthday.

"We have recently been reinstated to active duty by Commander Bringer of Good Tidings," Thinker said. "Authorization code zero-nine-nine-three-red-fifty-one-C-dash-three-dash-twelve-x-twenty."

The other guard leaned his flamethrower against the fence and pulled out a small handheld device. "That code checks out," he said, pushing a few buttons. "But where are you coming from? We saw you approach from atop the ridge. What were you doing up there?" His voice was reminiscent of David St. Hubbins' bandmate, Nigel Tufnel. It took everything in Joel's power not to laugh.

"Special border reconnaissance," Thinker replied. "We have been out on patrol since before your shift began this morning. You can check with the previous shift if you like."

"All right, you are clear." The Nigel Tufnel sound-alike guard nodded. He pushed another button on his device, and the gate swung open.

The team entered the compound and started toward the hangar. Once they were out of earshot, Felicity sidled up to Joel and said under her breath, "Dude, did you notice those guys' voices?"

Joel was about to respond enthusiastically before he remembered that he and Felicity had watched *This Is Spinal Tap* together in their tour bus. Saddened by that memory, he simply murmured "Yeah" before he turned to Thinker and asked, "So, um, how did you get that authorization code?"

"I hacked into their system on the way here, after Keeper of the Light and I came up with this plan," Thinker responded with glee, obviously struggling to keep his voice down. "That soulshifter salve was not the only thing I—*ahem*—harvested on my way out of this place. Oh no, I took all sorts of devices and technology with me. How do you think I have been able to continue researching your island all these past years?"

"Well, technically, Spectraland isn't *my* island, but, uh...anyway, good job."

"Thank you."

Felicity elbowed Joel in the arm. "Oh, so what, you're just gonna start ignoring me now?" she hissed.

"What? No, I—"

"Fine, whatever, Mister Passive Aggressive."

"Um...I don't even know what that means."

"This is probably not the best time for an argument," Thornleaf said out of the side of his mouth as a group of Mono Realm soldiers approached, marching in a single file line. The soldier at the head of the line made a hand motion that Joel assumed was a salute; Thinker returned the gesture, and the group passed on by.

"I wasn't ignoring you," Joel said when the coast was clear. "I was just...I dunno, it's hard to explain."

"Then don't bother," Felicity said in the frosty tone of voice she used when they had first met, seemingly so long (but actually only a little over six months) ago.

The team continued walking in uncomfortable silence until they reached the hangar. Thinker led them to a door at the back of the building that was unguarded but locked. Raising his right arm, he placed his fingertips on a recessed panel in the door and waited.

"What are you doing?" Thornleaf asked.

"Entering the combination," Thinker replied. Joel could see little flashes of light traveling down Thinker's fingers and into the panel. After a few seconds of this, the panel lit up with a faint beeping noise, and the door slowly slid aside.

"Interesting," Thornleaf said. "It is almost as if you have Aura energy of your own."

"It is nothing compared to what your people can do. Now, follow me."

Joel gave Felicity a side-eyed glance, expecting her to say something like "What do you think we've been doing" or "Not like we have a choice," but she remained silent, falling in behind Thinker with her lips pursed and her gaze fixed forward.

The immediate interior of the hangar facility was nothing like what Joel had pictured in his mind, which was a large, open-air space full of cryogenic tubes and other such accoutrements; instead, the team found itself in a narrow, dimly lit hallway with several doors on each side. The hallway continued for about twenty-five feet before it split off to the left and right in a T-shape.

"Stay close," Thinker whispered over his shoulder. "This facility can be rather tricky to navigate if you are unfamiliar with it."

Indeed, as they traveled through the various halls and corridors, Joel began to feel more and more like a mouse in a maze. Occasionally, they passed by other Mono Realmers, some of whom looked like soldiers and others who looked more like scientists, but fortunately, none of them paid much attention to the team beyond cursory nods of acknowledgment. They walked around for what felt like forever (but was, in reality, about thirteen minutes) until they came to a relatively large room and stopped in front of a door similar to the one they had entered the facility through. A keypad was on the wall next to the door; Thinker punched a few of the keys and then took a step back.

"Why is it not opening?" Thornleaf asked.

"Oh—this is a lift that will take us to the laboratory wing," Thinker replied. "We just have to wait for it to come down."

"A lift?"

"An elevator," Felicity said.

"What?"

"I'll explain it to you later."

"Soldiers!" a female voice snapped. Startled, Joel whirled around to see a tall Mono Realm woman approaching. She carried an air of authority about her; Joel assumed that she was a higher ranking officer of some sort.

"Ah, uh, yes, ma'am," Thinker stammered, giving the Mono Realm salute.

"What are you doing?"

"Routine patrol rounds, ma'am."

"In that case, the two of you"—she pointed at Thinker and Thornleaf—"come with me. I need assistance loading up some gear to be shipped out to Sector One."

"Well, ah...all four of us can help you," Thinker offered.

"That is unnecessary. I only need two. The others can continue your patrol rounds. Now come along." She turned and started to head out of the room.

This could be a problem, Joel thought as all four members of the team glanced at each other.

"Well, what are you waiting for?" the officer barked over her shoulder.

Joel heard a beeping noise behind him. He turned around. The elevator door had opened.

"Fourth floor," Thinker whispered before he and Thornleaf followed the officer out.

Acting on instinct, Joel got into the elevator. Felicity got in as well, and the door slid shut.

"I should've known this would happen," Felicity muttered, shaking her head. "Something like this *always* happens."

"Yeah, um, like in *Deathly Hallows*," Joel said. "When they were in the Ministry of Magic."

"Oh, so you're talking to me again?"

"Huh?"

"Forget it. What did he say? Fourth floor?"

"Um, yeah." Joel inspected a mosaic of small buttons on the wall of the elevator next to the door. Arranged in a circle and marked with glowing Mono Realm writing, it was basically impossible to tell which of them corresponded to the fourth floor. "I dunno, maybe we should just wait here for them."

"No, that would look too fishy. Let's just try to find Marshall. Maybe by then they'll catch up with us."

The elevator started to move.

"Hurry up and press a button!" Felicity exclaimed.

"But which one?"

"Just take your best guess!"

Okay, let's see, we were on the ground floor, but these buttons aren't lighting up, so I don't know which one is...well, maybe it's the one at the bottom of the circle. But then which way is the elevator going up, left or right? And what if there's a basement level or two? Or three? Or—

Felicity reached around him and pushed a button. "There," she said. "Let's hope that's right."

The elevator churned along as both of them stood there, facing the door. It definitely seemed to be on the slow side, quite unlike any of the other forms of Mono Realm transportation that Joel had experienced thus far. The only thing missing was some piped-in music.

"Hey, uh, so...sorry about ignoring you, and stuff," Joel said. "I didn't mean to do that."

"You don't have to apologize, dude," Felicity sighed. "I get it."

"You do?"

"Yeah. You're just jealous. That's natural."

"I am?"

"Sure. Of me and Thornleaf."

"Wait, what? No, no, it's not that."

"Yeah it is. Admit it."

Is it? "No, it's just that—I dunno, I guess it's like, I feel...I feel, you know—"

The elevator came to a stop and the door slid open, revealing another hallway. This one was short, only about ten feet long, and there was a Mono Realm soldier standing guard at the end of it.

"I'll do the talking," Felicity whispered as they exited the elevator.

"This is a restricted area," the soldier said. "What is your business here?"

"Special orders from Commander Bringer of Good Tidings," Felicity said.

"Orders to do what?"

"That's high-level, classified information. You need to let us through."

The soldier moved up close. "I do not recognize your energy signatures. What squadron are you from?"

"Er...Eight-Six-Four-A."

"Your regiment was discontinued."

"We were reinstated. Secretly. Like I said, we're carrying out classified orders."

The soldier paused and tilted his head. His antennae twitched. "I will need your authorization code."

"Sure." She glanced at Joel. "Tell him the code."

"But...I thought you said that you would do the—"

"*Just tell him the code.*"

"Okay, um, it's zero-nine-nine-three-red-fifty-one-C-dash-three-dash-twelve-x-twenty."

The soldier backed off a step. He took a device from his belt and pressed some buttons on it. "Very well," he said, looking at his device's screen. "You may proceed." He pushed another button, and the door behind him slid open. "Sorry to keep you."

"No problem," Felicity said as she strode past. "You're just doing your job. We'll put in a good word for you with the commander."

"I appreciate that."

"Oh, and don't forget—we're here on classified business. So don't tell anyone."

"Understood," the soldier said, and the door slid shut.

The pair found themselves in a tall, wide corridor that went on for about thirty feet before it took a left turn.

"That was awesome," Joel said as they walked.

"Yeah, I saw that routine in a movie once. Never thought it would come in handy one day."

"It was even better than a Jedi Mind Trick."

"Actually, I would've preferred that."

"How did you know I would remember that code?"

"I didn't." Felicity shrugged. "I just kinda figured you would."

"Okay, see, this is what I was trying to tell you in the elevator. It's like, you're the only one who—"

"Shh. I hear a bunch of noises up ahead."

After the turn, Joel could see that the corridor opened up into a large, brightly lit space that was more of what he was originally expecting when they first entered the facility. There were many doors along the walls, with soldiers standing guard at each one, along with blinded windows that concealed whatever was going on within the adjoining areas. The middle of the space was filled with desks, some of which had scientist-looking Mono Realmers seated at them, and around the desks were large pieces of equipment that appeared to be combinations of modern medical machinery and ancient torture devices. Beeping and hissing sounds filled the air.

"I'd say we're in the right place," Felicity whispered as they slowly approached.

"It seems like it, I guess. But how are we gonna find Marshall?"

"Hello—the Sight?"

"Oh—uh, right."

"Let's just stand over here," Felicity said, taking up a spot near the entrance. "Try to act casual."

Joel stopped next to her and looked around. None of the guards or scientists seemed to be paying them much mind. He figured that since the soldier at the previous door had let them in, probably everyone assumed that it was all right for them to be there. He cleared his mind and started up the Sight. It took nearly forty-five seconds before he finally saw flashes of Marshall, Darkeye, and the Lightsnakes being escorted around the room by Mono Realm soldiers; unfortunately, the images were blurry, sporadic, and seemingly out of sequence, so he couldn't tell exactly where they had been taken. He tried to relax and sharpen his focus, but as he did so, the images flickered and then disappeared altogether.

"Well, um, they were here, that's for sure," he said.

"Are they in one of those rooms?"

"What rooms?"

"You know, behind those doors."

"How do you know there are rooms behind those doors?"

"Dude, I'm just guessing. So where they did go?"

"I, uh, I don't know."

"What? What do you mean?"

"I mean that I couldn't see where they went."

"Ugh, I know that. I meant, why didn't the Sight work?"

"It worked, sort of, I just—I only saw brief flashes. I think I'm too tired or something."

"Didn't you sleep in the car?"

"Um...only a little."

"Great." Felicity rolled her eyes. "All right, I have an idea." She walked up to one of the scientist types behind a desk. "Excuse me."

The scientist type looked up. "Yes?"

"My comrade and I were assigned as additional guard detail for the rainbow folk. Can you tell me where they are being held?"

"The rainbow folk?" The scientist said, sounding puzzled. "They are no longer here."

"Where did they go?"

"They were transferred to Sector One last night. The Uniter himself requested it. Were you not informed?"

"Oh—no, we...there must have been some miscommunication, I suppose. Where in Sector One?"

"The Royal Tower."

"I see. Of course. We will go there right now. Thank you for your time."

The scientist's antennae twitched, as if she sensed that something was amiss. "You are very welcome."

Felicity turned and headed back for the corridor. Joel followed her until she rounded the corner and came to a stop.

"Okay, so *that's* a problem," she said.

"It is? What is?"

"That they were taken to Sector One, wherever that is! Unless it's, like, right next door to this place, we won't have enough fuel to make it there. Remember?"

"Oh—yeah. Well, um, there's probably a transit tube route that goes from here to there, don't you think?"

"Good point." She pulled out her countercom. "All right, I'll call Keeper and tell her to wait for us in that town, whatever it was called."

"Dwelling of the Lights?"

180

"Yeah, that one. Then we just need to find Thinker and Thornleaf and hope that they—"

All the lights in the corridor suddenly turned red. "Attention, all personnel," a voice sounded over hidden loudspeakers. "We have a potential security breach. Be on the lookout for soldiers claiming to be members of squadron Eight-Six-Four-A. They are believed to be imposters."

"Uh oh," Felicity said.

"If you encounter them, apprehend them immediately. Use lethal force if needed. I repeat, we have a potential..."

The door at the end of the corridor slid open, revealing the soldier that Felicity had talked into letting her and Joel pass. In one swift motion, she raised the countercom, aimed it at the soldier, and pressed a button. It emitted a high, squealing noise, and the soldier froze in the doorway with his rifle pointed directly at the two offworlders.

"Nice," Joel said.

"That's karate reflexes for ya," she said, pronouncing *karate* correctly.

"Help!" the immobilized soldier shouted. "The imposters are here!"

As the voice over the loudspeaker continued to repeat its warning, Joel and Felicity ran down the corridor toward the soldier.

"Grab his gun," Felicity said.

"It's stuck," Joel said, tugging at the weapon. "His grip is too tight."

"Figures." She yanked the soldier's device off his belt.

"Help!" the soldier shouted again.

"You can forget about that good word," Felicity said, pushing the soldier so that he fell face-first to the ground. She and Joel then stepped over him and into the adjoining hallway.

"That was a cool line," Joel said.

"Yeah, yeah." She held out the soldier's device. "Do you remember which button controls this door?"

"Sure, um, this one." Joel pressed a button on the device, and the door slid shut, leaving the soldier on the other side of it.

"Sweet. Okay, to the elevator."

"Right."

They hustled down the hallway. Recalling how Thinker had summoned the elevator earlier, Joel punched the same pattern into the keypad on the wall.

"I hope that works," he said.

"That makes two of us," Felicity said, pushing some buttons on her countercom. "I'm not sure this thing can freeze all the soldiers from that other room at once."

"Time to use the wavebows?"

"Thinker has the soulshifter-wiping-off-cloth, re-member?"

"Oh yeah."

Joel heard some muffled shouting sounds, and then the door at the other end of the hallway started to glow in the middle. The soldiers were probably trying to melt a hole in it, he figured.

"C'mon, c'mon, c'mon," Felicity muttered, tapping her foot.

Joel's mind raced. Was there anything else they could do?

"I swear," Felicity said, "if we die waiting for an ele-vator, I am going to *laaaaugh*."

A sharp screech rang out, and a spark ignited on the elevator door. The soldiers had succeeded in creating a small hole, one that they were now shooting through.

"Up against the wall!" Felicity exclaimed.

Following her example, Joel pressed his back to the wall, trying to make himself as flat as possible. Several more shots were fired.

"Why is this thing taking so long?" Felicity shrieked. "Are you sure you pressed the right buttons?"

"Um, pretty sure." Joel looked down the hall. The hole in the door was growing bigger. "What if you hold them off with the countercom?" he suggested.

"Okay, yeah, good idea," she said, sans sarcasm. She aimed the device and pressed a button. No sound came out of it. "Dude, I don't know if it's working."

"Low battery?"

"Or maybe they jammed it or something—I don't know!"

The shots were coming in a steady stream now. The hole continued to grow. Joel glanced over at Felicity who, in that moment, for whatever reason, seemed even prettier to him than usual, even though her face was currently contorted with panic.

"Okay, um," he blurted out, "so what I was gonna say was, I wasn't ignoring you, I just felt sad because—"

The elevator door slid open, revealing Thinker and Thornleaf. The latter already had a shield cast going, preventing the two men from being shot. He projected it out into the hall. Felicity slipped around the back of the shield and into the elevator. Joel did the same. Once they were both safely inside, Thornleaf withdrew the shield cast and the door slid shut.

"They are on to us," Thinker said.

"No kidding," Felicity exhaled.

Joel chuckled at that exchange. As he did so, he felt a searing pain in his side. He raised his arm and inspected himself. There was a large, smoking wound just below his ribcage.

"Oh, dude!" Felicity gasped, covering her mouth.

"I, uh, I think they got me," Joel managed to say before he suddenly grew light-headed and the world faded into nothingness.

CHAPTER 16: BUSKING

"Hey, Joel, get up, man!"
Just five more minutes...
"C'mon!"

Joel felt a hand shaking his shoulder. It took nearly three full seconds before he remembered that he had just been severely wounded in the Outpost Eight facility. He opened his eyes, expecting to see Felicity, Auravine, or another one of his fellow Wavemakers, but instead it was the face of Trevor, his bass player back on Earth, that greeted him.

"Wakey wakey!" Trevor grinned. "Man, I don't know how you can sleep at a time like this. I am so pumped!"

"What?" Joel said, clutching his side. It felt perfectly fine. "Why...what's going on?"

"Ha! Your sense of humor is really coming along, my friend."

Joel sat up. He was in some sort of dressing room; not the kind of grungy backstage storage closet that most small venues try to pass off as such, but a comfortable, spacious area complete with leather couches, lighted mirrors, and a long table topped off with deli trays and pitchers of ice water.

"I found him!" Trevor called out. "He was in here, napping! Can you believe it?"

"Oh, thank goodness," Julio said, breathless, as he ran into the room. "Joel, we've been looking all over for you! You're already ten minutes late!"

"Relax, man," Trevor said. "We're on rock and roll time. You've heard of it, right?"

"Hey, this isn't 1995 anymore," Julio retorted. "The Sugarblood people run a tight ship. They want things to happen on schedule."

Sugarblood? Joel thought. *So...this is our arena show*?

"Julio, man, I swear." Trevor chuckled. "You're gonna give yourself a heart attack one of these days."

"Then at least I won't have to listen to your—Joel, what's the matter? Are you all right? You look pale."

"Um, yeah, I'm fine." *Is this a vision*?

"Then let's go. Art's already on stage."

"What about Felicity?"

"Who?"

"You know, my...our other guitar player."

"Other guitar player?" Trevor laughed. "That's a good one!"

"Wait," Joel said, "so we hired someone else?"

"Okay, stop messing around already," Julio sighed. "You never *had* another guitar player."

What?

"Give him a break, man." Trevor spoke in that strange conspiratorial tone that people often used when they were talking about Joel in front of him as if he weren't there. "He's just trying to, you know, learn how to tell jokes, and stuff."

"Well, this is a really bad time for that. Now—"

Joel let out a loud moan as the pain in his side suddenly returned, stronger than before. He flopped back down on the couch and went into a fetal position.

"Joel!" Trevor said. "What's the matter? Are you joking again?"

"Aw, man, I *knew* he looked sick," Julio muttered.

Joel screwed his eyes shut and grimaced as the pain got even worse.

"Joel? Joel, can you hear me?"

That's weird, Joel thought, even though his side was killing him. *Why does Trevor sound like a girl all of a sudden?*

"What's happening? I thought you healed him!"

And Julio sounds like...Felicity?

"I did! I—I must have missed something—"

Joel heard the sounds of a wavebow. He opened his eyes a crack.

Auravine...?

Joel felt the pain start to recede as the music continued. Warm, soothing sensations reverberated throughout his body, as if he were lying on a loudspeaker. Eventually, the pain stopped, and so did the music.

"There," Auravine exhaled, "I think that should do it."

"Man, I hope so," Felicity said. "Dude—how do you feel?"

"Um...good."

"Okay, he's all right."

Joel sat up. The arena dressing room was gone, replaced by another room that was about the same size but much less luxurious. It was dark—the only light was coming from Felicity's illuminated wavebow, which she had propped up on top of a small crate so that it looked kind of like a lamp—and there were wood-and-metal boxes of various sizes everywhere, most of them stacked on top of each other all the way up to the ceiling. Joel realized that instead of a leather couch, he had been lying on a few of these boxes that had been pushed together to form a makeshift operating table.

"Don't strain yourself, though," Felicity warned him. "Not sure if little Miss M.D. here has much healing juice left."

"Where...where are we?" Joel asked.

"A storage room. In a motel. In...what was the name of this town again?"

"Dwelling of the Lights?" Auravine said.

"Right. That place."

"How did we get out of Outpost Eight?" Joel asked.

"Oh, dude, it was nuts. After you got shot, Thinker led us to the room where they have all the transit tube thingies. Turned out, though, they had shut them all down. I mean, of course, right? Fortunately, he knew the override code for the route that led here, since this is where he used to live and stuff. Guess they never updated it, or whatever. We almost got caught, but we managed to sneak out just in time. You know, like how we always do."

"But aren't they gonna follow us here?"

Felicity shrugged. "Thinker messed with the tube controls on the way out, so, according to him, it'll take them a while to figure out where we went. Something about having to analyze the tubes' residual usage patterns, blah, blah, blah. I dunno, I stopped listening to him after about a minute or so. Anyway, that was supposed to buy us enough time to fix you up and find some gas for the car. That's what everyone else is out doing right now. The gas thing."

Joel glanced over at Auravine, who was sitting on another nearby box with her eyes closed and her head bowed. She looked exhausted. He turned back to Felicity. "Well, um...thanks for staying here with us," he said.

"Of course, dude. Someone had to stand guard while she worked her magic. Besides, it gave us a chance to bond a little. Talk about stuff."

"Did you...did you guys talk about me?"

"Pfft, don't be silly," Felicity scoffed. "Why would we do that? No, man, we totally passed the Bechdel test."

"The what?"

"Look it up when we—I mean, you—I mean...you know what I mean."

He did. "That's what I was trying to talk about earlier. I wanted to tell you that...that I'm sad you're not going back. You're my best friend. Heck, you're my only friend. You're the only person who really...you know, gets me."

Felicity opened and closed her mouth a couple of times, as if she were about to say something but came up empty each time. Finally, she nodded in the direction of Auravine, who was snoring lightly, and said, "I think *she* gets you."

"What? Really?"

"Really. On a different level, maybe, but still." Felicity grinned. "Hey, I have an idea: why don't you move here too?"

"To the Mono Realm?"

"Dude."

"I know, I'm just kidding. You know I can't do that."

"Yeah, I guess not," she sighed. "It would be cool, though, wouldn't it?"

Before Joel could answer, a door to the room opened and Thinker came striding in, followed by everyone else.

They were all wearing a new shade of soulshifter salve, kind of a mustard yellow.

"Ah, I see Master Joel's wounds have been properly tended to," Thinker said. "But really, I expected nothing less."

"Yup, A.V.'s a miracle worker," Felicity said, taking a seat. "So, how'd it go?"

"Well," Keeper said, "we have what is known here in the Mono Realm as 'good news and bad news.'"

"Yeah, you know, I don't think you guys own the patent on that phrase," Felicity said. "All right, I'll play. What's the good news?"

"The town's refueling station is located right where it always has been, so it was very easy to find," Thinker answered.

"And the bad?"

"We cannot afford to buy enough fuel to make it to Sector One. Or anywhere else, for that matter."

"Of course we can't," Felicity muttered.

"So we spent whatever little we had left on some food," Keeper said, pulling out a small bag. "No sense in being hungry while we wait for the authorities to arrest us."

"We will not go down without a fight, I assure you that," Thornleaf said.

"You do recall what I told you about being hopelessly outnumbered, do you not?" Thinker said.

"If anything, we should just make our escape from this land now," Riverhand argued. "We can return another day, if necessary."

"I, uh, I really don't know if that's a good idea," Joel said, accepting a thin, wafer-like item from Keeper. "I think we need to find Marshall and the others soon."

"I recall you saying something like that earlier," Red-stem noted. "Why do you feel that way?"

Joel proceeded to describe, in between bites of the wafer (which was actually quite good—it was crispy and tasted like a sugar cookie), the vision he'd had back on the Firelight Highway about Marshall taking over the Mono Realm. Keeper reiterated her doubts, but then Joel theorized that Marshall would probably talk his way into an audience with the Uniter in order to get close enough for an assassination attempt. He summarized how the former Biledriver singer was able to seduce and manipulate many good people—including Auravine, Felicity, and Joel himself—into doing some very bad things. After that, Keeper was more or less convinced.

"Why would the Uniter's soldiers simply not arrest Byle, if he were to commit such an act?" Windblade asked.

"The Uniter is not...well-liked, to put it simply," Keeper replied. "Even among some of his closest advisors. They could very well be convinced to shift allegiances if he were taken out of the picture. Especially if this fugitive of yours is as devious and powerful as you make him out to be."

"Oh, he is, trust me," Felicity said around a mouthful of wafer. "And those other three guys with him aren't exactly the Jonas Brothers."

"The who?" Several in the room said at once.

"They're this—oh, forget it."

"All right," Thinker said, "so it sounds like we simply must get to Sector One soon, one way or another. But how? It would take us months on foot."

Nineteen seconds passed by. The only sound was the crunching of sugar cookie-flavored wafers. Then, as Felicity got up to renew the light cast on her wavebow, a puzzle piece fell into place in Joel's head.

"Oh—I have an idea," he declared.

♪♪♪

Like Keeper's coastal hometown, Dwelling of the Lights was a relatively small settlement, but it had a cleaner, more upbeat vibe that reminded Joel of some of the trendier neighborhoods in Seattle and Portland that his band had passed through on their way to play a gig. Buildings of various shapes and sizes lined the streets, which were paved with smooth, multicolored pebbles, and strings of white lights hung everywhere and from everything, making it seem like one big holiday party was going on. Mono Realmers of all ages were walking around, going about their daily business.

"I must admit," Redstem said as the whole nine-member party headed down a pebble-paved street, "I still do not quite understand how this plan is supposed to work."

"Just don't think about it too much," Felicity advised.

Joel was trying to do just that. Even though it was his idea, he was starting to feel a little nervous about it. Despite the fact that he was now a fairly seasoned performer, he had never done anything quite like this before.

"I think it is brilliant," Thinker enthused. "All citizens of the Six States—ah, I mean, the Mono Realm—love music, but the people of this town are especially appreciative. We should have what we need in no time."

"If that is the case, then could we not just barter for it?" Windblade asked.

"That is not quite how things work around here," Keeper answered.

They arrived at the town's main commercial district, which was uncannily reminiscent of Seattle's Pike Place Market. There was even one food stall where the vendors were throwing the orders to the customers and to each other, although what was being ordered looked more like miniature rhinos than fish. The party took up a spot in between several stalls where there seemed to be the most foot traffic.

"Actually, I'm not so sure about this now," Joel said, looking around. "Maybe there's a better way."

"What?" Felicity laughed. "Don't tell me you're getting cold feet. Confidence, remember?"

"No, I'm confident, it's just that..."

"Yeah, right. I can tell when you're freaking out."

"Well, *you* didn't want to sing earlier."

"I thought it was just silly at the time. This is different."

"It is, which is why I'm feeling like this."

"Relax, dude, it'll be just like caroling. You've done that before, right?"

"Um, no."

"Okay, well, c'mon, pretend it's just another show. How are you gonna play at the arena next month if you can't do this?"

She had a point, but there was a difference between performing with amplified instruments in front of an interested audience and singing a capella to a group of aliens who weren't expecting you. He'd done it for Keeper, sure, but that was one individual, in the privacy of her residence, in a seemingly critical situation.

"Are you sure we shouldn't do 'Down the Landvein River?'" Windblade asked the group. "After all, the offworlders are a bit more familiar with that one."

"I told you, I do not want to hear that song again for as long as I live," Redstem grumbled. "Let us just go with what we originally decided on."

"Very well."

Windblade counted off, and they all began singing "Lifepod Wine," a breezy little ditty extolling the virtues of said beverage. Most of the shoppers stopped and looked, their antennae twitching.

"Ah—er, yes," Keeper addressed the shoppers, obviously uncomfortable. "This is the...the Anthem Ensemble, a new musical group all the way from the City by the Lake. They are here today, performing for your listening pleasure. Donations will be graciously accepted."

More shoppers started to gather around as the song continued. A few of them even started to hum along. After the song was over they—led by Thinker, who was pretending to be part of the crowd—burst into applause. He came up to Keeper and touched his current disc to hers, creating something that sounded like a Super Mario coin chime; apparently, this was the way a payment was made between individuals in the Mono Realm. Joel had wondered why Thinker had suggested doing this, and Felicity had told him that it was because of some strange concept she had read about called "social proof," where people are influenced to do things based on the actions of others. Sure enough, after Thinker backed away, other Mono Realmers came up and touched their discs to Keeper's.

"Thank you, thank you!" Keeper said, warming to her role.

As his group continued to sing, Joel settled in as well, even while the crowd grew larger and larger; the enthusiastic response was the kind of positive feedback that he thrived on. The Mono Realmers seemed to especially enjoy the songs that were in a minor key and/or had multiple-part harmonies, like "The Ballad of Bluecrest," a dramatic tearjerker about a villager who lost his entire family to razorbears (which, as far as the Mono Realm citizens were concerned, must have been fictional creatures). After a while, they ran out of songs and had to repeat the set, but no one seemed to mind. Joel started to wonder if they already had enough currents to buy the fuel to get to Sector One and Keeper was just trying to milk the situation for her reward money.

Then, right as they were about to do "Down the Landvein River" (Redstem had relented since they had already sang all the other songs twice now), a tall Mono Realm woman walked up to Keeper and asked, "Excuse me, but do you folks have a permit?"

"We—uh—well, who are you, may I ask?"

"I am the manager of this marketplace," the tall woman replied, presenting what was probably her credentials. "You need a permit to conduct any sort of for-profit activity in this area."

Some members of the crowd began to boo. One of them sounded like Thinker.

"Well, we, er...we can certainly apply for one. Can you assist us with that?"

"Certainly. The expedited application process takes three weeks."

"Oh...I see."

"Let them sing!" someone in the crowd—probably Thinker—shouted.

"In the meantime," the manager said, unmoved, "I am afraid that you will have to cease your activity immediately and turn over any earnings that you have accrued. If your application is approved, I will be more than happy to return the entire sum to you."

Felicity stepped forward. "I'll handle this," she said. "Look, we're in kind of a tight situation here. We're doing this tour of the Mono Realm, see, and our manager, as awesome as she is, well, she forgot to..."

As Felicity continued talking, Joel saw, out of the corner of his eye, a trio of Mono Realm soldiers walking down the street. Headed in the direction of the marketplace, they were stopping everyone they came across and wiping the soulshifter salve off their faces.

Uh oh.

"...and so, if you just let us keep what we made for now, we'll come back right after our next stop and put in that application. Sound good?"

"I am sorry, but no," the manager replied. She pulled out a current disc and held it aloft. "Now, if you do not transfer your earnings to me right this instant, I will have no choice but to call security."

Joel moved up and tapped Felicity on the shoulder. "Hey, uh..."

"What? I'm busy here."

He nodded in the direction of the approaching soldiers.

"Oh...hmm."

"Very well, then." The manager put her current disc away and pushed a button on a device that she was wearing on her wrist. "Security? Please come to stall seven-C right away."

"I don't suppose we could bribe you with a sugar cookie, could we?" Felicity said.

Joel looked around as the members of his group started to back toward each other. Four heavyset Mono Realmers had emerged from different spots in the marketplace and were power-walking in their direction.

"What should we do?" Auravine said.

"Any good ideas?" Felicity asked Joel.

"Um..."

Thinker elbowed his way out of the crowd, which had actually become even larger for some reason, and leaned toward the group. "I suggest that we...*run!*"

And with that, everyone took off, to loud cheers from the assembled shoppers. With the security guards on their heels, Thinker led them through the throng, out of the marketplace, and down a series of pebble-paved streets until they arrived at what looked like a drive-in restaurant. Stalls framed by sets of short metal pillars were arranged in a circle around a small football-shaped building, and two of the stalls were taken up by occupied vehicles, both of them similar to Thinker's but in much better condition. The vehicles' occupants—one a single male, the other a family of four—all looked at the party with curious expressions.

"I think we lost 'em," Felicity panted.

"Actually," Joel said in between gasps, "they stopped following us a while ago."

"Oh? I didn't notice."

Thinker pushed a few buttons on one of the metal pillars next to an empty stall. A panel in the floor of the stall slid aside, and his vehicle rose up. "Give me the current disc," he said to Keeper.

"Just enough to get to Sector One, now," she said, handing the disc over.

"Yes, yes, I know," Thinker said, sounding like a harried husband. "There isn't much more beyond that, anyway." He inserted the disc into the pillar and pressed a few more buttons, and a low humming noise started up. "Everyone, get in."

As they all crammed into the vehicle, Joel heard a high *ding*, like the sound a toaster oven makes when your toast is ready. He looked around. Three stalls over, the family of four was pulling out—they drove away, their refueling done.

"How long is this going to take?" Thornleaf asked.

"Only a few minutes," Thinker replied.

"Excuse me," the single male in the other vehicle called out, "but do you folks have thirty-five extra currents I could borrow?"

"No," Thinker and Keeper said at the same time, not even looking over.

"I wonder why those guards stopped chasing us?" Riverhand said.

"They probably got tired," Redstem scoffed.

Then, from around the corner down the street, the three soldiers that Joel had seen earlier emerged. "I, uh, I think we have a bigger problem, though," he said.

"They will not recognize us," Thinker said, although he didn't sound entirely confident. "We are all wearing a different salve now."

"Yeah, but I saw them stopping people and wiping their salves off."

"What? But that is illegal!" Keeper exclaimed.

"They must have been granted special permission," Thinker said. "The government has its own supply of freecloths, expressly for purposes like this. That is how I got mine."

"Hey!" one of the soldiers shouted, looking over at the refueling lot. "You there, in the vehicle!"

"Are they talking to you?" the single male asked, sounding like he really hoped they were.

"See, now *this* would be a good time for a Jedi Mind Trick," Felicity grumbled.

The soldiers jogged up to Thinker's vehicle. "Are you the ones who caused the ruckus back at the market-place?" one of them asked. "The...the singers? Anthem Ensemble?"

"Ah...perhaps," Thinker said warily.

"Of course it is them, you fool," another soldier said to the first one. "They match the description the manager gave us."

Felicity leaned forward in the back seat. "Hey, look, we were gonna—"

"I just wanted to be sure," the first soldier snapped at his comrade. He turned back to the party. "We over-heard some of your performance while we were carrying out our duties, and I must say, you were absolutely bril-liant."

"Oh—er, thank you," Keeper said.

"Would you be willing to come back and continue? It certainly would make our jobs much less dreary, to be able to hear such fantastic music while we work."

"Well, we would, but..."

"You lack a permit, yes? Do not worry, the manager explained the whole situation to us. So we made a quick inquiry, and we were able to obtain a special government waiver for you. A benefit of our position."

"We...appreciate that," Keeper said. "Very much."

"Excellent! Oh, but before we go back, we just need to check something," the soldier said, pulling out a piece of fabric that looked a lot like Keeper's freecloth. "Merely a formality. You know, following orders, and so forth. Everyone who was in this town during the last several hours needs to have their identity confirmed. I am sure you understand."

Ding.

"Yes, of course," Thinker said. He pushed some buttons on the dashboard, and Joel heard the optical-drive whirring sound. "If you could, though, please begin with my tall friend in the backseat, here, while I run some routine tests on my vehicle."

Joel glanced over his shoulder at Thornleaf. The tall shaman seemed unfazed as he casually slipped a hand into his cloak, as if he needed to scratch himself. Thinker flipped a switch, and Joel felt himself pressed down into his seat.

"Very well," the soldier agreed. "Hold still, please." He proceeded to wipe the salve off of Thornleaf's face. A few seconds ticked by. The soldier's antennae twitched. "Wait a minute," he said, leaning in closer. "You are—"

Thinker flipped another switch and the vehicle shot backward out of the stall, its gravitational safety feature preventing the passengers in the front seat from either flying out or suffering from whiplash.

"Hey!" the soldier yelled.

Thinker whipped the vehicle around with a doughnut-like maneuver. The soldiers raised their weapons and fired, but Thornleaf, his wavebow already out, put up a golden Aura shield that deflected the shots into the ground. The soldiers shouted some mostly unintelligible things as Thinker punched a button, and the party zoomed away.

CHAPTER 17: THE REDIVISION

"They're gaining on us!" Felicity yelled.

Joel looked over his shoulder. Indeed, the single male's vehicle, now commandeered by the soldiers, had closed to within fifty feet or so. The soldiers fired off some shots, but Thornleaf, facing backward in his seat, continued to maintain his shield cast.

"Why are they catching up?" Keeper exclaimed. "You need to go faster!"

"This is a family vehicle!" Thinker said, weaving around some bowling-pin-shaped stone columns at nearly a hundred miles an hour.

"Take off someone else's salve so they can stun them!" Thornleaf insisted.

"And cause them to crash? I thought you people were not murderers!" Thinker said.

They had left Dwelling of the Lights behind and were now speeding through an adjoining area filled with the aforementioned stone columns and various other rock-like formations. About five hundred yards away stood a structure that looked like a giant amusement park ride set up in the middle of nowhere.

"Are we going back to the highway?" Joel asked.

"No," Thinker replied. "The authorities are on full alert now. The highways will all be blocked. I have another idea."

"If you will not let us stun them, then at least allow someone else to take over the shield!" Thornleaf said. "My energy is running low!"

Joel looked back again. The soldiers were now just twenty feet behind.

"I'll do it," Felicity volunteered. She stuck out her hand. "Keeper, gimme your cloth."

"Stop at once!" one of the soldiers barked through some kind of amplification device. They fired another round. Thornleaf's shield flickered for a moment, and one of the shots got through, barely missing him.

"Hurry!" Felicity shrieked.

As Keeper was passing the freecloth back, Thinker swerved to avoid another stone column. This had the unfortunate effect of causing the two women to fumble the exchange, and the cloth went flying away. "Why did you do that?" Keeper snapped at Thinker.

"I was trying not to get us all killed!"

Joel looked back once more. Thornleaf's shield was fading quickly, and the soldiers were right on their tail.

"I repeat, stop at once, or we will—"

Joel never found out what they were going to do, because at that moment, the commandeered vehicle abruptly slowed down and, within a handful of seconds, receded into the distance as the party continued on at full throttle. Some more shots were fired, but most of them were off line, and the few that did track the party's way were easily parried by whatever was left of Thornleaf's shield cast. Everyone seemed to breathe a collective sigh of relief.

"Those things may be fast, but they use a *lot* of fuel." Thinker snickered.

"Good thing you didn't lend that guy the thirty-five," Felicity said.

♪♪♪

In order to bypass the highway system, Thinker decided that they would reach Sector One by traversing a long stretch of barren territory known colloquially in the Mono Realm as The Vast Wasteland. Its appearance fit its name to a T; the flat ground was made up of nothing but dry, cracked rock, and the only features of the landscape were an occasional dirt mound and a range of small hills way off in the distance. Joel expected a tumbleweed to drift by at any second.

Auravine had gone back to sleep the minute they lost the soldiers, and the other Wavemakers all eventually drifted off one by one as the vehicle continued to speed along. Joel also tried to sleep, but either Auravine had cured his fatigue along with healing his wound or his state of unconsciousness after getting shot somehow counted as rest, because he found himself remaining wide awake despite his best efforts. Thinker put the vehicle on autopilot and dozed off as well, leaving Joel and Keeper as the only ones up. They sat in silence for a while, until Joel decided that this might be a good chance for him to practice his still-developing social and conversational skills.

"So, um, how did you get your name?" he said. "Is that your job, or something? Keeping lights?"

"No, I do not currently have an occupation. Keeper of the Light is my birth name. Apparently, the night I was born, a ray of moonlight broke through the shroud and cast its glow onto our home, signifying a life of good fortune. At least, that is the story I was told."

"Oh—that's, uh, that's a cool story."

"Thank you."

"That must be a rare thing—I haven't seen direct moonlight or sunlight since we got here."

"I have not seen either of them in my entire life. The elements in the sky above our land create the shroud and keep it trapped there at all times."

"That must get depressing."

"We are used to it."

"Are you sure you don't want to come back to Spectraland with us when this is all over? There's a lot of moonlight there."

Keeper sniffed. "I am beginning to think that I may have no choice."

"Oh, yeah...sorry about that."

"It is not your fault. Like your companion said, perhaps it is just destiny. Do your people truly believe in that?"

"In what?"

"Destiny."

"Um, I guess. Some of us do, anyway."

"Quite an odd concept. Almost frightening, really. If you believe in destiny, then, in effect, what you are saying is that you have no control over anything that happens to you. Your life is like this vehicle—on autopilot. You just sit back and let it take you where it will."

"Well, maybe, except that Thinker programmed the coordinates of where he wanted it to go."

Keeper laughed, a chime-like sound that was not unlike her regular, untranslated voice. "Indeed, a valid point! Your girlfriend is right, you are a rather wise young man."

"My what?"

"So, what you are saying," Keeper went on, "is that even though events happen that are beyond our control, ultimately, we are still the ones who decide upon our own direction."

"Uh...sure. Yeah."

"You know, it is curious...I was talking to your girl-friend when we were waiting for you outside of Outpost Eight. Remember how she convinced me to help you? By saying that I would be a hero?"

"Are...you talking about Auravine?"

"Yes," Keeper answered, undoing her ponytail and shaking her hair out. "I have to admit, there has always been a voice inside of me that said I was meant for bigger things. A restlessness, I guess you could call it. I was always just too afraid to take that chance, to step outside of my comfortable, mundane little existence. But when she said that word—hero—it triggered something, like per-haps this was my opportunity to finally break out of the rut I was in and make some kind of a difference."

"I, uh, I thought you just wanted that reward."

Keeper chuckled. "Well, that did not hurt, certainly. Please understand, I live a very meager life. But, as I was telling Auravine outside of Outpost Eight, the longer I remain with your group, the more I begin to feel...how should I put it...*alive*, I suppose. As if this is what I was supposed to have been doing all along."

"You mean, running away from soldiers?"

"The whole adventure. Making new friends. Sneak-ing into government bases. That entire scene back there...that was simply *exhilarating*. Scary, yes, but ex-hilarating. I felt positively giddy as we fled from every-one."

"You'll like it in Spectraland, then. We tend to get chased a lot over there."

Keeper chuckled once more. "Sounds wonderful."

"That reminds me—why didn't you just use your countercom on those soldiers?"

"Oh, it ran out of energy," Keeper answered, sounding somewhat sheepish. She took out the countercom and placed it up against various slots on the dashboard, like a toddler trying to figure out which hole the block should go into. "I left the battery pack at home...I was not expecting to be out this long."

"That happens to me sometimes too," Joel reassured her.

"I think I can charge it off the vehicle, though...ah, yes, there we go. Could you fetch me the other one, please?"

"The other one?"

"The one I lent your companion."

"Oh—right." Joel deactivated the gravitational safety feature and turned around in his seat. He was about to wake Felicity up and ask for the device when he noticed half a dozen vehicles on the horizon, apparently heading their way. "Um...I think we're being followed."

Keeper looked over her shoulder. "So we are," she sighed. "I suppose it was only a matter of time."

"At least it's more excitement."

"Well, I could have used just a *bit* more of a break." She nudged Thinker's shoulder. "Get up."

Thinker snapped awake. "What?"

"More soldiers," Keeper said, pointing.

Thinker turned. "Hmm," he said, following Keeper's gesture with his eyes. "I see."

"Hey," Joel said, "since now they know that we're rainbow folk—or at least one of us is—maybe we can just get rid of everyone's salve and use our wavebows."

"That would be a good idea," Keeper replied, "except that the freecloth that flew away back there was the only one I had. It was included with the purchase of the countercoms." She looked at Thinker. "Oh, but you have one."

Thinker reached into his tin foil suit. "Yes, I...oh. Hmm."

"What?"

"I believe I lost it back at Dwelling of the Lights," Thinker said, patting himself down. "While we were running."

"You cannot be serious."

"Unfortunately, I am."

"I'm hearing the sounds of a predicament," Felicity said, stretching. "What's going on?"

Joel explained it to her.

"That was a good summary of a bad situation," she remarked. "So, now what?"

"Is there a place around here that we can hide?" Redstem asked with her arms folded and her eyes still closed, apparently having been awake for at least the last minute or so.

"Let me see," Thinker said. He pushed a button on the dash, and a holographic map appeared on the vehicle's windshield. "If we can stay ahead of them for twenty more minutes or so, there is an area of scattered hills up ahead that we *might* be able to lose them in."

"I don't like how you put the emphasis on the word *might*, there," Felicity muttered.

"Will we have enough time?" Riverhand, also now awake, asked.

"I am not sure," Thinker replied.

"Do you know how fast they're going?" Joel asked Thinker.

"If those are standard military-grade pursuit vehicles, I would say...probably around a hundred and seventy miles per hour at top speed."

"And we're doing a hundred, right?"

"Yes, thereabouts."

Joel did a quick calculation in his head, estimating their pursuers' current position. "We'll make it," he declared.

"How do you know?" Windblade asked. Everyone was up now except for Auravine; her gentle snores sounded like the purring of a cat.

"Trust me, he does," Felicity said.

They changed course and headed, literally, for the hills (Joel made a joke to this effect, but no one laughed). As they drew closer, the military vehicles appeared to be gaining on them at an alarming rate, and Joel started to fear that one or more of the assumptions that went into his calculation were incorrect.

"I do not like the looks of this," Redstem said, glancing behind them.

"If they already have us in their sights, how will traveling through these hills help us?" Riverhand asked.

"It won't," Felicity said. "But I know what we can do." She instructed Thinker to drive the vehicle to a spot on the map where there were hills on all sides, sort of like a natural cul-de-sac. A little over two minutes later, they arrived at the spot and parked.

"Will we not get trapped here?" Auravine, who had finally woken up, asked.

"No, see, the good thing about this is that we won't get surrounded," Felicity said. "And they can only approach us from one direction, so we'll have a fighting chance of fending them off. Thornleaf can put up a shield while Keeper and I freeze 'em with the countercoms."

"It depends on how many of them there are, though," Keeper warned. "Together we can probably control up to twenty, twenty-five at the most. If they have more than that, we might be in trouble."

"I can take care of the rest," Thinker said, picking his rifle up off the floor of the vehicle.

"I thought you were opposed to that particular brand of violence," Thornleaf said.

"I did not want any of you to have to violate your principles," Thinker replied. "But as for me, I regret to say that this is something I have been forced to do before." He pushed a button on the rifle, and it started to charge up.

"Well, let's hope it doesn't come to that," Felicity said.

They took up positions in and around the vehicle and waited. Joel could hear the humming of the military vehicles getting louder. They would be here any minute now.

"You know, this'll actually work out well," Felicity said, sounding like she was trying to keep everyone's morale up. "After we handle these guys, we can borrow their rides. It'll be faster, and we won't be in a marked car anymore."

"I just hate feeling so helpless," Redstem griped. "I wish there at least was something I could throw at them."

"I doubt that would be very effective anyway," Riverhand said.

"Are you questioning my strength?"

"I just meant that—"

Riverhand was interrupted by a piercing whine, as if the emergency broadcast system tone were being played through a nearby P.A. system. Joel and everyone else covered their ears. A few seconds later, when it was over, the sound of the military vehicles was gone, replaced by indistinct talking and shouting. Then, after another several moments, those sounds were gone as well.

"What just happened?" Thinker asked as the party glanced around at each other.

"I was hoping *you* could tell *us*," Felicity responded.

The tone sounded again, albeit at a slightly lower volume. Joel tried to cover his ears once more, but he found that his arms were now frozen, along with the rest of his body below his neck. "Are—are you guys doing this?" he said, looking in Felicity and Keeper's direction.

"Oh, yeah, we totally are," Felicity replied, still facing forward. "No, dude, we're stuck too."

Joel heard a grinding noise, like rock on rock. He turned his head. A doorway was opening in the face of the hill to his left.

What the—

A gaunt male Mono Realmer with no soulshifter salve on his face walked out, holding something that looked like a tablet computer with a joystick attached to it. He fiddled with it for a bit, and then Joel felt his legs move involuntarily.

Well, here we go again.

"Who are you?" Thinker asked.

"Release us at once!" Keeper said.

Ignoring them, the gaunt male worked his device some more, causing the party to line up two-by-two, like animals boarding Noah's Ark (Windblade was the odd man out). They were made to walk through the doorway and into what evidently was not a hill at all, but a large transit-tube chamber with a multilevel platform. The door slid shut, and everyone marched up onto the platform's bottom level. Then, one long and bumpy tube ride later, everyone emerged into a large, dark factory-like space.

"What is this place?" Redstem said.

The gaunt male didn't answer.

"I see some familiar symbols," Keeper said, looking around as they walked. "Are you connected to the black market?"

The gaunt male remained silent.

"I guess I wouldn't admit that either," Felicity muttered.

They continued on, passing a number of similarly lean and non-salve-wearing Mono Realmers, both male and female, who were working at various machines of indeterminate purpose. Eventually, the Spectraland party and their friends were led into a small room within the factory where a Mono Realm woman with feathery silver hair—who, like her fellows, wore no salve—was sitting at a desk, examining what looked like a blueprint or a technical schematic. Joel immediately thought about Aunty Entity from *Mad Max Beyond Thunderdome*, a PG-13 movie that he hadn't seen until his post-birthday summer binge because he didn't want to watch it out of order (the first two Mad Max films being rated R).

"So," the woman said, not looking up from her blueprint, "you are not soldiers of the government, I assume?"

No one spoke for a moment. Then, after making a throat-clearing noise, Thinker replied, "That is correct, we are not."

"I figured as much," the silver-haired woman said, her speech slow and deliberate. "Your energy signatures are rather odd. Especially the tall one. And it would be unusual, in this day and age, for soldiers to be pursued by other soldiers. Multiple squadrons at that. Tell me, what did you do to warrant such attention?"

"We didn't have a busking permit at the marketplace," Felicity answered in her *all-right-I'm-taking-charge-of-this-situation* voice.

The woman put down her blueprint and chuckled. "Something tells me that is not the entire story. Were you involved in an unauthorized excursion into Outpost Eight, by any chance?"

"Maybe," Felicity said. "Or maybe not. Who's asking?"

The woman stood. "I am called Guider of the Worthy."

"By your friends, sure, but *I'm* just calling you Guider." Felicity said.

"Your spirited nature leads me to believe that you and your group are, in fact, the ones who successfully infiltrated the facility," Guider said. "We have been looking for you. It is fortunate that you decided to stop near one of our secret transit-tube terminals." She turned to the male who still had the party under energy lock. "Release them."

The male pressed something on his device, and Joel regained control of his body. Even so, he decided that the best course of action at the moment was to just continue standing perfectly still.

"Welcome to the headquarters of the Redivision movement," Guider continued. "We are a community of citizens who refused to go along with the Uniter's edicts after the Unification War. Sentenced to death, we managed to escape and hide out underground, where we have spent the intervening years working on our plans."

"Plans for what?" Keeper asked, even though it seemed like Guider was about to explain anyway.

"Overthrowing the Uniter. Abolishing the Mono Realm. Restoring the Six States to what they once were."

"Ah, standard-issue rebellion-type stuff," Felicity remarked.

"Yes, I suppose you could call it that." Guider smiled, stepping out from behind her desk. "So you can understand why I would be curious as to the purpose of your mission at Outpost Eight and how you were able to pull it off. Perhaps our causes can be...aligned."

Figuring that it was safe to tell Guider what she wanted to know, Joel decided to take the initiative. "Well, you see, we're, um, we're from the Land under the Rainbow. Five of us are, I mean—Keeper and Thinker are from here, they're just helping us. And we're"—he gestured at Felicity—"from another place altogether. But anyway, we're trying to catch some fugitives from Spectraland, I mean, the Land under the Rainbow. They were supposed to be at the Outpost Eight facility, but it turned out they were taken to Sector One."

"Rainbow folk?" Guider said, her antennae twitching so furiously that Joel thought she might be having some kind of a stroke. "So the rumors were true."

"Indeed they were," Thinker said. "I am Thinker of Deep Thoughts. I was the administrator of the rainbow folk bulletin system on the information exchange network. Perhaps you are familiar with some of my postings?"

"Oh yes, very much so." Guider nodded. "I must admit, though, I found them rather difficult to believe. A race of beings from an island across the sea, able to perform literal miracles through the power of their music..."

"Only a few of us have that ability," Thornleaf pointed out.

"Fascinating, nevertheless. Are your fugitives among those few?"

"One of them is," Joel answered. "And we're pretty sure that he's going to try to kill the Uniter."

Guider paused, tilting her head. "Is he now?"

"Yeah, um, so, we need to stop him. Can you help us?"

"Help you?" Guider laughed. "Why should I do that?"

Uh oh, Joel thought. *Did I say the wrong thing?* He glanced at Felicity, who was wearing her best McKayla Maroney scowl. "Uh, well, because—"

"If what you are telling me is true, then your fugitive will be doing our work for us. He will accomplish a goal that we have spent many long and difficult years dreaming about and striving toward, sometimes at great cost." Guider stepped up into Joel's face. "Are you familiar with what the Uniter has done? Have these two"—she gestured toward Thinker and Keeper—"told you the stories?"

"We have told him enough," Keeper said.

"During the war, entire cities were burned to the ground," Guider said, her tone turning acidic. "Thousands and thousands of innocent citizens, my entire family among them, were mercilessly slaughtered. And now, anyone found guilty of a so-called crime against the realm is put to death in the slowest and most painful way possible. This man is a monster. *He* is the criminal, not us. He rules by fear and fear alone. And you...you are telling me that you want to *save* him?"

"Well, no," Joel said. "I mean, not really. I mean...this guy who we think is gonna try to kill him—our fugitive—he's just as bad. Maybe worse, even."

Guider gave a derisive snort. "I find that very hard to believe."

"It is true," Auravine said. "Nineteen years ago, he almost destroyed the Land under the Rainbow. And he might have had a second chance, if it were not for..."

"That's kind of a long story," Felicity stepped in. "Anyway, trust us—he's a total jerk."

"Yeah," Joel said, "and after he kills the Uniter, he'll take over the Mono Realm."

"Take over?" Guider said.

"Yup." Felicity nodded. "And when that happens, you're gonna think that you've had it super easy up until now."

"How do you know he will be able to do that?"

"I, uh, I had a vision," Joel replied.

"A vision, you say."

"Yeah, um, so please, you have to let us go and stop him."

Guider paused. For a few seconds, Joel thought that she was going to say yes. But then she shook her head. "I cannot imagine such a scenario coming to pass," she said. "If the Uniter is somehow deposed, we have the means to swiftly fill that vacuum."

"Um, I don't think that—"

"I must allow your fugitive to continue with his plan to kill the Uniter," Guider said, stepping into Joel's personal space. "I would be doing my people a great disservice if I did not." She turned to the gaunt male. "Place them in the cells."

"But—" Joel started to protest, but then he felt his body seize up once more. Against his will, he turned around and started to walk out of the room.

"It is too bad," Guider sighed, sounding genuinely regretful. "I was hoping that we could work together."

Joel's mind spun.

Work together...work together...

"Wait!" he said. "What if we can?" His feet stopped in their tracks.

"What are you suggesting?" Guider asked.

"Yeah, what *are* you suggesting?" Felicity murmured out of the corner of her mouth.

"What if...what if *we* got rid of the Uniter instead? You know, while we're catching our fugitives? That way, neither of the bad guys would be in charge."

"You would kill the Uniter?" Guider said.

"No, not kill him, just...overthrow him, or whatever. Take him prisoner, since, like you said, he's a criminal."

Guider walked out and came face-to-face with Joel once more. "Are your people really so powerful that you could accomplish something like that?"

"Um...sure. We just need one thing, if you have it."

"And what would that be?"

"A freecloth."

Guider smiled. She reached into a pocket in her leggings and pulled out a long strip of white fabric, like a magician with an endless handkerchief. "I believe this should suffice."

"So you *are* connected to the black market!" Keeper exclaimed.

"Indeed we are," Guider said. "We manufacture the countercoms—my associate here has the latest, deluxe model—and sell them to finance our operations. And with every purchase, we give away a freecloth in hopes of encouraging new recruits."

"Why don't you just give those things away to every-one?" Felicity asked.

Guider shook her head. "Too risky. To prevent detection, our strategy is to grow our ranks a little at a time. We figured that anyone purchasing a self-defense device from a black-market agent would have a bit of a rebellious streak in them. Our hope was that they would use the cloth, get arrested, and then we would rescue them before they were executed."

"Were you always successful?" Keeper asked.

"We never had a chance to find out. As far as we know, no one has ever used the cloth."

"Well, most of us have a slight aversion to dying."

"An aversion you may have to soon overcome, if you truly intend to capture the Uniter."

CHAPTER 18: THE ROYAL TOWER

I f the City by the Lake was like downtown Camas, Washington, as Felicity had joked, then Sector One was the Mono Realm's equivalent of New York, Los Angeles, or, quite possibly, a combination of the two. Sprawling and immense, it was home to many large and exotic buildings—some of which seemed almost organic in nature—that were surrounded on all sides by twisting, looping strips of highway. Giant video billboards were scattered here and there, all of them showing the same thing: a propaganda loop of a blond Mono Realm woman (the same one that Joel had seen on the video monitor back in the Triplets' bar) praising the Uniter and reminding all citizens to always wear their soulshifter salve unless instructed otherwise by an authorized government representative.

"I think that's a good sign," Joel said, riding along with Keeper, Auravine, Riverhand, and Windblade in an appropriated military vehicle. Thinker, Thornleaf, Felicity, and Redstem were right behind in a second vehicle, while Guider and four of her lieutenants followed closely behind in a third. They were all wearing the last of Thinker's soulshifter salves, this one a dark blue that made them appear to be civilian workers for the government.

"A good sign?" Windblade said. "What do you mean?"

"Oh—uh, this video," Joel replied, pointing to one of the billboards. "If Marshall had already taken over, I'm sure he would be showing himself instead."

"So then we are not too late," Auravine said.

"Hopefully."

The Royal Tower, located at the heart of Sector One, appeared to be almost exactly like the tower Joel had seen in his Firelight Highway vision, except that it was larger and covered by a translucent energy dome similar to the one that protected the Wavemaker Temple back in Spectraland. Set in the middle of a circular paved area the size of a major league baseball field, it was visible from the road but not directly approachable, so Keeper had to settle for exiting the highway a little over a mile away. Her vehicle's navigation system led them to a nearby lot, where they parked the vehicles before splitting up into seven pairs—one Wavemaker with one Mono Realmer each—that would enter the tower grounds from different directions so as not to raise suspicion. It was like a grown-up, high-stakes version of a grade-school field trip, where each student was assigned a buddy. The hope was that they would be perceived simply as employees returning from a meal break. As he and Keeper walked, Joel hummed the *Mission: Impossible* theme song under his breath.

"What song is that?" Keeper asked.

"Huh? Oh—uh, just something from these movies I saw."

"Your homeland must be quite an interesting place."

"I guess. It's actually kinda similar to here. Parts of it are, anyway."

"Except that yours is still filled with the joy of music, while ours is not."

"Well, maybe that'll change. You know, if we can pull this off."

"That would be nice."

They strode as confidently as they could toward the dome-shaped energy barrier. The barrier crackled ominously, like some kind of high-voltage force field. Thinker told them that they should be able to walk right on through, since this particular soulshifter salve identified them as government staff, but then again, it *had* been a long time since he last used it. If it didn't work, then this had the possibility of being quite an impossible mission indeed. Out of the corner of his eye, Joel spotted Thinker and Thornleaf about thirty yards away, also casually heading toward the barrier. For a split second, he considered slowing down to see what became of them first, but he quickly banished that thought; if something bad was going to happen, it was going to happen to all of them together.

The closer they got, the louder the barrier crackled. It even gave off a little humming sound, like a fluorescent light. Joel held his breath and closed his eyes.

Here we go.

He stepped forward. He felt a little tingling sensation, but that was all, and when he opened his eyes again, he saw that he and the others had made it through unscathed.

Whew.

Inside the energy dome, workers and soldiers were everywhere. Most of the former were carrying documents or tablets and walking around like they really had somewhere important to be, while the latter were either standing guard by the tower or marching to and fro in formations, possibly participating in some kind of drill. It was a rather intimidating display, one that justified the party's decision to not just go charging in with guns and wavebows a-blazing.

Gaining access to the tower itself was their next challenge. There were numerous doors spread out at regular intervals along the base of the structure, and each of them had a recessed panel similar to the one on the back entrance to the Outpost Eight facility. With Joel following, Keeper walked up to one of the doors and placed her fingertips on the panel while both of them tried their best to ignore the pair of guards stationed on either side of the door. Using little flashes of energy from her fingers, Keeper entered a combination that Thinker had managed to obtain from the government's files. After an unnervingly long pause, the panel lit up and the door slid open.

"Have a good day," one of the guards said. "Long live the Uniter."

"Yes," Keeper replied. "Long live the Uniter."

Once inside, things got even trickier. Three of the groups, including the one composed of Joel and Keeper, were given the task of finding Marshall, Darkeye, and the Lightsnakes, while the other four attempted to locate and capture the Uniter, who, according to Guider, never left the tower these days out of concern for his own security. It was agreed that wavebows would probably come into play here sooner or later, as both a tracking device as well as an offensive weapon to stun any guards, but for the moment, employing them seemed rather impractical; the first level of the Royal Tower was doughnut shaped, like the ground floor of an Earthly arena, and there were more workers and soldiers walking about everywhere, as if they had just arrived for a concert and were heading for their seats. There were kiosks that resembled reception desks where the concession stands in an Earth arena would usually be, and, as he and Keeper circled around, Joel saw, in the center of the level beyond the kiosks, squads of soldiers engaged in various demonstrations and maneuvers. At every ten feet in between the kiosks, there was a large video monitor playing the propaganda loop.

"This is not what I was expecting," Keeper murmured after they had circled around one and a half times.

"Yeah, me neither," Joel said. "How are we gonna find them?"

"What about your special ability?"

"The Sight? That would only work if they'd passed through here," Joel replied. "I'll give it a shot, though." He did, but as he expected, the only things he saw were the ghostly images of more workers and soldiers. "No good."

"That is unfortunate," Keeper sighed.

"What if we just ask someone?"

"We could try that, I suppose."

They walked up to one of the kiosks, where three civilian workers were seated at terminals that looked like someone had grafted computer screens and keyboards onto some old-fashioned looms.

"Excuse me," Keeper said.

"Can I help you?" one of the workers replied.

"Yes, ah, my colleague and I are transfers from Outpost Eight. We were assigned to study the rainbow folk, who, I have been told, were recently sent here to the

Royal Tower by order of the Uniter himself. Can you tell me where I can find them?"

The three workers glanced at each other for a few seconds, their antennae twitching. Finally, one of them said, "If you were given such an assignment, your instructions should have included information about where and to whom you should report."

"Yes, ah, well, you see," Keeper stammered, "we must have...er..."

The worker stood up. "May I see your credentials, please?"

"We, ah, we forgot them in our vehicle," Keeper said. "We shall go and retrieve them now. And look over our instructions once more, as well. Uh, long live the Uniter."

She walked away hastily. Joel followed. Once they were out of sight of that particular kiosk, she stopped and grabbed Joel's arm.

"Ow!" Joel said. "What—"

"That was a terrible idea!" Keeper hissed.

"Well, um, I just thought—"

"Now they may already be on to us! And why did you not speak?"

Joel felt a lump develop in his throat. "Sorry, I, uh—"

"Attention, all citizens," an amplified voice said. It was the blond Mono Realm woman from the propaganda loop. Everyone stopped in their tracks and looked at one of the video monitors. For a nerve-racking moment, Joel thought that she was going to declare an intruder alert, but instead she said, "There will be an important announcement in twenty minutes. At that time, please make sure you are near a video monitor. Once again, there will be an important announcement in twenty minutes. Thank you." The loop resumed.

"I wonder what that could be about," Keeper said.

"I dunno," Joel said, just grateful that the report had distracted Keeper from scolding him any further.

"Hopefully it is something that—" She was interrupted by the sound of her countercom beeping. She took it out and covertly held it to her head. "Yes?"

Joel could hear Guider's voice coming from the device, but he couldn't make out what she was saying.

"Uh huh." Keeper nodded. "I see. All right. Yes...excellent. Very well, we shall meet you there." She pushed a button on the device before putting it away.

"What happened?" Joel asked. "Are they okay?"

"Very much so. They have located your fugitives."

♪♪♪

Eight minutes earlier

"This place reminds me of the Tacoma Dome," Felicity said, looking around as she walked.

"What is that?" Guider asked.

"It's an arena...a big building where they have concerts and sporting events and stuff," Felicity replied. For a moment, she felt an unfamiliar twinge of...regret? Doubt? Both?

Man, it would be really cool to play that Sugarblood show, wouldn't it?

"Ah, yes, before the war, we used to have large musical performances as well," Guider said. "Not in this structure, of course, but typically in wide-open outdoor areas. Oh, how I long for those days."

Guider's sentimentality made Felicity want to forget about her own, as she had no stomach for sappiness. "So, if we do what we're all here to do, those days will come back?"

"As the leader of the Redivision movement, I will personally see to it."

"Then let's get down to business. Can you tell if there's a bathroom around here?"

"Is that the kind of business you are referring to?"

"No, no—we just need some place where there're not as many people around."

"I think there is one just up ahead."

"Sweet."

Guider led the way to a narrow corridor in between a couple of reception desk-like kiosks. At the end of the corridor were two doors, one on either side, both of them marked with Mono Realm writing.

"You are a female, correct?" Guider asked.

A dizzying array of sarcastic responses flashed through Felicity's mind before she decided that now was probably not the right time for that sort of thing. "Correct."

Guider opened the door on the right, and they both went in. The room was remarkably similar to a public restroom back on Earth; on one side there were a number of stalls, each with their own door, and on the other side, a row of basins, above which hung a long mirror that reflected the viewer's internal energy signature (or so Felicity assumed, since she couldn't see her own external image in it). A soldier with frizzy blue hair was busy washing her hands. None of the stalls appeared to be occupied.

"So," Felicity said to Guider, "what did you think of that report?"

Guider's antennae twitched. "What report?"

"You know...that report that I asked you to look over yesterday."

"I do not recall—"

Felicity gave Guider what she hoped was a *just play along* expression.

"—oh, yes, that report. Well, I must say, I found it to be rather...detailed, I suppose, and, ah, quite comprehensive."

The blue-haired soldier, her hygienic duties completed, turned and walked out of the room. As soon as she was gone, Felicity pulled out a freecloth (Guider had provided one to each Wavemaker).

"If anyone comes in," she said, wiping her face with the cloth, "freeze 'em and then move 'em into one of these stalls."

"What if they call out for help?"

"I'm gonna take care of that here in a second."

"Are you sure this is wise?" Guider asked. "Remember, Thinker of Deep Thoughts does not have any more of this particular salve."

"Yeah, yeah, I know. Did I get it all off?"

"You did."

"Cool." Felicity pulled out her wavebow and moved to the far end of the room. She played a short riff. A white cloud of Aura energy streamed out of her instrument and spread out everywhere except for where she was standing. Guider's mouth moved as if she were saying something, but no sounds came out; everything within the cloud had been muted.

"Too bad I'll never get to use that one on Vicky," Felicity muttered to herself, recalling one of the many times when her sister wouldn't stop lecturing her about being more polite, less sarcastic, more feminine, less abrasive, blah, blah, blah, on and on ad nauseum. Victoria—she hated to be called Vicky—was so caught up in the drama of her own life that she never took the time to understand why Felicity acted the way she did.

Well, now that ignorant witch won't have to bother at all.

Shaking her head to get herself back in the moment, Felicity played another lick, and the headstock of her wavebow lit up with the shimmering green glow of a tracking cast. "All right, where are you bozos?" she said, moving the instrument around. After a few seconds, she got a hit; the green glow turned a few shades brighter as she aimed the headstock toward her feet. "Hey, I found them," she called out.

Guider tried to say something in response, but again, there was no sound.

"Come over here," Felicity said.

A civilian worker entered, but Guider, using a deluxe countercom, quickly froze her and walked her into one of the stalls before moving over to where Felicity stood.

"Nice job," Felicity said.

"Thank you. So, you have found your fugitives?"

"Yeah. They're, like, right underneath us. Does this place have a lower level or something?'

"It does." Guider nodded. "The prison level. That is where some of us escaped from, actually."

"Then you know how to get down there?"

"I do."

"Awesome. Okay, let's—"

Felicity stopped as she heard a voice coming from outside the restroom. For a moment, she thought that it was someone about to enter, but then she realized that it was the Mono Realm woman from the propaganda loop, apparently talking through a loudspeaker system. Felicity listened, but it was difficult to understand exactly what the woman was saying through the muting wavecast. Something about an "important announcement" and "twenty minutes."

"Hope that's not about us," Felicity muttered. "All right, I'll clean up in here and then wait in one of the stalls. Call me when it's safe to come out."

"Understood. What will you be doing in the meantime?"

"I've got a lot of thinking to do."

♫♫

Joel and Keeper met up with Guider in front of a narrow corridor, one of the few spaces in between kiosks that wasn't taken up by a video monitor. The Redivision leader was alone.

"Where's Felicity?" Joel asked, careful to keep his voice down.

"She removed her salve in order to perform some of her magic," Guider answered. "So now she is hiding in the restroom."

"Oh." Joel suppressed an urge to chuckle.

"We will need you to do the same here, shortly."

"Hide in the restroom?"

"No, perform some of your magic."

"Oh—okay."

"So, where are the rainbow folk fugitives?" Keeper asked.

"Down below, in the prison level," Guider replied.

"Did you inform the other team?"

"I tried to contact them, but got no response. Hopefully they were just occupied."

As Joel tried not to worry about Riverhand and Guider's lieutenant (the third team assigned to locate Marshall and the others), Guider led the way to another narrow passage that ended in a door with a recessed panel. Once there, she stopped and turned to Joel. "Remove your salve," she said.

"But then won't people see that I'm, you know, from the Land under the Rainbow?"

"Exactly. We are going to pretend that we are escorting you to the prison level."

"Oh—the fake prisoner thing. Okay, I understand." Joel took out his freecloth and began wiping his face.

"Two civilian workers escorting a prisoner seems rather odd, though," Keeper pointed out. "Are you sure this will work?"

Guider pressed her fingertips to the recessed panel and started entering the energy-combination. "No."

The door slid aside, revealing a small room with a transit-tube platform. The trio entered, and the door closed behind them. Off to the side of the platform was a lectern that looked old and medieval, except that it had a video screen monitor attached to it. A male Mono Realmer standing behind the lectern shifted his attention from the monitor to the trio.

"Excuse me," he said, "but...who are you?"

"Members of the Uniter's secret science division," Guider responded, pulling out a deluxe countercom. "We are returning this rainbow folk representative to his cell."

"I do not recognize any of you. And what is that you are holding? I will have to—"

Guider touched her device, creating a high-pitched squeal.

"Intruders!" the male Mono Realmer managed to shout before Guider, using her countercom's joystick, made his hands cover his mouth.

"Well, that was rather hasty, was it not?" Keeper said.

"He was about to broadcast our energy signatures for confirmation," Guider replied. She turned to Joel as the lectern attendant continued his muffled cries. "Could you silence him, please?"

"Oh—uh, sure." Joel took out his wavebow, aimed, and plucked out a quick note. A short red pulse of energy shot out and struck the attendant, sending him slumping to the ground, stunned.

"I meant just mute his voice, not render him unconscious," Guider said, running a hand through her silver hair. "I was going to make him operate the transit tubes for us. Can you revive him?"

"Um...well, that's more of a healer kind of thing."

Guider shook her head. "In that case, I will have to stay here and operate the tubes myself while the two of you go on. Try not to take too long."

"What will we find down there?" Keeper asked.

"Many cells, and at least twice as many guards. At this point, I recommend you bypass any talking and simply do what you did up here."

"You mean stun them?" Joel asked.

"Correct."

Joel and Keeper stepped up onto the platform while Guider worked the controls at the lectern. The instant Joel positioned himself on one of the platform's circles he was sucked down into the tube. Fortunately, it was a quick ride; barely three seconds had elapsed before the two found themselves deposited into another small room. A guard was standing next to a door, facing a video screen on the opposite wall.

"What the—?" the guard said, surprised. "I was not notified of any—"

Joel raised his instrument and strummed, firing out a wide stream of brilliant crimson light. The guard collapsed.

"I hope no one heard that," Keeper said.

The pair walked up to the door, which slid aside automatically. Beyond it was a dimly lit, Y-shaped hallway with three cells on each side. Each cell had, in lieu of a door or bars, a protective energy field similar to the one around the tower itself. Joel did a quick scan of the cells' inhabitants; all six of them were Mono Realmers. None of them seemed able to see Joel and Keeper as the two carefully made their way down the hall.

"We should stay together," Joel suggested once they reached the intersection. "I'll face the front, while you watch the back."

"Agreed."

They headed down the left side. There were more cells, each of them holding a single Mono Realmer inmate.

I wonder where all the guards are? Joel thought, unconcerned that he would jinx himself. If any were to show up, he was ready for them.

Keeper's countercom beeped. They stopped as she answered it. "No, we have not," she said after a pause, "but we believe that we are close…oh…all right…yes, very good…yes, we will contact you as soon as we do."

"Who was that?" Joel asked.

"Thinker of Deep Thoughts. He and Thornleaf have learned of the Uniter's present location, so they and the other three teams are going to rendezvous there."

"Oh—cool. Where?"

"The top floor of the tower, adjacent to the landing platform."

"That's perfect. They should just be able to fly away once they have him."

"I believe that is their plan. I hope we will be as fortunate."

"Don't worry, we got this."

They continued down the hall, which went on for another fifty feet or so before it took a sharp turn to the right. As he glanced into each cell (none of which contained Marshall, Darkeye, or either of the Lightsnakes), Joel could hear the anticipatory mutterings of a crowd, like an audience waiting for a show to start. After the turn, he found, the left side of the hall was still lined with cells, but the right side was open, with a railing. Joel backed up and peered around the corner while Keeper continued to watch the hall behind them. He saw that they were on the top of three levels, each of them connected by a short flight of stairs; it was like they were in a triangle-shaped shopping mall. In the middle of the area at the bottom stood twenty-five guards—much fewer than the number of cells, Joel realized; apparently, Guider had been exaggerating—all gathered around a large video monitor that was playing the propaganda loop.

"I think they're waiting for that important announcement," Joel said, turning to Keeper. "Check it out."

Keeper looked around the corner. "How fortunate," she said. "Would you able to stun them all from up here?"

"I should be able to," Joel said, fishing for his loudstone. "Just need to make sure I have enough energy."

The video monitor went black.

"Attention, all citizens," the voice of the blond Mono Realm woman said.

Joel located his loudstone in his cloak. He took it out and touched it to his temple. A surge of energy shot through him.

"Please cease your current activity and listen to this important announcement from your exalted leader, the Uniter. Thank you."

An image appeared on the video screen, one that nearly made Joel drop his loudstone. It was the male Mono Realmer that Blackspore had shown the Wavemakers—the one that resembled Joel's dad.

"Greetings, fellow Mono Realmers." He even sounded like Joel's dad, albeit with an English accent. "Today is a very historic occasion, one that is rivaled in significance only by the end of the war that unified our states into a single great nation." He paused for applause.

"What are you waiting for?" Keeper whispered. "Stun them already."

Joel was still getting over the shock. Apparently, his dad's doppelganger was the evil ruler of this land who was responsible for so much tragedy. "Um, right." He put away his loudstone, its energy now coursing throughout his body.

"As I am sure many of you are aware," the Uniter continued, "there have been rumors, much stronger as of late, that there are, in fact, people who live in the Land under the Rainbow, and that some of those people are actually here among us at this very moment."

Joel raised his wavebow and took aim.

"Well, I am here today to tell you that those rumors are true."

The camera panned out on the Uniter. He was standing on the landing platform of the tower, and next to him were Marshall, Darkeye, and the two Lightsnakes.

Uh oh.

"And I am proud to announce," the Uniter said, raising his voice, "that I have forged a divine alliance with them—one that will help usher in a new era of unparalleled prosperity for both of our lands!"

What the—

As more applause sounded, a door opened behind the video monitor. Some familiar faces, mixed in with additional guards, began to file in. Joel realized with horror that they were the other members of his party, Felicity included, wearing fancy, glowing handcuffs.

"The leader of the rainbow folk," the Uniter went on, "is now hereby, officially, my coregent. Tomorrow morning, we will be setting off on a tour to all the cities of the realm, at which point every citizen shall be required to publicly swear their allegiance to him."

"I do not understand," Keeper said, sounding aghast. "I thought that..."

"After the tour, per my coregent's request, we will be sending a contingent of soldiers and scientists to visit the Land under the Rainbow. As some of you may already know, it has always been protected by huge, unpassable waves. But thanks to him, we now have the means and the knowledge by which to overcome them."

Okay, that doesn't sound good.

"So, without further ado, I would like to ask that he step forward and say a few words about himself and his entourage."

Marshall stepped forward. All of his remaining disfigurements appeared to have been healed, or at least covered up somehow, and he had been fitted with a prosthetic right arm that looked like something straight out of *The Terminator*. "Yes, hello, greetings, everyone," he said with a smug grin. "Before I begin, I want to thank the Uniter and his security forces for their brilliant work in helping me foil an outlaw band of insurgents who followed me here, intent on ruining my mission of peaceful outreach and cooperation."

"Joel!" Keeper exclaimed, grabbing his shoulder.

Joel whirled around. Another group of guards was at the far end of the enclosed hall, coming their way. *It's a trap*, he thought to himself in his best Admiral Ackbar voice. He couldn't help it.

"Halt!" one of the guards shouted.

Flush with energy, Joel gave his instrument a furious strum that flooded the entire hallway with red light. The approaching guards dropped like giant sacks of wheat.

"More are coming!" Keeper said. "This side!"

Joel turned to see lines of guards and soldiers streaming down the open hall and up the stairs from the lower levels, as if a dam had been broken. All of them were headed toward him and Keeper with their weapons raised. A quick glance to the other side revealed that the group of guards he had just stunned was merely the initial wave; many more were now following, filling up the hallway as they marched shoulder to shoulder.

"...and as you will see," Marshall babbled on, "my followers and I possess many extraordinary abilities that will allow us to..."

Joel created a dome of Aura energy around him and Keeper just before the first volley of shots arrived. Keeper used her countercom to freeze a few of the guards, but this was as useful as swatting the first couple of locusts in a swarm. Drawing on his augmented power, Joel was able to maintain the shield cast while he sprayed more stunning casts in all directions.

"Downstairs!" he shouted to Keeper.

With her right behind him, he cut a swath through the guards and soldiers who were now beginning to fill up the place like fans at a Sugarblood show in a drastically undersized venue. Seizing their opportunity, the other members of Joel's party charged forward through the chaos—Felicity took out a couple of guards with some well-placed roundhouse kicks along the way—and Joel breathed a quick sigh of relief when he realized that they were all apparently wanted alive, since it would have been easy for the guards to have simply killed their prisoners as soon as the melee broke out.

"Over here!" he called out to them.

Wavemakers and Mono Realm allies alike all started to wade their way through the mass of bodies toward Joel and Keeper. Joel's extra energy, combined with his Sight ability, had the effect of slowing things down—*this must be what veteran professional athletes are always talking about,* he thought—to the extent that he was able to pick off, with pinpoint precision, the guards and soldiers who posed the most immediate threats to the members of his party less skilled in self-defense. Eventually, all of them made it under the relative safety of Joel's shield-dome, where they huddled together as close as fourteen people could possibly get.

"This whole thing was a setup," Felicity said.

"Um, yeah, you think?" Joel said, still firing away.

"That's—that's good. You're really getting it."

"Where are your wavebows and loudstones?"

"They took them all, dude."

The soldiers, seemingly endless in number, continued to pour in. For every one that Joel stunned, two took his or her place up against the shield, pounding it with their fists, stabbing at it with their bayonets.

"I don't know how much longer I'll be able to keep this up," Joel said.

"I have an idea," Felicity said. "Play the transfer cast."

"The what?"

"You know, the one to send us back to Earth."

"But what about—"

"I know, I know, everyone else looks like aliens. We'll just pass it off as a late Halloween or something."

"But will it work from here? Don't we need to be at the Rift?"

"I don't think we have a choice—Marshall might come down here at any minute."

"Okay, yeah, you're right." Joel took a deep breath. "Here we go." He started to play the notes of the transfer wavecast. The shield flickered a little, but it held firm against the blows of the soldiers surrounding it.

C'mon, Suzuki, you can do this.

He could feel his energy draining away at an exponential rate, like a tub with the stopper taken out; loudstone or not, the amount of power needed to send fourteen people across time, space, and possibly dimensions while simultaneously holding up a shield cast was enormous.

He stole a glance at Felicity and was reminded of that moment on Crownrock, right before they were about to confront Marshall for the first time. She had the same look in her eyes, the look that said she was relying on him, counting on him to come up with some brilliant plan to save the day. It was an amazing look. *She* was amazing.

Is this what love is?

He finished the song. The shield cast fell away. Everything went dark.

CHAPTER 19: IN LIMBO

The first thing Joel saw was the coffee shop.

We made it, he thought.

He quickly glanced around, looking for the others. They weren't there.

Oh no. Where did they—

Then Joel realized that he wasn't on Earth at all. The coffee shop was just an image, like a mirage, and together they were floating in the middle of teal-tinted space. Other images were there as well: video game consoles, cans of soda, a baseball glove. But there was no sign of Felicity, Keeper, or anyone else.

I've gotta get back, he thought, frantic.

His wavebow was still in his hand, so he strummed it. Nothing happened. He took out his loudstone. There was a faint light inside it, but otherwise, it felt cold and dead. He pressed it to his temple. Again, nothing.

"Okay, okay," he said out loud, trying to quell a rising sense of panic, "let's just stay calm here. No need to freak out. Everything's gonna be all right. They'll all probably show up in a few minutes, like how Felicity did the last time, and then Thornleaf can help me recharge the loudstone, and then we can go back to Spectraland.

No problem. I'll just wait here patiently until that happens."

And so he waited, reciting an alphabetical list of Piers Anthony novels in his head as he did so. He got as far as *On a Pale Horse* before his patience started to wear thin.

"Okay, now I remember," he continued talking to himself. "The last time I was here, I moved around for a bit before Felicity appeared. Maybe I just need to do that again."

He flapped his arms and air-swam past the coffee shop image. Beyond it, there were more images, but none of them were of people. He activated the Sight and kept going until his shoulders started to hurt from all the flapping. Along the way, he had seen nothing but ghostly inanimate objects.

Something's definitely wrong. Last time I was here for six minutes and thirty-three seconds before Felicity showed up. Now, it's been...what, almost twenty minutes? Man, I can't even estimate the time anymore.

Unable to come up with another course of action, he resumed propelling himself around. His feelings of panic started to escalate. Was he going to be trapped in here forever? What happened to everyone else? Were they okay?

I need to calm down somehow. Thinking of a list didn't really work this time...what else can I do?

He looked at his wavebow, and an idea struck him. Even though its magic was gone, he could still play music on it, and hopefully, like when he practiced his guitar in his room back home, doing so would at least alleviate his anxiety enough that he would be able to come up with another plan.

He returned to the coffee shop image, parked himself in front of it, and started to play some scales. More objects drifted by: a Rubik's Cube, a thumb drive, one of the full-size arcade versions of *Mario Kart*. Switching from scales to songs, he decided that he would run through the entire catalog of all his favorite bands, starting with Alice in Chains and then going from there. He was in the middle of "Rooster" when a nineteen-inch flat screen computer monitor that was floating past him suddenly crackled to life.

"Joel?" the monitor said.

Joel stopped playing. "Whoa—wait, what?"

A blurry image on the monitor struggled to gain focus, like a Skype call with a lousy Internet connection. "Joel, can you hear me?"

"Um, yeah, but who...who are you?" Joel asked, swimming after the monitor. "Are you for real? Is this a vision? Did I fall asleep?"

"Hold on, let me adjust something." A pause, and then the image suddenly became crystal clear, almost hi-def. It was Blackspore. "Ah, there we go. Can you see me now?"

Joel nodded, dumbstruck.

"Excellent." The monitor slowed, and then it stopped. "Thank the Aura I was able to find you. Good thinking, there, playing your wavebow."

"How did—where did you..."

"After you and the others departed, I found that I still had some of the Aura energy I borrowed from the healer girl left over," Blackspore said. "So I dug out the remains of my wavebow and decided to...well, keep tabs on you, I suppose."

"You were spying on us?"

Blackspore chuckled. "You could call it that. I prefer to think of it as...watching over. Looking out for you."

"I dunno...it still seems kinda creepy to me."

"But now you must be glad that I did, are you not?"

"Well, yeah, I guess." Joel *was* relieved that someone had found him, but in all honesty, he had done such a good job of distracting himself with his music that he wouldn't have minded if Blackspore had taken a bit longer to do so. That was, of course, until he remembered another, larger concern. "Do you know where the others are?"

"Unfortunately, I was only able to focus on one person, so I selected you, since you are the one with the Sight. Did Fireflower tell you about all the visions that master Wavemakers have had about you over the years?"

"No, not really."

"Ah, too bad. Then again, she *was* still just an apprentice when the Fourfoot War ended. She probably did not have a chance to access those records before they were destroyed."

"Um, okay."

"One of those visions in particular talks about how the Sight will grow over time, until you become more powerful than any other Wavemaker who has ever lived, either on this world or another."

"Will that happen in time for me to get out of here and save my friends?"

"Not completely," Blackspore said with another chuckle. "But you will not need that much power to rescue them."

"I'm confused."

"What I am trying to tell you is that your training is woefully inadequate. I feel that the Aura has brought the two of us together so that I may play a part in guiding you toward your eventual destiny."

A ghostly glazed doughnut drifted in front of the monitor. Joel waved it away. "But...aren't you a war criminal, or whatever? How do I know you'll be giving me good advice?"

"There were reasons for what I did, beyond simply wanting to help my village. After I explain them to you, I think you will understand." Blackspore made the little sideways head motion that was the Spectraland equivalent of a shrug. "Besides, I am not sure you have any better options at this point."

"True."

♫♫

Felicity felt the point of a rifle jab her in the back. "Hey, watch it with that thing," she snapped.

"Quiet," the guard behind her said.

Surrounded by dozens of guards and soldiers, Felicity and the others—sans Joel, who seemed to have succeeded in only transporting himself—were forced to walk up a short flight of stairs and toward what looked like the only empty cell in the whole prison level.

This must've been where Marshall was hanging out just a few minutes ago, she groused to herself. *Can't believe I fell for that. Stupid, stupid, stupid.*

One of the guards pressed a button on the wall, and the cell's force-field barrier disappeared. The thirteen remaining members of the party were then shoved into the cell, which had enough room to comfortably accommodate four, maybe five people at the most. After everyone was jammed in like rush hour subway commuters, the barrier came back up.

"What happened to Joel?" Keeper asked.

"He abandoned us," Thornleaf grumbled.

"No," Felicity said, "he wouldn't do that. I think he just messed up the cast or something. Wouldn't be the first time."

"I am sure he will be back soon," Auravine said.

"You are stepping on my foot," one of Guider's lieutenants said.

"Apologies," Riverhand said.

"So, what are we going to do now?" Windblade asked.

"How about *you* suggest something, for once?" Redstem said.

"What are you talking about? I always have ideas."

"Name one."

"Stop it, both of you," Thornleaf snapped.

"They cannot keep us in here like this forever," Thinker said. "Eventually, they will have to relocate us to other cells. That will be our opportunity."

"Unless they continue to station as many guards around us as they have now," Guider said.

"You gotta admit, it's kinda flattering," Felicity said.

"What is?" Redstem said.

"This whole fifteen-to-one guard-to-us ratio, or whatever it is. They must think we're pretty dangerous."

"I am not sure that is much consolation at the moment," Thornleaf said.

"I didn't say it was."

The guards standing in front of the cell moved aside. Felicity frowned as she saw who they were making way for: Marshall Byle and the Uniter, the two of them coming up the stairway side by side like a couple of old high school buddies.

"...truly a fascinating device," the Uniter was saying. He was holding Guider's deluxe countercom. "I have dispatched many undercover agents over the past few months in an effort to obtain one of these, but none of them were successful. And now, several have been hand-delivered to my front door!"

"You're not the only one who's made out, mate." Marshall grinned. Auravine's wavebow hung from a strap around his shoulder, and he was casually tossing a loudstone up in the air and letting it fall back down into his hand. "These are some very valuable and powerful artifacts that these outlaws had stolen from me. I'm glad to have them back in my possession."

"I think our partnership will prove to be quite fruitful."

"Indeed."

"Yo—dirtbags," Felicity said.

"I would refrain from antagonizing the Uniter," Guider warned.

"Well, hello again, my dear," Marshall said, stepping up to the force field. "Nice to see that you still have some of your fighting spirit left."

"Let us outta here, would ya?" Felicity said. "It's getting kinda smelly."

"Oh, we will, we will." Marshall nodded. "In fact"—he glanced at the Uniter—"why don't we do that right now?"

Felicity tensed herself, figuring that she would have a split second after the force field came down to attack Marshall and grab the wavebow. It would be close, but she was pretty sure she could do it.

"Very well," the Uniter said. He turned to a civilian worker who was standing behind him and handed over the countercom. "You finally got this figured out, did you not?"

"Yes, Your Majesty."

Oh, crud, Felicity thought. *Wait, why am I not swearing to myself? Joel must really be rubbing off on me.*

The worker fiddled with the device, obviously not as proficient with it as Guider or her lieutenants, but after a few seconds, Felicity felt her body freeze up below her neck. The force field came down, but there was nothing she could do. Some more fiddling, and everyone in the cell was made to face forward.

"So," the Uniter said, looking at Marshall, "as per our agreement, the outlaws from your land will be transferred to the facility at Outpost Eight, where they will be dissected and experimented on before they are ultimately disposed of."

"Yes," Marshall said. "And your local rebels shall be taken to the public square in Sector One, where they will be publicly tortured and executed, providing a most effective deterrent to any more misguided insurgencies."

Felicity rolled her eyes. "What, did you guys, like, rehearse that whole bit beforehand or something?"

"But what about the boy?" the Uniter asked, ignoring her.

"Not to worry." Marshall smirked. "He won't be bothering us anymore."

♪♪♪

"Your problem is distraction," Blackspore said.

"But...my teachers at school say that I'm improving," Joel responded.

"I would claim just the opposite."

"What? Why?"

"Did you notice how many mistakes you made in the Mono Realm?"

"Um..."

"Your failure with the game machine, getting shot in the hallway, miscalculating the position of the soldiers in the wasteland—"

"Okay, okay, yeah, I know. But I did some good stuff too."

"Not nearly enough." Blackspore shook his head. "Not nearly enough to be the hero that you need to be."

"So, what, I just need to focus some more? Is that it?"

"There is a bit more to it than that. For you see, what you are distracted by...is love."

Joel furrowed his brow. "Love?"

"Yes, love. You have feelings for your fellow offworlder, but she prefers another and will soon be an offworlder no longer. You have feelings for the healer girl, but she is fated to return to prison for the rest of her life. You want love, you crave it, and so you are afraid. Afraid that your best opportunity for it is slipping away, and that you will never have another one like it ever again."

To most seventeen-year-olds, that declaration would seem silly, but deep down, Joel had to admit that Blackspore was right. He knew that finding love was difficult for anyone, let alone a shy guy on the autism spectrum like himself, and so yes, he *was* afraid that he would never make another connection with someone the way he had with Felicity and Auravine. The fact that he had even made those two in the first place seemed, to him, almost like a minor miracle.

"I see my words are having an effect," Blackspore continued. "Understand, Joel, I was like you once. Because of my feelings for someone, I disobeyed the Elders' directive to remain neutral in the Fourfoot War. I loved her so much that, in order to impress her, I took the drastic step of searching elsewhere for help when it seemed that all was lost. If I had not done these things, if I had stayed focused and concentrated on what I was supposed to have been doing, none of the tragedies that followed would have taken place. Byle would have never come over to Spectraland, and many innocent lives would have been spared. Do you know why I was so afraid of returning to the island? It was not the fear of imprisonment. No, it was because of these memories."

"Um...I'm not sure that's the same thing as my situation, though."

"Oh, but it is, it is!" Blackspore said, his tone turning dark. "The circumstances are different, but the core lesson is the same—love is like the sun: it seems bright and warm, but when you look at it too closely, it blinds you. When you bask in it for too long, it burns you. It makes you lazy and weary, careless and complacent. Prone to mistakes. Those are not good things to be, Joel, when you need to be the hero. The hero does not get the girl. The hero gets the job done."

"So...you're saying that to be a hero, you have to be lonely?"

"Ultimately, yes. That is what heroes do. That is what leaders do. They walk a separate path by themselves. When you are the hero, everyone is depending on you. You cannot afford to feel fear, doubt, love, or anything else that makes you weak and vulnerable. If you are experiencing hardship, you cannot show it. You must bear the burden alone."

Joel pursed his lips. This certainly wasn't what being a hero was like in the movies. Or was it? Luke Skywalker ended up alone, if you didn't count all that Mara Jade business from the Expanded Universe. And Jiro from *Kikaida*, that old 1970s tokusatsu series, was always riding off into the sunset on his motorcycle by himself at the end of each episode. So maybe there was something to what Blackspore was saying after all.

"I know that all of this may be hard to hear," the middle-aged Wavemaker went on. "Being a hero is, without a doubt, the most difficult job in the universe. But these are the realities that you must accept if you are going to take the next step in your journey. You must put aside your feelings and focus solely on the task at hand. Can you do that?"

Joel nodded. "I can."

♫♫♫

Felicity discovered that she was right about the Uniter's forces considering her and the other Wavemakers to be dangerous. They weren't sent to Outpost Eight via transit tube, since that would mean they would be unattended for a period of time, however short; instead, they were sealed—still under energy lock and cuffed at the wrists and ankles—into individual coffin-like containers and loaded up into large covered vehicles filled with armed guards that would transport them via the highway. It seemed like overkill to her, but she wasn't about to complain. She knew that they were making a fatal mistake in giving Joel more time to get his act together and come back to rescue them. That was her hope, anyway.

Part of her resented the fact that *she* had to be the one in this particular predicament, depending on Joel to save the day, but then she reminded herself of all the other times that she had been the hero. And really, she realized, it was kind of silly and pointless to think about it like that; it wasn't a competition, and it wasn't a matter of gender roles, it was the just the two of them, two people, doing whatever they could to help the good guys win in the end. Throughout every sticky situation in Spectraland, every precarious mess in the Mono Realm, and even every concert that they played back home, they always seemed able to bail each other out when one of them faltered for whatever reason. They were a team, and a pretty good one at that.

"Felicity," a voice said. It was Thornleaf, one of the rare times when he called her by her actual name. Apparently they had placed his coffin-container close to hers.

"What?" she replied. "You're gonna get us gagged, you know."

Something clanged against her coffin-container. Probably a rifle. "No talking," a guard said. They always said stuff like that.

"There is something...that I want to ask you." Thornleaf sounded tentative, almost nervous. Very uncharacteristic.

I suppose I should be nervous too, since we're on our way to be dissected. Maybe I'm getting too used to this kind of thing. "Fire away."

"In the event that we somehow make it out of this alive, I would like to—"

"I said, no talking!"

Sure enough, as Felicity expected, the lid of her container flew open, and a guard bent down and placed what seemed like a large bandage over her mouth. It was more comfortable and better-smelling than your typical gag back in Spectraland, so there was that, at least.

♪♪♪

"So, like, how does this work, exactly?" Joel asked. "I just forget about love, and then, ta-da, I'm good to go?"

"Ah, if only it were that simple." Blackspore chuckled. "Training your mind to achieve the necessary level of clarity requires many years of solitary meditation and effort."

"I, uh, I don't think I have that much time."

"You are right, you do not. But fortunately, there is a shortcut that we can employ." Blackspore reached his hand out through the monitor screen.

"Whoa, cool."

"I have spent nearly two decades in exile doing all of the training that I have just told you about. Using whatever little Aura energy I have left, I can transfer these experiences to you. It will be temporary, but it should last long enough for you to save your friends and complete your current mission. And after that, you will have a baseline of knowledge upon which you can build as you mature. Now, take my hand."

Joel extended his hand.

"No, no—the wrist," Blackspore said.

"What? But you said—"

"Just grab my wrist, like how the healer girl did. Remember?"

After a little awkward positioning, Joel took hold of Blackspore's wrist, and the master shaman did the same to Joel.

"Close your eyes."

Joel closed his eyes. Nothing happened for a moment, but then a flood of memories and emotions came rushing into his mind, so intense that it made him gasp. He instinctively tried to pull away, but his fingers were locked around Blackspore's wrist as if they were being held in place by some kind of magnetic force.

"Relax," Blackspore said. "Let it all in."

Joel took a deep breath. As the memories sorted themselves out, he could see a younger Blackspore, talking to a female Spectraland native dressed in a pale yellow tunic. Her features were blurry, but somehow she was still the most beautiful woman Joel had ever seen. He yearned for her. He wanted nothing more than to go to her, to embrace her, to tell her that everything was going to be all right.

A moment later, the scene shifted. Streaks of light were flying everywhere. There were screams, explosions, sounds of pain and despair, and, in the middle of it all, an unsettlingly familiar laugh. Joel shuddered, consumed with escalating sensations of rage, guilt, and sorrow that were each threatening to tear him apart.

Just as they were about to do so, a calm set in—not a serene, peaceful calm, but that dull, numb ache that lives at the border between depression and acceptance. This was followed by a gradual hardening, as if his heart was literally changing from living tissue into a mineral substance, impervious to all forces of nature. A portrait in his hands burned and then crumbled into ashes. Darkness engulfed him. He felt like curling up into a ball and dying.

But then something strange happened. A single, solitary spot of light broke through the gloom. He was alone, but he was not lonely. The yearning was gone. He was free.

"Open your eyes," Blackspore said.

Joel opened his eyes. The ghostly images of the limbo plane were still there, but now they were surrounded by colorful wisps of light that swirled around them like orbiting electrons.

"What do you see?" Blackspore asked.

"I see...the Aura. It's—it's everywhere."

Blackspore smiled. "You are ready."

CHAPTER 20: THE FACILITY

The vehicle came to a stop. Felicity could feel her coffin-container being unloaded.

Okay, Joel, any time now.

"Did you experience any problems on the trip over here?" a voice said.

"The prisoners began talking, but we gagged them before they could say anything of significance," came the reply. "Other than that, nothing to report."

"Excellent. Take them upstairs. They have some special guests."

Hmm. Wonder who that could be.

The lid of the container opened. A guard knelt down and removed Felicity's ankle-cuffs. Then, against her will, she rose up and stepped out of the container, like some kind of remote-controlled vampire. She saw that she was in a dusty lot adjacent to the hangar-like facility in Outpost Eight, surrounded by the other Wavemakers, a few civilian scientist-types, and more soldiers than she could count. She tried to catch Thornleaf's eye, but the tall shaman just kept staring forward.

What's his problem?

The civilian with Guider's countercom made the Wavemakers line up single file, shortest to tallest, before they began to march toward the facility. They walked through a pair of sliding glass doors, which Felicity assumed was the front entrance, and into a lobby-like area teeming with Mono Realm military personnel. There were video monitors everywhere, but instead of the propaganda loop they were now showing footage of a large stage in the middle of a gravel pit with a big crowd in front of it; it reminded Felicity of an outdoor music festival she had attended a few years ago.

That must be one of the old concert venues that Guider was telling me about.

She and the others were made to stop as the camera zoomed in on the stage. Sounds of cheering and applause started up, although they didn't seem like they were coming from the assembled crowd. Then, a moment later, the blond woman from the propaganda loop walked out, carrying what looked like one of the karaoke microphones from the Triplets' bar.

Is she gonna sing? Felicity wondered.

"Greetings, everyone," the woman said. "Thank you for your attention. We are coming to you live from the Public Yards outside of Sector One. Now, as many of you already know, a number of intruders were apprehended last night in the Royal Tower as they attempted to carry out a coup against the Uniter and his new coregent. This group included a band of criminals from the Land under the Rainbow, working in conjunction with members of the underground insurgency movement."

Yeah, I don't think I like this song.

"The rainbow folk criminals have been taken to a secure military facility, where they will be experimented on by the finest scientists of the realm in an effort to expand

and advance our vast stores of knowledge, all for the continued betterment of our citizens' way of life."

Felicity was glad that the energy lock didn't prevent her from rolling her eyes. *Oh, give me a break. What a load of—*

"And now, before I announce the fates of the local insurgents, I would like to introduce you to our new Minister of Information. Please welcome, Maker of Magical Fluids."

Eww, what a gross name...wait, is that who I think it is?

More (now obviously canned) applause sounded as the camera panned out to reveal Darkeye walking out on stage and taking the microphone from the blond woman.

Yup, it sure is.

"Thank you—*hic*—very much," Darkeye purred. "I would like to say that I am—*hic*—very honored to be part of the Mono Realm's royal council, and that I will strive to—*hic*—provide the Uniter and his coregent with the best possible advice and—*hic*—guidance."

Who is writing all these corny speeches, anyway?

Darkeye handed the microphone back to the woman, who resumed talking. "As you all know," she said, "earlier today the Uniter and the coregent embarked on a royal tour of the realm. In the more remote areas, they will not arrive until much later on tonight. But fear not, because in the meantime, we have a special treat for you: a public ceremony featuring the captured insurgents that will be broadcast to all corners of the land."

Thinker, Keeper, Guider, and the four lieutenants all walked out onto the stage, obviously under energy control. They lined up left to right and kneeled down, facing the audience.

"With the help of our Minister of Information, these despicable outlaws shall be subjected to a constant stream of torture until tomorrow morning when the royal procession returns. Then, at that time, they will be formally executed during the final ceremonies, providing a fitting conclusion to a most triumphant period in Mono Realm history."

C'mon, Joel, where are you?

♪♪♪

Filled with Aura energy and a single-minded sense of purpose, Joel zoomed through the sky like a heat-seeking missile. Thanks to the temporary boost in power provided to him by Blackspore's lesson, he was now able to perform all sorts of incredible feats not normally possible, like flying above the clouds at a near-hypersonic rate of speed. He couldn't transport himself directly back to the Mono Realm, but he was at least able to return to Blackspore's atoll via the limbo plane portal, thus saving him from having to start all the way back at Spectraland.

"I found them," Blackspore said in Joel's ear. Using a fishing hook and some natural adhesive, they were able to fashion Joel's loudstone into an earpiece of sorts that served as both a means of communication between the two of them and a way to keep the loudstone up against Joel's head, so that he could constantly reload, and draw from, its stores of energy. "They are in a...a large hut, of sorts, in the middle of a dry plain next to a ridge."

"Okay, I know where that is."

Joel looked down at the dark cloud below. People in the Mono Realm wouldn't be able to see him up here, but thanks to his enhanced Sight, *he* could see *them*, as well as all of the Realm's buildings, roads, and landmarks. In addition, as in the limbo plane, he could perceive streams and pockets of Aura energy everywhere he turned; it wasn't confined only to Spectraland after all. It was different, but just as useable.

"I have also located the Mono Realm citizens who were helping you," Blackspore said. Joel had lent him a lot of energy, allowing the middle-aged Wavemaker to use his long-distance viewing cast much more effectively and efficiently while talking to Joel at the same time.

"Yeah, I'll save them next."

"You are not letting your feelings affect this decision, are you?"

"No. It just makes the most logical sense." *Man, now I sound like Mister Spock.*

"Good."

Joel's eyes followed the Firelight Highway to where it terminated near Outpost Eight. He knew that despite his increased abilities, he couldn't afford to just go charging in, as that might provoke the Uniter's forces into to prematurely killing their captives. He would have to do this in stealth mode, ninja-style, without the benefit of any soulshifter salve.

Time for some serious first-person shooter skills.

"I'm gonna go dark here for a bit," he said.

"Understood," Blackspore replied.

Joel came to a stop above a small fleet of vehicles near the Outpost Eight facility. Then, after performing a muting cast on himself, he dropped straight down, feet-first, through the dark cloud and onto the dusty surface below, like a silent meteorite. He landed in between two of the vehicles and crouched down. Immediately, he saw an image of twenty-nine Mono Realm soldiers escorting the other Wavemakers toward the facility. The image was quite vivid, so he knew that this event had occurred not too long ago.

Cool. Hopefully I'm not too late.

A Mono Realm soldier, this one in present time, appeared in front of Joel, apparently checking out the mysterious *whoosh* of movement he must have just witnessed a few seconds earlier. Joel plucked his wavebow and, despite the fact that he was casting from inside of a muting cloud, the soldier fell over face-first, stunned. It was like shooting a gun with a silencer on it.

Man, these new powers are awesome, Joel thought. *Too bad most of them are temporary.*

He carefully peered around the back of one of the vehicles. The next closest soldiers—five of them—were fifteen feet away, and, of course, there were many more walking around the compound. Squinting, Joel took aim at an unoccupied refueling station about half a mile from his current position and strummed his wavebow.

And...boom.

The refueling station exploded. An alarm began to sound as most of the soldiers, now in a state of high alert, charged toward the smoke and flames. Joel crept out from behind the vehicle and saw more soldiers streaming out of what appeared to be the facility's front entrance.

Okay, not gonna go that way.

He fired up a flying cast but remained upright, hovering just a couple of inches above the ground. Using his additional speed, he zipped across the compound, unnoticed, toward the back of the facility. The entrance there was now guarded by a pair of soldiers who apparently were under orders not to abandon their post, explosions or no. Joel fast-glided over—it wasn't exactly Quicksilver-fast, but it would do—and stopped right in front of the soldiers before they even noticed him approaching.

Hello, he mouthed, along with a little wave of his hand.

"What? Who are—"

Another quick stunning cast, and both soldiers crumpled to the ground.

All right, now let's see about this lock.

♪♪♪

After being forced to watch the first few minutes of Keeper and the others' ordeal on the Public Yards stage (it began with Darkeye pouring some kind of potion on their heads that seemed to cause excruciating pain), Felicity and the rest of the Wavemakers were made to walk through the lobby area and toward a large elevator door, which opened as soon as they got near.

Oh, sure, now *it's fast.*

"You can handle it from here, I assume?" one of the soldiers said.

"Yes, ma'am," another one replied.

Most of the soldiers and civilian scientists peeled off from the group at that point, leaving eight of them (six soldiers, two scientists) with the Wavemakers, who were then herded into the elevator. The door closed. One of soldiers pressed a button. Twelve excruciating seconds passed, during which no one said anything—Felicity wanted to ("you guys need to invent deodorant"), but her mouth was still gagged—while the elevator moved toward its destination. Then, finally, the door opened, revealing the large, brightly lit space with all of the medical/torture-device-looking pieces of equipment.

Somehow I just knew I was gonna end up back here, Felicity thought.

As her eyes scanned the various pieces of equipment, wondering which one of them her captors were going to place her in (her bet was on a particularly hideous contraption that looked like a cross between a dentist's chair and a medieval rack), she noticed a couple of familiar faces—if you considered an alligator's visage to be a face—emerging from one of the side rooms.

The Lightsnakes. So those are our special guests. Great.

The two Lightsnakes walked up to the group. Then, to Felicity's surprise, one of them spoke.

"Finally, at last," it said in an elegant English accent, addressing her directly, "we have you, the Queenslayer, in our grasp."

"You may remove her gag," the other Lightsnake said to one of the soldiers. "We would like to have a conversation with her."

The soldier did so, ripping off the gag like the bandage it resembled. Felicity wasted no time in teeing off.

"I see you jerks finally figured out the translation cast," she said. "'Bout time. Too bad all you have to say are tired clichés."

"I am surprised that you do not show us a little more courtesy and respect," the first Lightsnake said. "After all, we did save you from your burning temple, remember?"

"And *we* saved *you* from that collapsing alternate plane," Felicity retorted. "Tactical error on our part, obviously."

"Well then, I suppose we shall call it even. Allow me to introduce myself. I am known as One-Zero-One-One-Zero."

"And I am Zero-One-Zero-Zero-One," the other Lightsnake said.

"Your names are binary numbers?" Felicity snorted. "Forget it, I'm just gonna call you Tweedledee and Tweedledum."

"I suppose it really does not matter," Tweedledee said. "We just thought that you might like to know how to address us when you are begging us for mercy."

"Wow, you guys have been hanging around Marshall *way* too much."

"He is a wise man and a kindred spirit. We have learned much from each other. We are happy to serve him in place of our Queen."

"Who, as you may recall," Tweedledum said, looking at Felicity, "was brutally murdered by the very same individual we are talking to right now."

"Yeah, not that I need to defend myself here, but *she* was trying to kill *me*."

"Regardless," Tweedledee said, "the time has come for you to pay the price for your actions. We had hoped that your energy could have been used to help restore our master, but I must say, this will be even better."

"Yes," Tweedledum agreed. "Because now, we can extinguish your life with our own hands, thus avenging our queen once and for all."

"Man, you guys sound like you really did your homework at Bad Guy University. You both majored in Mustache Twirling, I assume?"

Tweedledum turned to the soldiers and scientists. "You may begin with the others," he said, grabbing Felicity's arms with his pincers. "And release this one from her energy lock. We will take care of her personally."

♫♫♫

Joel stared at the recessed panel in the door as a past vision of it being opened played out before his eyes.

Okay, I see the pattern now. Easy enough.

He touched the headstock of his wavebow to the panel and played, pumping in the necessary energy charges. After he was done, the panel lit up with a faint beeping noise and the door slowly slid aside.

Nice, he congratulated himself.

Dispelling the muting cast, he stepped into the narrow T-shaped hall, keeping his instrument raised.

"I'm in," he whispered.

"Very good," Blackspore said. "Do you need my help navigating the hut? It appears to have a rather complex set of passageways."

"Nah, I got it," Joel replied.

Recalling the path that Thinker had followed when they were last here, Joel began to make his way through the labyrinthine corridors.

"Can you check on the others?" he asked under his breath.

"Of course," Blackspore said.

A door in the hallway opened and a scientist type carrying a deluxe countercom stepped out right in front of Joel. Startled, she pushed a button on the device, causing a loud squealing sound to ring out. Joel grimaced, expecting to be placed under energy lock, but to his pleasant surprise, he retained control over his entire body.

Huh. Must be thanks to the temporary energy boost, he figured.

"Help!" the scientist cried. "An intruder has entered the—"

Joel plucked a string and the scientist went down. After glancing around, he looked into the room that she had just exited; fortunately, there was no one else in there to sound an alarm—just a few tables and some displays that looked like high school science fair projects.

"The others are now in a large room filled with odd and dangerous-looking apparatus," Blackspore said. "And the two Lightsnakes are there as well."

"The Lightsnakes?" Joel said, dragging the unconscious scientist into the room.

"Yes. You may want to hurry."

"Okay."

Joel went back out into the hall and closed the door behind him. He picked up his pace, stunning a couple of soldiers along the way, and eventually reached the large room with the elevator. Before he had a chance to enter the keypad combination, the elevator doors opened on their own, revealing four more soldiers. None of them even got a word in edgewise as Joel dispatched them all in the blink of an eye.

Man, I am gonna rock at Halo 4 *when I get back. Just three more days 'til it's released...*

He stepped into the elevator and around the fallen bodies. As the doors closed, he pressed the appropriate button and then stood off to the side. After what felt like a very long time, the elevator stopped and the doors opened once more. The short hallway outside was filled with guards (seven of them, to be precise); Joel flooded the area with a broad wave of stunning energy, instantly knocking the entire group out.

"Not to alarm you," Blackspore said, "but the Mono Realm scientists have begun their experiments."

"All right, I'm almost there."

♪♪♪

While the rest of the Wavemakers were being forced into the various devices stationed about the area, Tweedledee waved his three arms around in an elliptical pattern, as if he were doing a warm-up exercise. This movement appeared to have the effect of creating a tone not unlike that of a wavebow playing a middle G.

"What the heck are you doing?" Felicity said.

"The members of our race used to be powerful users of the Aura," Tweedledum answered as tiny sparks began to emanate from his comrade's pincers. "Regretfully, we lost most of our abilities a long time ago. But now, thanks to your Songshell fragments, those abilities have returned, stronger than ever."

"Yeah, you're welcome," Felicity muttered.

A cloud of green-tinted energy formed in front of Tweedledee, which he then cast onto Felicity. She caught her breath as she rose up a foot into the air.

"Ah, it is truly wonderful to be able to do things like this again," the Lightsnake said. He pointed toward one of the side rooms, and Felicity began to float in that direction.

"Aw, but I wanted that one over there," she said, nodding toward the aberrant dentist chair.

"Under no circumstances are we to be interrupted, is that clear?" Tweedledum snapped at a group of nearby guards. All of them nodded in agreement as he went on ahead and opened the door to the room.

"Wow, what a gentleman," Felicity quipped as she floated in. The room was small, about the size of a typical exam room in a doctor's office, and it was empty save for a flat, nondescript table in the middle. Tweedledee fol-

equipment and being fussed over by a small contingent of government scientists. More guards lined the walls.

"Where's Felicity?" he whispered.

A pause, and then: "The Lightsnakes have her in one of the side rooms. They are...they are siphoning off her Aura energy. She only has a few minutes left. You need to act now."

"Okay. There are too many guards and scientists for me to zip in there and stun a few at a time, but I can't stun the whole place at once either, because then I'll hit the other Wavemakers. Any suggestions?"

"What about a sleep cast? That way, you can simply wake the others afterward."

"Oh—yeah, good idea. What about the Lightsnakes, though? Will they notice everyone falling asleep?"

"I doubt it. They are completely engrossed in the siphoning process."

"Cool. I mean, not cool, but—you know what I mean."

"Just hurry."

"Right."

Joel played a soft, ballad-like melody on his instrument, generating a cloud of faint powder-blue light. He then sent the cloud around the corner and into the area ahead so quickly that everyone within it nodded off before they even knew what was happening.

"Well done," Blackspore said.

"Thanks. Now, which room are they in?"

"I do not know."

"What?"

"Unfortunately, I cannot see the room in relation to the rest of the area."

"All right, no problem. I know what to do."

Joel charged ahead, engaging the Sight along the way. He saw a relatively fresh image of one of the Lightsnakes levitating Felicity into a room near the far right hand corner. Once she was inside, both Lightsnakes entered the room and closed the door.

Gotcha.

"Thirty seconds," Blackspore said.

Joel ran up to the room. He gave his wavebow a good strum, and the door burst open. Felicity was lying on a flat table in the middle of the room, and the Lightsnakes were standing on either side of her, slowly waving their pincers around. Joel could see Aura energy rising off of her like steam. The Lightsnakes barely registered his presence before he hit each of them with a quick stunning cast.

"Felicity!" Joel said, rushing over to her. She was pale and shivering, the latter of which meant that she was, at least, still alive.

"She needs her energy restored," Blackspore said. "Quickly—find the loudstones."

"Right." Joel looked at one of the fallen Lightsnakes. The loudstone was not readily apparent, but he caught a small spark of light coming from inside the creature's mouth. He crouched down and pried open the alligator-like jaws. The glowing stone was there, embedded in between two of the Lightsnake's fangs, like a gold false tooth. He plucked it out and then repeated the process on the other one.

"Five seconds," Blackspore said.

Joel stood up and pressed the loudstones to Felicity's temples, one on each side. For a brief and frightening moment, he thought that he was too late, but then warmth and color returned to her face and she opened her eyes.

"Dude," she rasped, "That kinda hurt."

"What? What did?"

"The loudstones." She mustered up a weak grin. "You, like, poked me with the pointy ends."

Joel returned her smile. "Don't be such a wimp."

It took about three and a half minutes for all of Felicity's strength to return, during which time Joel noticed that the bodies of the Lightsnakes were beginning to char and disintegrate like burning paper.

"No wonder they had to close the door," Felicity said, sitting up and rubbing her head after she had mostly recovered. "Guess interrupting the process is fatal, or something."

"Well, too bad for them," Joel said, putting the now-spent loudstones into a fold in his cloak.

"Hey, can you give me one of those?"

"They're totally drained," Joel said. "Can't use them again until we get back to Spectraland."

"Ugh, of course."

The pair then stepped over the ashen remains of their reptilian adversaries and back into the main area, where they roused the other Wavemakers and released them from their energy locks before making their way to the exit.

CHAPTER 21: THE PUBLIC YARDS

Towing six other people—at a high altitude, at that—was definitely a bit taxing, but thanks to his temporarily enhanced power, that just meant that Joel could only soar along at a mere supersonic rate of speed (rather than hypersonic). After making his way back over to Sector One, he came to a stop above the Royal Tower, which is where Blackspore had located the rest of the wavebows except for Auravine's.

"All right," Joel exhaled. "I hope this works."

"It will," Blackspore said in Joel's ear.

Joel played a short note. A few seconds went by. Nothing happened.

"Try again," Blackspore said.

Joel played the note once more. This time, after another pause, five wavebows zoomed up out of the dark cloud and into their respective owners' hands.

"Wow, cool!" Felicity said, looking her instrument over. "When did you learn that one?"

"Blackspore taught it to me on the way here."

"Wait, what? Blackspore?"

"Yeah."

"How?"

"Long story," Joel said. Between sneaking out of the facility and jetting over to Sector One, there had been neither time nor opportunity for him to explain everything that had happened since he teleported out of the Royal Tower. "I'll tell you later."

"Fine," Felicity fake-grumbled.

Then, with Blackspore giving him directions like a Spectraland version of GPS, Joel made the short flight over to the space above the Public Yards. Hovering in midair, he looked down and saw, through the dark cloud, a large stage with nine people on it and a lot more down on the ground in front of it—nine hundred and eighty-seven more, to be exact. If he didn't know any better, he would have thought that this was a concert by an over-sized ensemble band like Arcade Fire or Jamiroquai.

"Most of the audience members appear to be heavily armed military personnel," Blackspore observed.

Joel set his jaw. He knew that even with his increased energy, he wouldn't be able to stun the entire crowd at once. *Looks like the time for stealth is over.* He turned to the other Wavemakers. "There's a big army down there," he announced, pointing. "Almost a thousand soldiers. That's going to make this rescue mission a bit complicated."

"Yeah, just a little," Felicity said.

"So here's what we'll do. There's Aura energy in the air here, but not a whole lot, so I'll give you all some of mine. Then Felicity, Riverhand, Redstem, and I will engage the soldiers while Thornleaf, Windblade, and Auravine go around the back of the stage to get Thinker and the others."

"Those teams are unbalanced," Thornleaf objected. "The strongest offensive Wavemakers should be the ones to take on the army. Thus, Riverhand and I should switch places."

"I am perfectly capable of performing combat wavecasts," Riverhand said.

"Capable, perhaps, but not proficient," Redstem said.

"What are you talking about?" Riverhand said, indignant. "Do you not recall the time when we had to rescue that villager boy from the Singing Swamp?"

"While they are busy arguing," Blackspore said in Joel's ear, "your Mono Realm friends continue to suffer down below. You need to take charge of this situation."

"Right, I got it." Joel turned to Thornleaf. "Look, those teams *are* balanced. I divided us up that way because the rescue group needs at least one Wavemaker who's really good at offensive casts, just in case something unexpected happens, which it usually does. I mean, Darkeye's down there, on the stage. What if he has more of those grenade things, or worse? That's why you need to be in that group."

Thornleaf furrowed his brow and glanced at Felicity.

"Makes sense to me." She shrugged.

"Very well," Thornleaf sighed. "But I want Windblade to be the one carrying Auravine along. And lending her his wavebow if any healing is needed."

Windblade nodded. "I can do that."

"Okay, then it's settled," Joel said. "I guess, uh, everyone form a line and hold each other's wrists." He extended his hands. Felicity grabbed his left wrist, while Auravine took the right. He glanced at each of them in turn as the others formed up. Their hands felt impossibly soft, as if they had been soaking them in moisturizer.

"Remember—no distractions," Blackspore said.

Joel looked down at the cloud. "I know, I know."

"Who are you talking to?" Felicity asked. "And is that a loudstone in your ear?"

Joel didn't respond. Instead he took a deep breath, allowing the supercharged Aura energy that was within him to flow down his arms and out through his fingertips. As the energy made its way across both sides of the line, the other Wavemakers began to glow, almost like they were a string of Christmas lights.

The whole process took exactly one full minute, after which Felicity turned to Joel and said with a rare earnest expression, "Okay, you don't need to tell me what you were up to while you were gone. I saw it."

"What...what did you see?"

"Pretty much everything."

Joel winced, feeling slightly embarrassed. "Even the part when Blackspore said that I had feelings for..."

"Yeah. Don't worry, it's cool. I...I already knew. I've known for a while now."

"You did? How?"

"I've been studying body language, remember? Now let's go save our friends."

Joel looked at Auravine, who simply smiled at him before she was whisked away by Windblade's flying Aura.

Remember—no distractions.

Joel flew down through the cloud, flanked by Felicity, Riverhand, and Redstem. Like a squadron of fighter planes, they split up and began to launch stunning casts into the crowd, which, after a few scattered exclamations of surprise, retaliated with skyward blasts of laser and flame. Sharing his energy with the others had caused Joel to lose most of his advanced speed, but he still had enough juice to continue performing multiple casts sim-

LEGEND OF THE LOUDSTONE

ultaneously while dodging the soldiers' shots, at least for a little while longer.

"Woo!" Felicity shouted as she mowed down a row of fifty-two soldiers with a single cast.

Joel zipped past her and the other two, yelling "Lead them away from the stage!" at each of them as he went.

Following his instruction, the Wavemakers gradually moved toward the edges of the gravel pit as they flew around, trying to draw both fire and attention away from the stage area. While doing so, they continued to fell huge swaths of the army, thinning its ranks considerably. The plan seemed to be working until—

"Rainbow folk!" an amplified voice exclaimed. It was the blond Mono Realm woman. "Surrender yourselves, or we will have no choice but to execute your insurgent allies!"

Joel looked toward the stage. A dozen soldiers had joined the woman and Darkeye there; all of them were pointing weapons at the prisoners. There was no sign of Thornleaf, Windblade, or Auravine.

"Blackspore!" Joel said, narrowly evading a volley. "What happened to the other group?"

"Hold on," came the reply. "Let me see...hmm...ah, yes, there they are. They are lurking somewhere behind the stage."

"What are they doing? Are they all right?"

"They appear to be...arguing."

Dangit. Maybe putting Thornleaf with that group wasn't such a good idea after all.

"You have one minute to comply!" the blond woman said.

Joel stopped firing and put up a spherical shield cast instead. The others noticed and did the same before flying over to him.

"What's going on?" Felicity said, hovering in place.

"Are we surrendering?" Riverhand asked.

"What about the other group?" Redstem said.

Joel blinked as he tried to process the multiple questions. "They're, um, they're a little held up. We need to give them more time. Any ideas?"

"Blondie over there might be bluffing," Felicity said as a continued barrage of shots from the soldiers reflected off of everyone's shield casts. "Maybe they're not supposed to actually kill them until Marshall and the Uniter get back."

"Maybe," Joel said. "I don't wanna take that chance, though."

"Thirty seconds!"

"Then I say we turn ourselves in," Riverhand suggested.

"You cannot be serious!" Redstem protested.

"It will buy the other group some additional time," Riverhand responded.

"But then they will have to rescue us as well as the Mono Realmers."

"I have faith in them."

"Even Thornleaf?" Felicity smirked.

"Especially Thornleaf," Riverhand answered. "The two of us may not always see eye to eye, but that does not mean I do not believe in him."

"Ten seconds!"

"Blackspore, what do you think?" Joel asked.

"I leave it up to you."

Joel took the fishhook off his ear and pocketed it, along with the loudstone. "All right," he said, looking at Riverhand, "sounds good to me."

"I'm down." Felicity nodded.

Redstem shrugged, Spectraland style. "I hope you are right, Riverhand."

The four Wavemakers raised their hands above their heads, letting their instruments drop to their sides. As their shields and their flying Auras dissipated, they slowly floated to the ground, where they were instantly surrounded by the remaining soldiers.

"Hey, easy there," Felicity snapped as one of the soldiers gruffly confiscated her wavebow.

Joel's wavebow was taken from him as well, but fortunately, no one thought to perform a detailed check for anything smaller than perhaps a countercom (a soldier gave him a brief pat-down, but that was all), so the loudstone remained in his possession.

"A wise decision," the blond woman said as the four of them, hands still in the air, were forced to walk toward the stage. "You have bought your friends a few more hours of precious life. It is too bad they will have to spend them in pure agony."

Joel looked at Thinker and the others. From what he could tell, it did seem as though they wished they had been allowed to die rather than suffer any additional torture.

Don't worry, he thought emphatically, as if by doing so he could establish some kind of telepathic link with his Mono Realmer allies. *We're gonna get you guys out of this, I swear.*

He and the other three Wavemakers dragged their feet as much as they could until they finally arrived at the stage. Along the way, there still had been no sign of Thornleaf, Windblade, or Auravine. Joel decided to take this as a good thing; if any or all of them had been caught, surely they would have been paraded up onto the stage with everyone else.

"Resume the broadcast," the blond woman said to some unseen technician. Then, after clearing her throat, she resumed speaking into the microphone. "We apologize for the interruption. A change of plans has occurred, one that I am sure you will all find most entertaining."

Joel, Felicity, Riverhand, and Redstem were marched up a short flight of stairs, placed under energy lock, and made to kneel down next to the other prisoners. Joel tried to catch their eye, but none of them looked his way; with their heads bowed, it seemed as though they barely had enough strength left to breathe.

"The experiments on some of the renegade rainbow folk have been concluded ahead of schedule. Thus, they have been transferred here, so that they may have the privilege of taking part in our grand celebration."

"Hello, Wavemakers."

Joel turned his head. Darkeye was standing behind them, holding a vial in each hand.

"Believe me when I tell you that—*hic*—I gain no pleasure from this whatsoever," the wizened old potion-maker said, sounding oddly sincere. "Personally, I find torture to be—*hic*—an abhorrent practice. I am simply following the wishes of—*hic*—my new overlords."

"Doesn't make you any less of a sleaze-bucket," Felicity said.

"Maker of Magical Fluids," the blond woman said, "you may proceed."

Joel squeezed his eyes shut and braced himself. Then, a moment later, he heard the sounds of a wave-bow, followed by the *thunk* of someone falling to the stage floor.

"Sorry we are late!" Windblade shouted.

Joel felt the release of the energy lock as weapons' fire rang out around him. He stood up and turned.

Thornleaf, Windblade, and Auravine were there, on the stage, with a large shield cast out in front of them. Thornleaf was firing stunning casts over and around the shield, knocking out soldiers left and right, while Auravine was crouched down behind the other two. Darkeye was on the ground, prone, the contents of his vials seeping out.

"It took us a while to find the best way to get up here without being noticed," Windblade continued yelling over the din, "and then we ran into some guards, and then—"

"Be quiet and focus on maintaining the shield!" Thornleaf snapped.

A few of the other soldiers turned on Joel, including the one that had his wavebow, but then Thornleaf played a different note and Joel's wavebow broke out of the soldier's grip and zipped back into his hands. He immediately set up a shield cast as shots were fired his way.

"Cease the broadcast!" the blond woman wailed.

Joel enlarged his shield, creating an energy bunker of sorts that protected Thinker and the rest of the Mono Realm allies on his end. He glanced around to his left and saw that Riverhand, with his wavebow returned to him as well, had done the same thing on the other side. Next to Riverhand stood Redstem, who began firing at the soldiers that were trying to get up onto the stage.

"Duck!" Felicity exclaimed, kneeling behind Joel's shield with her wavebow in hand.

Joel turned back around and ducked as a laser blast whizzed over his head. He saw the blond woman aiming a small pistol-like weapon directly at him. Before he had a chance to enlarge his shield any further, Felicity stood up and fired a stunning cast that hit the woman right between the antennae.

"You give blonds a bad name," she spat as the woman crumpled.

"Hey, that's a good one!" Joel said.

"I know, right? I actually thought of it a while ago. I was hoping I'd have a chance to use it."

"Oh, and uh, thanks for the warning there."

"No prob. Let's get back to it, shall we?"

The remaining soldiers kept trying to close in, so while Joel, Riverhand, and Windblade maintained their shields, Thornleaf, Felicity, and Redstem continued to knock out as many of them as possible. Just when it seemed like they were nearing the end of the assault, Joel looked out at the gravel pit and spotted something off in the distance.

"Um...I think we should get out of here," he said.

"What? Why?" Felicity said.

"There's, like, a big convoy of military vehicles coming our way."

"How big?"

"Really big."

"Geez, how many soldiers does this place have, anyway?"

"Well, if you add up all the ones that we've seen so far, I think it's probably around—oh, wait, that was a whatcha-call-it..."

"Rhetorical question."

"Right."

Joel turned to the other Wavemakers. "I'll keep a shield up," he said. "The rest of you—grab one or two of the Mono Realmers and get a flying cast ready."

Everyone nodded in acknowledgment.

"What about Darkeye?" Auravine said.

"Oh yeah," Joel said, looking over at the unconscious potion-maker. "Someone scoop him up too."

"I got him," Felicity said.

Joel changed his shield into a dome that surrounded everyone while each of the others, minus Auravine, conjured up the green Aura of a flying cast. The remaining soldiers kept firing; apparently, their weapons never ran out of ammunition.

"Um, while I'm doing this, someone also needs to—"

"Yeah, yeah," Felicity said. "I got you too."

Joel glanced at her and wondered for a moment how, even though he knew that happiness was just a state of mind, he could ever truly be happy again without her around. Then his shield flickered, so he shook his head and banished that thought.

No distractions.

Focusing harder, he expanded the shield into a giant hamster ball-like sphere just a split second before the others, towing two people each, rose up into the air and flew away.

CHAPTER 22: TOWN BELOW THE MOUNTAIN

Anyone in Sector One who looked up at the sky at that point probably noticed a rather curious sight: a big yellow-green bubble that contained possibly up to fifteen people floating through the air right below the dark cloud.

"The Sector One village and the entire area around it is completely infested with soldiers," Blackspore reported. "You need to get out of there before they figure out a way to bring you down."

"Okay," Joel said, "but we need to land somewhere soon. We're starting to run low on energy, and the Mono Realmers are dying."

"Understood. You might just have to—"

"The...the town," Guider rasped.

"Hold on, Blackspore," Joel said. "Guider? Are you all right? What did you say?"

"The town," she repeated, her voice barely above a whisper. "Town...below the mountain."

"What?"

"I'm guessing that's where we need to go," Felicity said. "A place called Town below the Mountain. Keeper mentioned it before."

"Oh—okay," Joel said. "Blackspore, can you see something like that? A town below a mountain?"

"Give me a moment...ah, yes, I think I have it. A small settlement next to the mountain range, about twenty-five miles due north."

"He found it!" Joel announced. "Everyone, fly north."

"Thank goodness for literal translations," Felicity muttered.

The Wavemakers flew north as quickly as they could while Joel kept his shield cast up, just in case. After a few minutes, the town came into view; consisting of just a dozen brain-shaped buildings and a few other, even stranger-looking structures (giant upside-down bird claws was the closest description Joel could think of), it stood in stark contrast to the shiny, modern enormity of its neighboring city to the south.

"Is there anyone here in particular we should be looking for?" Thornleaf asked, but there was no response; Guider had lost consciousness.

"Guess we'll just have to wing it," Felicity said.

As they approached, a number—thirty-five, to be exact—of Mono Realmers came out of the various buildings and congregated together near the edge of the town, all of them looking up at the giant bubble that was heading their way.

"I think it's safe," Joel said. "No one's pointing any weapons or anything at us."

"Just keep the shield going until we can confirm that," Thornleaf said.

"Right."

They landed in front of the gathered townsfolk, all of whom appeared shabby, disheveled, and possibly undernourished. One of them, a lean, middle-aged-looking male with no hair, stepped forward.

"Rainbow folk," he said, "we saw what happened at the Public Yards. Thank you for saving Guider of the Worthy. Please, let us tend to her and the others."

"How do we know we can trust you?" Redstem asked.

"You do not have to," the man replied. "You can keep your shield up and your weapons trained on us. Please, just allow us to assist the ones you rescued. A few of us are proficient in medical arts."

"What do you think, Thornleaf?" Redstem said. "Should we perform a truth cast on him?"

"Hmm," Thornleaf said, apparently mulling it over.

"I don't think we need to," Joel said, letting the shield cast fall away. "Okay," he addressed the man. "We have a healer in our group—maybe she can help too."

"Thank you," the man said. He motioned to the other townsfolk, most of whom came up to carry Guider and the rest. Turning back to the Wavemakers, he continued, "I am called Runner of the Fields. I would be honored if you would join me in my residence. I have some important information to share with you."

Joel nodded. "All right, sounds good." He turned to Auravine and handed her his wavebow and his loudstone. "Can you go with the others while we talk to this guy?"

"Of course," she replied.

The remaining six Wavemakers followed Runner of the Fields to one of the brain-shaped buildings, introducing themselves along the way (with Felicity adding that she was going to refer to their new host only as Runner).

"I must admit," Runner said after introductions were over, "we have been rather shocked by all of the recent events that we have witnessed on the video feed: the rainbow folk—you—being real, the Uniter agreeing to make your comrade his coregent—"

"He's not our comrade," Felicity interrupted.

"Oh, yes, apologies—I misspoke," Runner said, manually opening the door of the brain-building. "The fact that you are not in league with him was made quite evident by the subsequent events. What all of you did was very brave and impressive, taking on an entire regiment like that."

"Well, you know, all in a day's work," Felicity said.

They entered the building. The interior was spacious but austere; there was only a small table in the middle with three other objects arranged around it. One of those objects was a video monitor, currently showing just a blank screen.

"Forgive me—I would offer you some sustenance, but unfortunately my stores are rather empty at the moment," Runner said, sounding more bitter than apologetic. "Prior to the war, this used to be a prosperous, self-sufficient little town. Now, however, the Uniter's forces routinely raid us for our resources. In fact, the only reason he allows our continued existence is because we can grow things here that cannot be grown anywhere else in the realm."

"Okay, I'll connect the dots here," Felicity said. "That's how you know Guider. You're secretly supporting the Redivision."

"Very perceptive," Runner said, a wan smile crossing his face. "Believe me, we would join her outright—as would many citizens of the realm—were it not for one thing."

"What's that?" Joel asked.

"To put it simply—fear."

"After what we have experienced, I certainly do not blame you," Riverhand said.

"I appreciate that." Runner walked over to the video monitor. "Now, though, thanks to you, that fear has been replaced by a very different emotion: hope." He pushed a button on the monitor, and footage of the Public Yards scene began to play. Joel saw himself on the stage, maintaining his shield cast while Felicity stunned soldier after soldier after soldier. "You see," Runner went on, "these visuals were broadcast to every single town and city in the entire Mono Realm. By the time the Uniter's loyalists censored them, it was too late. The message was delivered. Now the populace knows that the Uniter *can* be toppled. That it *can* be done."

"You mean, that it can be done by us," Redstem said.

"Well, yes. We have all witnessed the incredible power that you possess."

"Um, there's a problem with that, though," Joel said. "We had—how do I put this—we had some extra strength when we did that, and we still couldn't take out all the soldiers. If the Uniter has even, like, I dunno, half, or thirty-five percent, or whatever, of the amount of soldiers protecting him on his tour, we could be in trouble."

"Not to mention," Felicity added, "Marshall's with him, and Marshall has three of our loudstones."

"Oh yeah," Joel said. "He'll be even more powerful now."

"But!" Runner's antennae twitched as he stepped into Joel's personal space. "You do not have to do it alone. Now the people will be with you."

"Meaning what?" Thornleaf said. "That the citizens of the Mono Realm will attack the Uniter's soldiers?"

"Exactly. For you see, the hope you have given them will overcome their fear."

"But does Guider really have enough supporters to defeat the Uniter's armies?" Windblade asked.

"No, of course not," Runner replied. "But she does not have to. They will borrow the strategy that you employed at the Public Yards—occupy the soldiers long enough so that you have a chance to capture the Uniter without exhausting your energies first. Once that is done, the soldiers will no longer fight for him."

"Oh, just like chess," Joel said.

Everyone turned to look at him.

"Chess—it's this game back on Earth. You can actually win it just by cornering your opponent's king, without taking any of their other pieces. I've done it a few times."

"I am glad to hear that," Runner said. "There is one small problem, however."

"Of course there is," Felicity sighed.

"In order for this strategy to have the greatest chance of success, we need to know well in advance what route the royal procession is taking—which cities they are heading to, and in what order. That way, we can ensure that the Redivision supporters in one particular area are organized and prepared enough to mount an effective attack at the right moment. If we mobilize too many areas at once prematurely, word could get out. Do any of you happen to have such information?"

"We don't," Joel said, "But I think I know who might."

♪♪♪

With Felicity and Thornleaf accompanying him, Joel headed for the bird-claw structure where Guider and the others were being tended to (he had wanted to go by himself, but Felicity said that she would tag along, which prompted Thornleaf—in true annoying-couple fashion—to join them, under the pretense that his presence would be helpful for what Joel wanted to do). The structure had a rusty metal door that Joel proceeded to knock on. It opened a few seconds later, revealing a tired-looking Mono Realm woman.

"Oh—yes, rainbow folk, please, come in," she said.

"How is everyone?" Joel asked as he entered.

"Stable. They are going to make it. Your healer friend was a great help."

"Cool."

The trio followed the woman down a short passage into an open area that was filled with piles of what looked like purple hay; Thinker, Keeper, Guider and her lieutenants were each lying on one of them (since beds were not a thing here in the Mono Realm). Two other townsfolk were there, along with Auravine, who was standing next to one of the lieutenants and playing a soft melody on Joel's wavebow. She stopped and turned when she saw Joel and the others enter.

"I apologize," she said, glancing at Joel. "I had to use up most of whatever energy was left in your loudstone."

"That's okay," Joel said. "I heard you were a great help."

"I did what I could. Their physiologies are similar to ours, but there are still some significant differences."

"She is being modest," the townswoman said. "If it were not for her, we surely would have lost them."

"It was your guidance that made what I did possible," Auravine said.

"All right, all right, you're all awesome," Felicity said. "The main thing is that everyone is fine. Good to know. Now—where's Darkeye?"

Auravine blinked several times, as if she needed a moment to adjust to the abrupt change in subject. "In the adjoining room," she answered.

"Is he still stunned?"

"Yes."

"We need you to revive him," Thornleaf said.

"Oh—of course."

The Wavemakers walked into the adjoining room, which was more like a storage closet with a single small window. Darkeye was lying unceremoniously on the ground between two broken wooden boxes. Auravine played a brief note, and the wizened old potion-maker's eyes snapped open.

"*Hic!* Ah—where—what—"

"Sit up, Darkeye," Thornleaf said, his wavebow raised.

"Oh...hello, Thornleaf," Darkeye said, quickly regaining his composure as he pulled himself into a sitting position. "Auravine...and the—*hic*—offworlders, as well. I see you were able to—*hic*—successfully extricate yourselves from that precarious situation at the—*hic*—Public Yards. I suppose I should have expected no less. In fact, I am actually rather—*hic*—relieved that you—"

"Enough jabber," Thornleaf interrupted. "We need some information from you."

Darkeye's lips curled into a toothless smile. "Is that so? Well, information is—*hic*—my specialty. What do you wish to know?"

"We need to know what route the royal procession is taking," Joel replied. "Which cities they're heading to, and in what order."

"Ah, planning an ambush, are—*hic*—we? Well, you are correct in assuming that I am—*hic*—intimately familiar with the details of the Uniter's itinerary. It was a distinct—*hic*—pleasure to learn about all of the various settlements that—"

"Just tell us," Thornleaf demanded.

"And why, pray tell, should I—*hic*—do that?" Darkeye said, his smile vanishing. "If I recall correctly, you reneged on the—*hic*—terms of our last deal. My freedom in exchange for the—*hic*—mind control antidote, remember?"

"*You* took it upon yourself to escape, and then *you* freed Byle and the Lightsnakes," Thornleaf said. "That alone invalidates our agreement, not to mention the other atrocities you committed once you arrived here."

"That sounds to me like you are—*hic*—changing the terms of the deal after the fact. I am not sure I want to make any more bargains with—*hic*—someone who goes back on his word."

"How dare you accuse me of—"

"Hey, uh, why don't we just do a mind control cast on him?" Joel suggested. "Or a truth cast?"

"He has always been immune to mind control for some reason, and a truth cast will be of no use if he does not talk," Thornleaf replied. "But I will take care of that." He jabbed the headstock of his wavebow into Darkeye's chest and strummed a loud chord, shooting out a direct pulse of Aura energy.

"Ah!" Darkeye cried out.

"Tell us!" Thornleaf barked.

"You...you must first—*hic*—give me—"

Thornleaf strummed again. "I said, tell us!"

"Whoa, whoa, okay, stop," Felicity said, grabbing Thornleaf's arm. "What are you doing? This isn't the way we do things. Just chill, all right?" She glanced at Joel and Auravine. "Why don't you guys handle this—me and Thornleaf have to go talk about some stuff."

"Um, okay," Joel said. He looked down at Darkeye as Felicity pulled Thornleaf out of the room; the old potion-maker was back on his elbows, wincing in obvious pain.

"How are you going to get him to talk?" Auravine asked.

"I dunno...not that way, though, that's for sure. Even though he totally deserves it."

"Very...*hic*—honorable of you, offworlder," Darkeye croaked. "I appreciate your—*hic*—adherence to your principles."

"We still need that information," Joel said.

"Of—*hic*—course. I might be willing to strike a deal with you, since—*hic*—you seem to be of slightly higher moral character than your—*hic*—taller comrade. I will give you the information you want, if you—*hic*—meet my terms."

What do people in the movies usually say at this point? Oh yeah: "I'm listening."

"First of all, if your ambush is—*hic*—successful and you capture both the Uniter and Chief Byle, you will take me back—*hic*—to Spectraland with you, whereupon I will be immediately pardoned of—*hic*—all alleged crimes."

"Well, I don't know if I—"

"Secondly, you will grant me—*hic*—full access to the Wavemaker archives, allowing me to peruse them at—*hic*—my leisure whenever I so desire."

"Um, I'd have to check with—"

"And finally," Darkeye said, sitting up fully (he didn't seem to be in much pain anymore), "you will agree to serve as my—*hic*—ongoing personal information re-source, answering, while under the—*hic*—influence of a truth cast, any questions that I may have regarding—*hic*—your homeworld."

I guess Felicity could do that, since she's going to stay in Spectraland, but... "None of those are really my calls to make, though."

"You are the legendary—*hic*—offworlder. I am sure you will find a way to get it done. That is, if you—*hic*—really want your information."

Joel glanced at Auravine. "What do you think?" he asked.

"It is your decision," she replied. "Obviously, Fire-flower and the chiefs will not listen to anything I have to say. It would be on you to convince them."

Joel considered checking with Blackspore, but he knew that the answer would probably be the same. To help clear his mind, he looked out the window. To his surprise, he saw Felicity and Thornleaf outside, apparently having some kind of serious discussion.

She looks stressed. I wonder what they're talking about? Maybe she's mad about what Thornleaf just did to Darkeye. Maybe she's having second thoughts about moving. Maybe they're...maybe they're breaking up?

The sight filled Joel with a jumble of mixed emotions: sympathy for Thornleaf, relief and happiness that Felicity might be going home with him after all, and a small twinge of guilt about said happiness.

"Well, offworlder, what do you—*hic*—say?"

"Huh? Oh—uh, yeah, okay, deal."

"Do you promise that you will be able to fulfill—*hic*—all of my demands?"

"I promise."

"Excellent."

"One condition, though—if you do anything else bad, then the whole thing is off."

"*Bad* could have—*hic*—all sorts of definitions."

"*Bad* meaning illegal under Spectraland law."

"Very well. Agreed."

"Okay. Auravine, can you do a truth cast on him?"

She held out Joel's wavebow. "I think you should have the honors."

Joel placed Darkeye under a truth cast, and the old potion-maker proceeded to divulge all the details of the royal procession's itinerary. After he was done, Joel (who had memorized everything Darkeye had just told him) performed a binding cast on him before leaving the bird-claw structure with Auravine.

"That was very well done," she said.

"What?" Joel said, looking around for Felicity and Thornleaf; they were nowhere to be seen. "Oh—uh, thanks."

"I must admit, at first I was concerned about whether or not you would be able to convince Fireflower and the chiefs to agree to Darkeye's terms, but then I remembered how persuasive you can be when you really set your mind to it."

"Um, okay."

"I have also been thinking about what you said back on the Firelight Highway, about how I should have a chance to redeem myself." She looked down at the ground. "Tell me...do you still feel that way?"

"Well, sure, yeah."

She looked back up at Joel. "Then I want to help you capture Chief Byle and the Uniter."

"But...you don't have a wavebow." Joel shook his head. "No, I think it'd be safer for you to stay here."

"I do not need a wavebow to be of help. I can serve as a distraction, or a diversion. I can join the other Redivision members. I can also borrow an instrument if anyone were to require healing. Please, Joel, I have to go along with you."

"I dunno...this is gonna be pretty dangerous, and you've already redeemed yourself enough, I think."

"I must respectfully disagree. However, it seems as though the Aura has now given me an opportunity to change that. To tilt the scales the other way."

"It has? How?"

"If I am able to help you not only capture Chief Byle but also liberate an entire land from its cruel and oppressive ruler, then I think I might have a chance, however small, of forgiving myself...and also, quite possibly, Fireflower and the chiefs might be a bit more open to entertaining your idea."

"Um...what idea?"

"That I be allowed to move to your world with you."

Joel's breath caught in his throat. "Oh—um, wow."

"Is that offer still open?"

"Yeah, uh...sure. Of course."

"I was not sure how you felt before, but when you lent us energy at the Public Yards, I saw your conversation with Blackspore...when he said that you have feelings for me...when he said that you want love. I am very flattered, Joel, and unlike your fellow offworlder, I can return those feelings. I can give you what you want. It is what I want as well. We can be together. Please, just allow me to help you. Give me—give *us*—this chance."

Joel's mind whirled. Sure, he had feelings for Auravine, but what about Felicity? Now that it seemed like she was no longer going to be with Thornleaf, would he have a chance with her? Because as nice and as pretty as Auravine was, he didn't really feel like they connected on quite the same level as he and Felicity did...or did they? After all, her nature *was* more in tune with his—sensitive, reserved, thoughtful.

This was all so confusing and new. Joel never had a girlfriend before. Up until now, no girl had ever even told him that she liked him. He had zero experience with this sort of thing. What was he going to do?

Sometimes, you just gotta say...what the heck.

"Okay, yeah, you can come."

Auravine's eyes lit up. "Thank you."

"Just...be careful. Please."

"I will. I promise."

♫♫♫

Joel and Auravine looked around for Felicity and Thornleaf, but they had no luck finding them until they returned to Runner's house, where they discovered the pair, along with the rest of the Wavemakers, Runner, and three other townsfolk.

"So, how'd it go?" Felicity asked, seemingly in a normal mood.

"How'd what go?" Joel responded.

"You know, with Darkeye. Did you get the info?"

"Oh—uh, yeah."

"Nice. I figured you would. All right, let's hear it."

"Okay, well—"

"And try to summarize, if you can."

"Right. So, Marshall and the Uniter are traveling in some big vehicle with a see-through bubble top that supposedly deflects all kinds of stuff. They're being escorted by two armored troop-transport vehicles that are each carrying exactly one hundred soldiers. They're using the standard highway system, and their next stop is tonight at some place called Five-Point Province."

"That is a location in the middle of five adjoining towns," Runner noted. "There is a coliseum there. I am sure that is where they will be."

"Yeah, Darkeye mentioned that," Joel said.

"Let me see if the people there have been made aware," Runner said. He took out a deluxe countercom and pushed a few buttons on it.

"Yes?" a voice said through the device.

"AN-26? This is RF-7," Runner said, apparently using code names.

"Go ahead, RF-7."

"Have your people been told to go to the coliseum at Five-Point Province tonight?"

"No. We only just received word that there will be a special broadcast announcement this evening."

Runner looked around the room. "As we suspected—they are keeping the location secret until the last possible minute." He turned back to his device. "AN-26, the government will be instructing your people to report to the coliseum tonight to pay tribute to the royal procession. Mobilize all members of the Redivision in each of the five towns. We will meet you there."

"Understood. AN-26 out."

"We cannot carry out the attack there," one of the townsfolk, an older male with droopy antennae, insisted. "With such a large gathering present, casualties could run very high."

"According to Darkeye, though, all of their public appearances are at places like that," Joel said.

"Perhaps we could we ambush them on the highway," one of the other townsfolk, a woman, suggested. "We could distract them on the ground while the rainbow folk drop out of the sky."

"That would work if I could still fly above the cloud," Joel said. "Unfortunately, I don't have the energy to do that anymore. They'll see us coming from miles away."

"Then tonight, at the Five-Point coliseum, represents our best chance," Runner declared. "We can still have the element of surprise on our side." He looked at Joel. "Are you familiar with soulshifter salve?"

"Yeah, but we can't do any wavecasts if we have that stuff on."

"We have extra freecloths."

"What are you thinking?" Riverhand asked.

"You will pose as normal citizens and enter the coliseum with us and the rest of the Redividers. Then, once we all get in close enough, we will engage the soldiers while you remove the salve, enabling you to use your powers to capture the Uniter and his coregent. With any luck, it will be over with quickly."

"What about their protective bubble?" Windblade said.

"It was made for deflecting shots from Mono Realm weapons," Runner said. "I am sure it will stand no chance against your magic."

"I agree with that assessment." Thornleaf nodded.

"All right, so how are we going to get there?" Redstem asked.

"The fastest way will be via transit tube," Runner replied. "It will take multiple transfers, but we should still be able to arrive in time."

"And we are going with you," a newcomer to the room said. It was Guider, who had let herself in. She was followed by Thinker, Keeper, and her lieutenants. Each of them looked healthy, albeit a bit tired.

"No," Auravine protested. "You all need more time to rest."

"Yes, this will be a very hazardous operation," Runner said. "If you are not fully recovered, then all of you should remain here, for your own safety."

"I appreciate your concern, but I would not miss this for the world," Guider said, a look of grim determination on her face.

"Nor would I," Thinker said.

"Besides," Keeper said, "we do not need your permission. We are going whether any of you like it or not. This is our choice. Our decision."

Everyone was silent. Then, after a few moments, Felicity spoke up. "You know, she's got a good point there."

Auravine flashed Joel a small, possibly mischievous smile. "Perhaps that is what I should have told you in the first place."

Joel felt himself blush, although he wasn't entirely sure why.

CHAPTER 23: FIVE-POINT PROVINCE

Walking up a broad stairway leading to the front entrance of the coliseum, Joel looked around at the surrounding flocks of Mono Realm citizens. He had never been to a live sporting event before, but based on what he'd seen on TV, he assumed that it felt something like this. The coliseum itself seemed like a near-perfect cross between an ancient Roman arena and a modern-day open-air stadium: engraved stone columns were framed with metal railings, ten-foot-tall wooden statues of Mono Realmers in full battle gear seemed ready to come alive at any moment, and a ring of white lights at the top of the structure cast a glow like moonlight on the surface below. It had been built, Joel was told, near the site of an old cryovolcano, where rivers of near-frozen liquid chemicals—kind of like slush—flowed deep underground. These rivers served as a natural coolant for the coliseum as well as a source of special effects; man-made vents would release plumes of slush-generated vapor at appropriate times during performances.

"This could be interesting," Felicity muttered in Joel's ear as they—along with the other Wavemakers and

Redividers, the latter of which now numbered close to one hundred—approached the entrance. Wide and high, with an arch over it that was covered in Mono Realm writing, the entrance was flanked by eight soldiers, four on each side. Based on the information gleaned from Darkeye (and corroborated by reports that Runner had received from Redividers in other towns), no one would be checking the attendees for wavebows, countercoms, or anything else—but, Joel supposed, there could always have been a last-minute change of plans. Much to his relief, though, there didn't seem to be one, as the soldiers were simply handing out freecloths to everyone entering, like ushers passing out programs.

"Oh—uh, no thanks," Joel said to one of the soldiers attempting to give him a cloth, "I already have one."

"You do?" the soldier said, antennae twitching. "How did you acquire—"

"He's kidding," Felicity said, accepting the cloth and giving it to Joel before taking one for herself. "Such a joker. And thank you for this."

"Um, yeah, thanks," Joel said.

The moment they were out of earshot, Felicity hissed, "Dude, we're not supposed to have these things, remember?"

"Sorry, I forgot. But that's weird, right? Since we're not supposed to have these, why are they just giving them out like that?"

"Maybe for some kind of symbolic gesture or something."

"Like what?"

"I dunno, like, maybe they'll have us burn them or tear them up, you know, to show that we'll never need them, or whatever. Who knows?"

Joel continued wondering about it as they made their way inside. Some of the Mono Realm citizens were streaming into the surrounding rows of stone bleachers, while others—his party included—headed down into the main "playing field" area. Over at what Joel figured was the rough equivalent of the north end zone, under a glaring spotlight, he saw three parked vehicles: the two armored troop transports and, in between them, something that resembled a giant double-decker tour bus. Mounted on top of the bus was a flying-saucer-like contraption, complete with a clear, bubble-top cockpit. No one was inside of it at the moment.

"Guess they're planning on making a dramatic rock 'n' roll entrance," Felicity remarked.

The swarming crowds made it difficult for the entire contingent to stick close together, but that had been expected; the plan was simply for the Redividers to advance as close to the vehicles as they could, and then, once there, wait until Guider gave the signal. A pulse would be transmitted through the countercoms—one of which every member of the contingent, Wavemakers included, now had—and they would strike. Then the Wavemakers, who would have positioned themselves farther back and on the fringes so as not to be prematurely spotted by Marshall (they considered using invisibility casts, but that would put too much of a drain on their already-limited energies), would charge forth and try to stun the two regents while everyone was still distracted by the ensuing mayhem.

Elbowing his way through the throng, Joel eventually reached a spot near the "fifty-yard line," where he proceeded to skulk behind some tall Mono Realm citizens. As the crowd buzzed with muted anticipation, he remembered something.

Aw, man, I should've been wearing my loudstone!

He pulled the loudstone out of his cloak and hung its connected fishhook over his ear. Almost instantly, a voice sounded out of it: Blackspore's.

"You have allowed yourself to become distracted again."

"What? Uh—no, no, I haven't."

"Yes, you have. I saw that conversation you had with the healer girl back in the mountain town."

"Have you been watching *everything* I do?"

"For the most part, yes. It is my responsibility to guide you through this stage of your evolution."

"Look, I...I don't know how I feel, or what I think, about Auravine, or Felicity, or any of that stuff. It's all just really confusing right now. It gives me a headache."

"Which is exactly why you must purge it from your mind."

"Well, remember, I did that, which helped with the temporary power boost, but then after that ran out, I could still see the Aura here in the Mono Realm, and so I figured that everything was..." Joel trailed off, noticing that one of the tall Mono Realmers standing in front of him had turned around and was looking at him quizzically.

"Everything was what? Fine?" Blackspore said. "Therefore, you could just forget the entire lesson that I taught you? Joel, please, you have to trust me when I tell you that this will only lead to—"

"Um...hold on." Joel waved at the Mono Realmer. "Hi there," he said. "I'm just...you know, talking to myself. I do that. A lot. Especially when I'm bored. Like now, when we're all...waiting...you know, for the...for the thing."

The Mono Realmer's antennae twitched. "That is a very nice piece of jewelry you are wearing," he said. "It has such a unique energy signature."

"What, this?" Joel put a finger to his ear. "Oh—uh, yeah, um, thanks."

"Do you know where can I obtain something like that?"

"Well, it's...it's very rare. I actually don't think that you could, um, really get it from—"

Joel was bailed out by the amplified sound of a riff that he recognized as the intro to "Let Me Hear You Scream," the lead track off of Biledriver's Grammy-nominated fourth album, *Conquer and Divide*. The lights dimmed, and bursts of vapor shot out from the vents that were scattered all around the perimeter of the coliseum's inner surface.

Dramatic rock 'n' roll entrance, indeed.

"Good evening, Five-Point Province!" Marshall's voice boomed.

Joel craned his neck. Now he could see Marshall standing under the bubble top along with the Uniter.

"Greetings, everyone," the Uniter said as the "Let Me Hear You Scream" riff faded away. "Your presence here tonight is greatly appreciated."

Required, more like. Under penalty of death.

"As you know, this tour was arranged so that you would all have the chance to see—and swear fealty to—your new coregent live and in person. It is also a celebration of the new alliance between the Mono Realm and the Land under the Rainbow, an alliance that I am positive will pay rich dividends for the citizens of both countries."

Joel caught himself tuning out the Uniter's speech. He really didn't want to have to suffer through what was undoubtedly going to be a long and boring spiel about how great Marshall was, but he knew that the others needed as much time as they could get to maneuver themselves into the best possible positions.

"And with any new partnership comes the influx of new ideas," the Uniter continued. "I realize that, in the past, I may have held steadfast to some of my beliefs—a few of which, I will confess, were more popular than others. But, as an enlightened ruler, I certainly consider myself open to any suggestions that will help my land and my people reach the highest states of fulfillment."

Man, this is so bogus, Joel groaned silently. *No wonder he and Marshall get along.*

"One of those suggestions in particular has been adopted into a new law that I think you will all find to be most agreeable. To talk about that law, I give you your new coregent, a man known simply as...The Orchestrator."

Joel nearly broke out laughing. *The Orchestrator? So that's Marshall's Mono Realm name? I guess it's appropriate...still sounds silly, though.* Joel was sorely tempted to call Felicity on his countercom so that he could hear her take on it, but he was able to restrain himself.

"Yes, thank you, hello," Marshall—The Orchestrator—said. "I'd like to preface this by saying that diversity and individuality are concepts that we value very highly back in the Land under the Rainbow. You may not have been able to perceive this exactly the way we do, but I'm sure you've all noticed that my lieutenants and I differ somewhat in appearance."

A human zombie, a green Spectraland native missing an eye, and two creatures with gator heads and multiple limbs...yeah, I'd say they differ quite a lot.

"But I believe that it is not appearance, but rather, the feelings and the convictions of the individual *beneath* the surface—or, in your case, the energy signatures—that matter the most," Marshall said, making one of those Earth-politician type of hand gestures. "I have shared this opinion with the Uniter, and after some careful consideration, he has grown to accept and embrace my point of view."

That actually sounds...good, Joel thought, puzzled. *What is he up to?*

"And so," Marshall went on, "I am happy to announce that from this night forward, the soulshifter salve"—he paused here for dramatic effect—"*will no longer be required!* Go ahead, wipe it off, Five-Point Province!"

After a moment, the crowd erupted into loud, boisterous cheers. Joel looked around at the surrounding Mono Realm citizens, all of whom were eagerly wiping their faces and then throwing the freecloths into the air like mortarboards at a graduation.

"And now, because I know how much you all love music, I will perform a song for you," Marshall said. "Rejoice, my people! Dance and rejoice!"

"There is something wrong going on here," Blackspore said in Joel's ear.

"Yeah, I know, but what?" Joel responded as the crowd chanted *wipe it off, wipe it off.* "Why is he doing this?"

"Hold on, I think I see...oh, yes, now I understand."

"What?"

"Byle is performing a massive mind-control incantation."

"But...I thought mind-control casts don't work on Mono Realmers. Thornleaf tried it on Keeper when we first got here."

"I believe the soulshifter salve had made them immune, but now..."

Uh oh.

Joel looked back up at the double-decker tour bus. The bubble top had been opened, and sure enough, Marshall was using Auravine's wavebow to conjure up an immense, billowing cloud of dark-blue Aura energy. It was the same wavecast that he had used on Spectraland's people after he killed off the Wavemakers many years earlier, and before Fireflower had adjusted the brainwave frequencies of all the island's inhabitants to make them resistant to any further mind-control attempts.

"Oh no, no—this is not good," Joel muttered as the cloud began to quickly spread around the coliseum. He pulled out his countercom and punched up Guider's number. "Guider! It's Joel. Can you hear me?"

No response.

Dangit. Joel pressed the button to call Runner.

"Joel?" Runner's voice sounded.

"Yeah, hi, it's me. Did you wipe off the salve?"

"No, not yet, although I am under tremendous pressure to do so. I was not sure if—"

"Don't do it. It's a trick. He's performing a mind control cast. The salve will protect you from it."

"All right. I will try to inform the others."

"Okay. Oh, and also, I couldn't reach Guider, so give the signal to attack. We need to do it now."

"Understood."

Being already immune to mind-control casts, Joel wiped off his own salve and fired up a flying cast. As he sped through the air toward Marshall, he saw that the other Wavemakers were also airborne and heading for the double-decker tour bus, each of them approaching it from a different direction.

"Blimey, it's the insurgents!" Marshall exclaimed, sounding more amused than alarmed. It was almost as if he had been expecting them—which, Joel now realized, was probably the case.

"The situation has gotten worse," Blackspore said.

"Um, no kidding," Joel replied, letting his sarcasm practice kick in. He was close enough to the tour bus now to see that Marshall was wearing a necklace made from the three remaining stolen loudstones and that the Uniter had vanished from sight. Marshall replaced his vehicle's bubble top with a dome of shield-Aura and began firing blasts of dark-violet energy at his attackers.

"The mind-control cast has taken over a large number of Redividers," Blackspore said. "It seems that they were too eager to remove their soulshifter salve."

"Great," Joel muttered as he dodged one of Marshall's shots. "So what do you think we should—"

"There are more insurgents down below as well!" Marshall shouted. "Get them, my followers! Protect your rulers!"

Joel looked down. Many of the Redividers—as well as members of the general crowd—were joining forces with the soldiers to attack those who had not yet removed their salve.

No wonder they didn't check us for weapons, Joel realized. *They* wanted *everyone to be armed. Runner's gonna need some reinforcements.*

He flew over to the nearest Wavemaker, who happened to be Redstem. "Grab Riverhand and Windblade and help out on the ground!" he shouted as a dark Aura energy blast whizzed past them. "The rest of us will handle Marshall!"

"But—the loudstones! He has—"

"We'll handle it!"

Redstem nodded and flew off. Another blast missed Joel's head by three inches.

At least, I hope we will.

"Surrender now, you vile criminals!" Marshall yelled. "You have no chance! More of my forces are on their way!"

"He is right," Blackspore said. "Armored vehicles from all of the neighboring towns are approaching the coliseum."

Seriously? As if he needs more *help,* Joel grumbled to himself.

"Your little insurgency has come to an end!" Marshall started to spin around, spraying streams of dark Aura everywhere like some kind of evil Wavemaker sprinkler.

"We're doing this all wrong!" Felicity shouted as she swerved around a dark energy stream and zoomed up to Joel. "We have to get inside that tour bus!"

"Good idea." Joel nodded. "I'll do it."

"What, by yourself? No, I'll come with you."

"No, seriously, I got it. You and Thornleaf keep him busy out here. That way he'll be distracted and I can sneak in."

"But I...okay, yeah, you're right. That does make sense."

"I know."

Felicity smirked. "Oh, and hey—stay focused, all right? Just like Blackspore told you."

"I will."

Joel turned and flew toward the ground, where the melee had become completely chaotic: soldiers were shooting, Redividers were fighting each other with hand-held weapons, and in between it all, Redstem, River-hand, and Windblade were firing stunning casts everywhere, trying desperately to gain control of the situation.

"Your offworld companion is rather wise," Blackspore said.

"Yeah, she is," Joel said as he landed. A group of mind-controlled citizens converged on him, but he quickly dispatched them with a few bursts of Aura energy.

"Are you going to the vehicle now?" Blackspore asked.

"I am," Joel replied.

"Good. Now, remember that—" Blackspore's voice cut off, like a telephone call being disconnected.

"Blackspore?" Joel said, touching his loudstone. "Blackspore, can you hear me? Are you still there?"

There was no response. The loudstone felt cold.

Aw, man, it ran out of energy!

Looking around, Joel spotted Runner and one of Guider's lieutenants. They were using their countercoms to freeze some of their surrounding assailants, but it was obvious that they—and the entire group who hadn't wiped off their salve—were hopelessly outnumbered.

All right, well, loudstone or not, I need to do this now, Joel thought, setting his jaw. He turned and dashed toward the tour bus. Weaving his way through the fray, he got to within fifteen feet of the vehicle when suddenly someone grabbed his arm.

"Joel!"

Joel whirled around. It was Auravine.

"Where are you going?" she asked.

"To the—to Marshall's vehicle," he answered. "I'm gonna try to take him down from the inside while Felicity and Thornleaf occupy him up top."

"Do you have your loudstone?"

"I do, but it ran out of energy."

"Then you will need my help."

Out of the corner of his eye, Joel saw a group of soldiers heading his way with their weapons raised. He put up a shield cast around himself and Auravine that barely managed to deflect an incoming volley of shots. "But you don't have a wavebow," he pointed out once again.

"I told you before, I *do not need* a wavebow," she insisted, her expression turning steely. "I have one of those countercom devices, lent to me by Guider's people."

"Yeah, I know, me too, but that's not gonna work on Marshall. Not when he has all those loudstones to boost his strength."

"Then there is another way I can help."

"How?"

"I can be your loudstone."

Joel furrowed his brow. "Wait, what?"

"You can borrow my Aura energy. Since I have not been wavecasting, I am currently at full strength. With the additional power, you should be able to overcome Chief Byle."

"I—I just...I don't know. I don't think it's a good idea."

"Why?"

"Because, well..."

"Because it is dangerous? It does not matter, Joel. I will be in danger whether I go with you or remain out here. And my going with you will give us the best chance to stop him. To be the heroes. What do you say?"

Joel looked at her as the battle raged on outside of his shield. For a moment it felt like they were the only two people in the universe.

"Okay, yeah, you're right."

Auravine smiled. "I am glad you agree. Now, take my wrist."

Joel clasped her wrist, and she clasped his. A jolt of energy surged through him, and along with it, memories of a young girl back on Spectraland losing her parents, training to be a Wavemaker, and conspiring with Marshall Byle before ultimately turning her back on him, even though she knew that doing so would lead to her having to pay the price for her crimes. Joel felt everything she had felt: the sadness, the anger, the desperation. But he also knew that despite it all, Auravine had a good heart and the best of intentions. She felt sincere remorse for her actions. She had simply been trying to do what she thought was right for her brother and for future Spectraland generations. Sure, she had gone about it in a twisted, misguided kind of way, but at the time—before Joel convinced her that there was an alternative—she honestly believed that she had no other choice.

He also sensed the strong sense of affection and admiration that she felt for him. It flooded his mind and body with a warm, ecstatic sensation that was not unlike the kind he got when he solved a particularly difficult puzzle or came up with the perfect lyric to finish off a new song. He still wasn't exactly sure what love was, or what it truly felt like, but he thought that, perhaps, just maybe, it might feel something like this.

"Are you ready?" she said, releasing her grip.

Joel nodded. "Let's get him."

CHAPTER 24: THE ANGRY FOG

The soldiers guarding the tour bus had no chance. Fueled by the additional boost from Auravine's energy (as well as something more?), Joel was able to maintain his shield cast while simultaneously firing out a broad wave of stunning energy that knocked all of them down at once like a set of bowling pins.

Strike.

The entrance to the tour bus wasn't readily apparent, so Joel engaged the Sight.

Gravity Falls *episodes, in order: "Tourist Trapped," "The Legend of the Gobblewonker," "Headhunters," "The Hand That Rocks the Mabel"...*

A past image appeared, one of Marshall and the Uniter entering the bus through a well-camouflaged door near the back of the vehicle.

Gotcha.

Joel followed the image. Then, stopping in front of where the door was, he performed a muting cast that deadened all sound within a ten-foot radius before he blasted the door open with an exploding cast. He charged in, Auravine right behind him. The inside of the vehicle was spacious and luxurious, much more so than

Joel's own tour bus back home. With leather couches, furry carpeting, and huge video monitors, it looked like something that only the most successful and decadent rock bands on Earth would even dream of having. On one of the couches near the far end sat the Uniter, with a Mono Realm woman on either side of him. Startled, the two women stood up and drew small, pistol-like weapons, but Joel stunned them both before they had a chance to fire.

"Please, do not hurt me!" the Uniter said, raising his hands in surrender.

Joel was about to explain that he wasn't going to hurt him, he was just going to stun him, but then he remembered the muting cast, so he simply shrugged and shot a small burst of red light directly into the Uniter's chest. As the Mono Realm ruler slumped over, Joel spotted a staircase that led up to the vehicle's second level. He started to walk toward it when he felt Auravine tapping him on the shoulder. He turned around. She pointed to the Uniter and the two women, made a twirling motion with her finger, and then wrapped her arms around herself. Joel looked at her quizzically for a moment before he realized what she was trying to say.

Binding cast. Good idea.

After that was done, the pair carefully stalked up the stairs. The second level was even nicer than the first; it contained a king-sized bed (for Marshall, Joel assumed, since Mono Realmers didn't use beds), a hot tub, and even something that resembled a recording studio setup, complete with huge speaker cabinets. No one was there. In the middle of the area was a ladder leading up to a circular panel in the ceiling that Joel assumed was the entrance to the bubble-top cockpit.

Let's see, how should we do this? he wondered, staring at the panel. *Climb up normally and then surprise him? Using an invisibility cast? Depending on which way he's facing, though, he might see the panel opening. Hmm...*

Auravine tugged at his sleeve. He looked at her. She pointed to the ceiling, made a wide circular motion with her finger, and then waved both hands toward the ground, like she was quickly pushing down on something. It wasn't exactly sign language, but Joel got it.

Ohh—if I cut open a hole in the ceiling, then the whole flying-saucer-thing will come crashing down, and we'll have him. Great idea.

Auravine grabbed Joel's wrist to give him another boost of energy. Then he aimed his wavebow at the ceiling and fired out a powerful, concentrated heat cast. Based on what he had seen from the outside, he had a pretty good idea of how big a hole he would need to carve in order to encompass the entire rooftop car. He would also have to put some levitation pressure against the ceiling at the same time, to prevent the hole from creaking open prematurely and tipping Marshall off. It would take a lot of energy, but with Auravine here, he was sure that he could do it.

And indeed, when his circle was about halfway complete, he could feel himself starting to wear down. So he held the neck of his wavebow with his left hand while his right hand held onto Auravine's wrist. With her feeding him a continuous stream of energy, he was able to resume carving. After another minute or so, the circle had reached the ten o' clock mark.

Almost there...

Eleven o'clock. To give himself even more energy (and since he was almost done anyway), Joel dismissed the muting cast.

Almost there...

The panel popped open.

Wait, that's not supposed to—

Marshall dropped down out of the hole made by the open panel, landing on his feet in front of Joel and Auravine. "'Ello, 'ello, you two!" he said, grinning as he strummed his stolen wavebow.

Joel barely had enough time to let go of Auravine's wrist and play the note for a shield cast. The shield deflected Marshall's attack, but it was struck with such force that Joel and Auravine were both blown backward, bouncing off of Marshall's bed and landing behind it.

"I must say, I'm rather proud of you, Joel." Marshall chuckled. "You had quite a brilliant plan going on there. You almost had me." He shot off another cast that turned his own bed into dust, forcing Joel and Auravine to scramble behind the hot tub. "You forgot to take one thing into account, however. Even though I couldn't hear you, I could still *feel* you—or, more accurately, I could feel it when you blasted open my door, and when you were cutting a hole in my roof. With my dulled hearing, I've grown quite attuned to vibrations, you know." He fired a cast that shattered the hot tub and sent water flying everywhere. Joel and Auravine crawled swiftly over toward the speakers. Marshall fired at them, but— probably thanks to the momentary cover provided by the water—he missed and blew open a huge hole in the vehicle's wall instead.

"So you see, in the end, I'm still the grandmaster. The Orchestrator. No one can out-plan me."

Hiding behind the speakers, Joel looked at Auravine. They were both almost out of energy. He probably had enough left for one more cast. Auravine's eyes moved toward the hole in the wall.

We can fly out of here, she seemed to be saying. Joel could almost hear her talking in his head.

The hole is too far away, Joel thought. *We'll never make it.*

Yes, we will. Trust me.

"Well, I'd love to hang around here and monologue some more, especially seeing as how we're archenemies and all, but I've got some cleaning up to do outside, so I'm afraid I'll have to kill you both right now. Farewell, you two."

Joel started up a flying cast just as Marshall hit the speakers with a stream of Aura, splintering the cabinets into tiny fragments. The flying cast surrounded both Joel and Auravine, and then, the moment they took off, she engulfed him in a tight embrace. Marshall got off three more shots, but to Joel's amazement, none of them seemed to land. He zoomed out of the hole and back into the coliseum, where the battle was still going on.

"You were right—we made it!" Joel enthused as he flew up toward a platform area near the top of the structure.

"Joel," Auravine said.

"Wait here," he said as they landed. "I need to check if Felicity and Thornleaf are okay. But don't worry, I won't be—"

The flying cast dissipated, and Auravine collapsed.

"What the—Auravine?" Joel looked down at her. There were three large, gruesome spots on her back, smoking and pulsing with dark Aura energy. "Auravine!"

he exclaimed, kneeling down and setting his wavebow aside.

"Joel," she said weakly, turning her head. "Please..."

"Quick, um—teach me a healing cast!" he said, even though he knew it didn't quite work that way. "Or—or—"

"Please...forgive..."

"Auravine! C'mon, look at me, you're gonna be all right! You have to be..."

"Dude, what happened?" a voice said from behind. It was Felicity. She and Thornleaf had flown up to the platform. "We are *so* sorry. We were distracting him, but then he—oh no. Is she okay?"

The Sight seemed to engage itself, and Joel could see that the personal Aura field surrounding the young healer had faded away. "No," he said, hot tears forming in his eyes. "She's...she's gone."

Thornleaf rushed up, knelt down, and began to play a melody that represented the extent of his healing skills, but it was too late.

"Oh, Joel," Felicity said, "I...I don't know what to say."

Joel didn't either. All he knew was that there was a cold, empty feeling at the bottom of his stomach. He wished for a miracle—some amazing, improbable event that would bring Auravine back to life—but none came.

"Finish them, my followers!" Marshall's amplified voice boomed. "Eliminate your traitor countrymen! I will handle the rainbow folk criminals myself!"

"Aw, man," Felicity said, "and now he can fly."

Joel looked away from Auravine's still form just in time to see Marshall, in a green Aura cloud of his own, rising up out of the tour bus through the now-collapsed hole in its roof.

Marshall. You *did this.*

Joel felt his grief turn into rage. He clenched his jaw as an angry fog began to roll into his head.

This is all your fault.

Joel's sight blurred; everything seemed to be covered in a red haze. A new kind of energy filled him—not one that was derived from personal Aura, or the Aura surrounding him, but from some powerful and terrible source, as if he had tapped directly into the flames of the underworld.

I'm gonna get you.

He picked up his wavebow and launched himself into the air.

"Joel! Wait!" Felicity shouted.

But there was to be no waiting. Marshall was going to pay, and he was going to pay *now*, once and for all. Joel let out a furious scream as he zoomed toward the man who was the cause of so much suffering, suffering that no one expected or deserved. Now, after everything that had happened, it was going to be that man's turn to suffer.

"Ah, Joel, there you are," Marshall said, his voice still amplified like he had forgotten to turn off his microphone. "I was wondering where you had gotten to." He fired off a couple of casts, but Joel, instead of slowing down and creating a shield, simply swerved around them and sped up. "Whoa, that's some fancy flying there, mate. Where did you learn—"

Joel made a last-second turn, after which his extended fist struck Marshall square in the face. As fast as he was going, such an impact should probably have shattered Marshall's skull, but, protected somewhat by his own flying Aura, Biledriver's ex-singer simply flipped over backward a few times.

"Bloody hell!" Marshall exclaimed, clutching at his nose. "All right, then, a fight it is."

Joel came back around for another pass. Marshall was ready for him this time, though, and, with all of the loudstones on his necklace glowing like a set of miniature suns, he shot out a wide, thunderous cast that would have been impossible to dodge. So, instead, Joel screeched to a halt and threw up a large shield of Aura at the last moment. The shield deflected Marshall's cast and sent it crashing into the ground below, where it cracked open a long, smoking crevice that nearly swallowed up a few of the fighting Mono Realmers.

"Ha-*ha*!" Marshall cackled. "How do you like *that* one, eh? I composed it myself!"

Joel withdrew the shield and speed-picked a furious riff. He wasn't quite sure what he was playing, exactly; the only thing he knew was that in his mind, he was picturing Marshall exploding into millions of little pieces. Multiple streams of Aura jetted out of his instrument. Marshall countered with multiple streams of his own that collided head-on with Joel's, creating a deafening, dissonant blast of sound.

"Yeah!" Marshall shouted. "Oh, we're having fun now!"

Joel was getting set for another cast when Marshall replayed his previous one, once again forcing Joel to go on the defensive and put up a shield. Like before, the cast bounced off the shield and hit the ground, breaking open a fissure that, this time, ended up claiming a handful of screaming victims.

"Look, Joel, collateral damage!" Marshall said.

Joel looked down. Through the red haze in his eyes and the white vapors billowing out of the fractures, he could see a number of Mono Realm citizens—Runner among them—plunging to their deaths in the cold, fast-flowing slurry below. Even if he flew as fast as he could, there was no way he would be able to save any of them.

"So, who's the bad guy now?" Marshall asked, tauntingly. "Hard to tell, innit?"

Joel's entire body shook with anger. Despite the growing chill, he felt hotter than ever. He knew that this needed to end, and soon. Drawing even deeper from his reservoir of rage-fueled energy, he played a series of notes on his wavebow that created a sonic shell of Aura in the air surrounding both him and Marshall. Marshall tried to perform a cast as well, but his instrument was drowned out. Then, after a moment that felt far longer than its actual duration, the space inside of Joel's sonic shell warped, and, like a pair of polar opposite magnets, the two adversaries came together, face-to-face, in a flash. Marshall barely had time to register a shocked look on his face before Joel ripped the loudstone necklace off of his neck.

"That belongs to us," Joel roared. His voice was demonic, dripping with reverb and distortion.

"Oh—uh, er, yes, of course," Marshall stammered, eyes darting left and right as if he would find some answers there. His voice, no longer amplified, sounded small and tinny in comparison to Joel's. "By all means, take it."

Joel thrust the headstock of his wavebow under Marshall's chin. *"And now* you're *gonna know what pain feels like."* He started up a steady strum, one that would feed a constant stream of agonizing shockwaves throughout the body of his former idol.

"My word," Marshall grunted, grimacing. "You...you certainly have grown...quite powerful..."

The sonic shell—now an egg-shaped ellipsoid of swirling, crackling energy—started to rise up toward the dark cloud above.

"By the way," Marshall grunted through clenched teeth, "sorry I had to fridge your little girlfriend back there. But, you know, in my defense, I was actually aiming for you."

As the shell neared the cloud, lightning flashed, thunder roared, and buckets of rain began to fall.

"And on that subject," Marshall said, somehow able to continue blathering on through the pain, "I think I actually did you a favor. You know, by killing her."

"Why don't you do me a favor and shut up."

"Ah, yes, good one there. Very clever. But no, really, Joel, listen to me. I spared you an *incredible* amount of pain. You think you're hurting me right now? I assure you, this is nothing compared to what she—or any woman, really—would have done to you. She would have broken your heart. Left you for someone else. Turned you into a cold, bitter shell of a man. She betrayed me, and she would have betrayed you too."

"She wouldn't have done that. She loved me."

"Love?" Marshall said, forcing a chuckle. "Let me tell you something about love. Love is a losing proposition. Love is like global thermonuclear war. To paraphrase a popular movie: 'the only way to win is not to play.' Trust me, you are so much better off, my friend."

"You don't know anything about love."

Marshall's expression turned hard. "Oh no? All right, then, I'll let you in on a little secret. All those years as a famous rock star, I never once had a proper girlfriend. Not a single one. None of the birds I fancied ever reciprocated my feelings for them. All I ever experienced was rejection. And so I figured out that the one and only thing about love that anyone ever needs to know is that *love is a lie.* There is no such thing as love, Joel, and the sooner you learn that lesson, the better."

Joel's head was spinning, the angry fog quickly growing into a hurricane. "*Stop trying to distract me! It's not going to work!*" he growled, raising the intensity of his wavecast as the sonic shell moved up into the cloud itself. He didn't want anyone to see what he was about to do.

"Well go on, then, kill me!" Marshall snapped, defiant. "Just remember what I told you!"

Joel bared his teeth and strummed his instrument again. A stream of Aura poured out, wrapped itself around Marshall like a python, and then stretched out nearly fifteen feet to the far edge of the sonic shell. Marshall writhed and groaned as the part of the stream that was wrapped around him started to constrict, slowly crushing the life out of him.

"*This is for Auravine!*" Joel spat, channeling the entirety of his hate and his hurt and his anger into his wavecast. He could see Marshall's Aura slowly leaving his body. Sixty-six more seconds, and it would be all over.

"*And Runner! And everyone else you've killed!*"

Sixty seconds.

"*You'll never hurt anyone again!*"

"Joel," a voice said, seemingly from very far away.

Joel glanced in the direction of the voice. It was coming from his left. He saw a faint green glow outside the sonic shell.

"Joel, it's me."

Felicity.

"Can I come in? It's super cold and wet out here."

"*I'm busy. Go away.*"

"Joel, listen to me. I know what you're doing in there. You need to stop."

"*No. He needs to die. It's what he deserves.*"

"Maybe it is, and maybe it isn't," Felicity said, her voice steady and even. "I don't know. All I know is that it shouldn't be like this. Not this way. You have him. We got what we came for. Now let's just take him back to Spectraland, like we planned."

"*But he killed Auravine.*"

"I know. And he'll be punished for that one way or another. But you can honor her memory by doing it the right way, just like how you told her. Remember?"

Joel glanced at Marshall, who was turning paler by the second.

"Please, Joel," Felicity said. "Try to remember. I know you can. Your memory is, like, amazing."

Joel's mind flashed back to the moment when, just as Auravine was about to kill him and Felicity, he was able to convince her that what she was doing was wrong, and that there was another way, a better way for her to be the hero that she had always wanted to be.

A better way...the right way.

The moment played out in Joel's mind. Then, after it was over, he eased up on the constrictor cast just ever so slightly and allowed an opening to form in the sonic shell. Felicity drifted through the opening, drenched and weary looking.

"So...you remembered, right?" she said, wiping rainwater out of her eyes.

"Um, yeah, but...how did you know I told her that?" Joel asked, his voice returning to normal. "I thought no one could hear that conversation."

"She told me, back at Dwelling of the Lights." Felicity smirked. "I mean, we did talk about you *a little*, after all."

Joel grinned, feeling a bit sheepish. "Well, um, thanks for stopping me there. I can get a little carried away with my emotions sometimes."

"I know, dude. And believe me, I totally understand."

Just then, Joel spotted a flash of movement over Felicity's shoulder. Marshall had somehow recovered enough strength to wriggle his arms free of the constrictor cast. He was raising Auravine's wavebow and getting ready to fire.

"Look out!" Joel shouted.

Everything after that seemed to happen in slow motion.

Marshall shot out a wavecast.

Joel moved in front of Felicity. He withdrew the constrictor cast and replaced it with a large shield of Aura. Marshall's cast bounced off the shield and reverberated within the sonic shell a few times until it struck its originator.

The shell began to break apart. Marshall screamed as what was left of his personal Aura scattered into the air like a swarm of frightened flies. The shell disintegrated.

Marshall's body hung suspended for a moment before it fell down through the cloud and toward the coliseum below. Joel, his anger-fueled energy gone, fell as well, but Felicity swooped down and caught him with her flying Aura. She played a note, and Auravine's wavebow zipped back up into Joel's free hand. The two of them then watched as Marshall's lifeless form dropped into one of the cracks in the coliseum's surface.

"You know, we make a pretty good team," Joel said.

"Yeah, we do," Felicity replied.

They flew down and landed near the remains of the tour bus, where the other Wavemakers and some of their Mono Realm allies, including Thinker and Keeper, had congregated. All of the fighting had stopped. Still, no one seemed happy.

"So, yeah, I talked Joel out of it," Felicity announced to the group.

"But...Byle," Redstem said, looking puzzled, "we saw him—he—"

"He did that to himself," Joel said.

"Well, either way, it is over," Riverhand declared. "Now we can go home."

Joel looked around and saw a blanket, probably taken from the tour bus, draped over a body on the ground next to Windblade. He walked over to it, knelt down, and pulled the blanket back. Auravine's eyes were closed, and she had a peaceful expression on her face. She could have easily been sleeping.

"I'm sorry," Joel whispered, trying not to cry. He placed her wavebow beside her and, after one more moment of waiting for a miracle, pulled the blanket back up.

"Thank you, rainbow folk," someone said as they approached. Joel turned. It was Guider, her feathery silver locks waving in the chilly breeze. "The Mono Realm is no more. We are the Six States beneath the Shroud once again."

"You are welcome," Thornleaf replied. "Although, our actions were not completely altruistic. We also saved our own land from what sounded like a possible invasion."

"Indeed." Guider nodded, then looked toward Auravine's body. "I am sorry for your loss."

"You suffered casualties as well," Thornleaf said.

"Yes. And they will be mourned in a manner befitting individuals who have performed at the highest levels of honor and valor. I trust she will be, as well."

Thornleaf paused before responding. "She will."

"What of the mind-control effect?" Keeper asked. "That was such a terrible feeling...like the energy control, only much worse."

"It only lasts while its original caster is alive," Thornleaf explained. "With Byle gone, it will not return."

"Good," Keeper muttered. "I never want to experience anything like that ever again."

"If you wish, we could return with our leader, Fireflower," Riverhand offered. "She should be able to adjust your energy signatures so that you will be permanently protected, without having to use the soulshifter salve."

"Should we be concerned that one of you may attempt something like that again?" Guider asked.

"Well, no, but—"

"Then I do not see that as a priority. Your leader is certainly welcome to visit, however. And all of you are welcome to stay here as long as you like."

"We appreciate that," Thornleaf said, "but we should depart as soon as possible. Fireflower and our chiefs will be anxious to hear the results of our mission."

"Understood. Is there anything we can do for you before you leave?"

"Well, we still have to pick up Darkeye and our supply packs," Felicity said. "Oh, and buy back my loudstone from that bartender lady. Think you could spot us two hundred and fifty currents?"

"Consider it done."

At that moment, a hole opened up in the cloud above, and a ray of moonlight came shining through. Everyone gazed up at it in wonder. Joel wasn't sure if it was a natural occurrence or a result of his battle with Marshall, but right now, it didn't really matter.

CHAPTER 25: GOOD NEWS AND BAD NEWS

Joel opened his eyes. The afternoon sky above Spectraland was clear and cloudless, and the brilliant orange sun shone brightly as it made its daily trek down toward the horizon. The Aura seemed to sing a soft hymn as it drifted by on a warm, gentle breeze, carrying with it the smoke from a small pyre in the middle of the grass field behind the Wavemaker Temple. Fireflower was standing in front of the pyre, facing a small crowd that consisted of the four island chiefs, the Wavemakers (including Blackspore, whom the chiefs had pardoned upon hearing of his contributions to the Mono Realm mission), Yellowpetal, Starpollen, Sammy the silvertail, Thinker, Keeper, and a few other island denizens who had known Auravine during her short lifetime.

"And so," the Wavemaker leader said, concluding her eulogy, "we will choose to remember her as a friend, a daughter, a sister, and most of all...a hero."

Joel's gaze turned to the portrait—expertly rendered by Windblade on a large piece of parchment—that hung from a wooden stand next to the pyre. A tear rolled down his face.

Bye, Auravine. I'll miss you.

"Would anyone else like to say something?" Fire-flower asked. "Joel?"

"Um, no thanks," Joel replied, looking at the ground.

"Very well," Fireflower said understandingly. "In that case, this portion of the ceremony is over. In accordance with Spectraland tradition, the deceased's closest kin will deliver her ashes to the ocean at dawn. Since Starpollen is not of age yet, my mother and I will"— Sammy gave a little chirp here—"pardon me, and Sammy, will accompany him to the north coast. The rest of you, please stay and partake of some food and beverages. Thank you."

Joel turned and started across the field toward the refreshment tables. Having no intention of eating or drinking anything, he would have much preferred to simply return home to Earth, but he decided that leaving right this minute would probably be disrespectful. And besides, neither he nor Felicity had broached the subject of what her plans were at this point, so he figured that maybe now would be a decent time to do so.

"You okay?" she said, suddenly appearing at his side like she knew what he had been thinking.

"Yeah. I guess."

"Look, I'm sad she's gone too, even though it may not seem like it. I think you just have to think about it like...you have feel that...I dunno. You know I'm really bad at consoling people, right?"

Joel gave a soft chuckle. "Yeah, I know. Thanks for trying."

"Any time, dude."

Any time? Does that mean...

"So, um," he said, bucking up his courage, "what happened to you and Thornleaf?"

"Huh? What do you mean?"

327

"Did you guys...break up?"

"What? What gave you that idea?"

"Oh, well...back at the Town below the Mountain, after he was hurting Darkeye and you guys went outside...it looked like you were arguing, or something."

"Ohh...that," Felicity said, a strange expression crossing her face. "Yeah, actually, I was just trying to get him out of that room, you know, to kinda defuse the situation. He had told me earlier that he had something he wanted to ask me, so I figured I'd bring that up—thought maybe it'd distract him, calm him down a bit. And that's when..."

"What?"

"He, uh...he asked me to marry him."

Whoa. "What did you say?"

"I said...yes."

Joel's heart sank into his stomach. "Oh."

They arrived at the tables. Felicity helped herself to a small plate of sliced lifepods, while Joel, numbly going through the motions, grabbed a wooden cup filled with plain water. As he took a sip, the realization sunk in and hit him like a ton of bricks.

She's marrying Thornleaf. She's not going home after all.

Before he could say or think anything else, Blackspore came up to him.

"Joel, can I talk to you for a moment?"

"Um, sure." Joel blinked, still in shock.

Blackspore led him off to the side. "I did not have a chance to ask you this earlier, but—what, exactly, was happening to you during your final battle with Byle?"

"I dunno." Joel shrugged. "Lots of things."

"Well, specifically, where did you get the energy for the casts that you were performing?"

"I was just...I was angry, I guess. Like, really angry. That used to happen to me sometimes back home too. Not the wavecasting. Just the angry part."

"I see." Blackspore's brow furrowed.

"Why?"

"Oh—well, no reason, really. I was just curious."

"Okay." Joel took another sip of water. "By the way, I think you're wrong."

"Hmm? About what?"

"About love. I mean, Auravine felt love for me, and Felicity feels love for Thornleaf, and yet both of them are heroes, too. In fact, throughout this whole thing, the two of them were probably better heroes than I was. They did so many good things, and they didn't seem distracted at all. So, yeah, I think you're wrong."

Blackspore looked like he was about to respond in a challenging manner, but then, after a pause, his expression softened, and he said, simply, "I hope you are right, my boy. I hope you are right."

Felicity came sauntering over. "I heard my name," she said around a mouthful of lifepod. "What're you guys talking about?"

"Your fellow offworlder was just telling me about how you were able to perform many heroic feats while managing your feelings of affection at the same time," Blackspore replied. "Perhaps you could share some of your wisdom with us."

"Oh—yeah, well, you see, that's something my therapist taught me when I was a kid." She looked at Joel. "Yes, I had a therapist."

"Um, okay."

"Basically," she continued, "it's like—you make these little boxes in your head to put the different parts of your life in. So, like, there was one box for school, one box for family, one box for music and karate, and one box for all of my...I dunno, other nerdy interests, I guess. That way, whenever something was stressing me out, like a test, or my sister, or whatever, but I had to focus on something else, I could just put that thing in its box and forget about it until I had time to come back to it later. It really helped. It kept me from getting stuck. And man, I gotta tell ya, Vicky spent a *lot* of time in that box."

"Wow...that sounds pretty good," Joel said.

"Yeah, you should try it. Oh, and that reminds me of something I wanted to tell you earlier: I'm not just staying here because of Thornleaf. It's also because this place gives me a chance to do some really awesome stuff and, you know, make a difference, I guess. I mean, being in the band's cool and all, but here, as part of the Wavemaker Order or whatever, I get to help fix villages, settle disputes, rescue people from razorbears...it's like how people say 'music saved my life,' but literally. You know what I mean?"

"I do."

Felicity took another bite of her fruit. "I wish you could stay here too, but I know you've got your family, and the band, and...oh, hey, you should *totally* go hang out with that girl...you know, the one from the coffee shop. What was her name again?"

"Suzi?"

"Yeah, Suzi. I think she kinda likes you. I mean, I know it'll be a little awkward at first, seeing as how she looks so much like Auravine and all, but I dunno, maybe just wait a little while, you know, give it some time, like an appropriate mourning period or something be-fore...ah, you know what, I'm just gonna stop talking now." She turned and headed back for the tables.

"She is quite an amazing individual," Blackspore said once Felicity was out of earshot. "Thornleaf is a lucky man."

"Yeah," Joel said. "Yeah, he is."

♪♪♪

Later, after all the appropriate farewells were exchanged and nearly everyone had departed, Felicity stood with Thornleaf, Thinker, and Keeper in front of the temple's main entrance at the top of the stairs. She watched as Joel walked down into the clearing, turned, waved, and then turned around again. She wondered, as she had numerous times now, if she was making the right decision, but then she put that thought away in a little box and sealed it, vowing at that moment never to open it again. This was her home now. Now and forever.

"He will come back to visit, will he not?" Thinker asked.

"He'd better," Felicity said.

"Why does he have to leave from this particular spot?" Keeper asked. "I thought you could just fly into the air from anywhere."

"You can," Felicity answered. "He just likes doing it this way."

Joel stopped next to the river that bisected the clearing and played the flying cast melody on his wavebow. A cloud of green Aura billowed out of his instrument's headstock and engulfed him within its shimmering borders. He looked up at the sky for a moment before taking off, leaving a trail of sparks in his wake as he soared toward the horizon.

"Wait—Crownrock is in the other direction," Thorn-leaf said. "Does he know that he is going the wrong way?"

"Yeah, he knows," Felicity said, smiling as she watched Joel's outline disappear into the setting sun. "He knows."

EPILOGUE

Marshall had been here before. Well, not *here*, exactly, but in a similar state of disembodiment, caught between what most people commonly think of as "alive" and "dead." It was a familiar, almost comforting place to be, and, as his cognitive abilities slowly returned, he came to a sudden realization that filled him with a delicious sense of delight.

The Lightsnakes were right.

The first time he "died" was back on Spectraland when that little git, Joel Suzuki, threw the Songshell to him just as it was about to explode. But instead of either entering some traditional form of an afterlife or fading away into eternal darkness, he'd ended up suspended in an alternate plane of existence as a sentient collection of energy particles—a ghost, if you will—that eventually regained the entire consciousness of the man known as Marshall Byle.

He'd wandered that plane for what felt like an eternity until he stumbled upon a nexus between his plane and the ruined remains of Prism Valley, another parallel state, this one suspended above Spectraland and home to an ancient race of beings known as the Lightsnakes. That other git, Felicity Smith, had taken out the Lightsnakes' queen, causing their near-total destruction, but a few of them had survived.

At first Marshall thought of these creatures either as ignorant things to be avoided (at best) or savage enemies to be destroyed (at worst). Over time, however, he discovered that they were actually quite brilliant—a proud group of once-powerful Aura users capable of tremendous wisdom and insight. Marshall struck up an alliance with them, and eventually they made him their ruler, finally replacing their long-vanquished monarch.

One day one of the Lightsnakes—a particularly clever fellow—posited a theory about what had caused Marshall to turn into a ghost. At the end of an old, long war between the Lightsnakes and a race of tiger-ram creatures known as the Fourtails, a large explosion of Aura had permanently altered their personal energy structures and physically banished them to the Prism Valley. Based on that experience, the Lightsnake reasoned that a similar event had occurred to Marshall when the Songshell blew up. In Marshall's case, however, his personal energy had left his body altogether and *merged with the Aura*, effectively making him immortal, albeit confined to his alternate plane. This train of thought eventually led to the idea that, even if Marshall were to somehow repossess his corporeal form, as long as there was Aura present, he would be unable to truly die, since his energy was already a part of the greater whole.

Taking it even further, the Lightsnake postulated that an even larger explosion of concentrated Aura on an exponentially greater scale would turn someone not into a mere ghost, tethered to one place, but a superwraith of sorts that could go anywhere, be anyone, and do anything. That individual would be so powerful as to be nearly omnipotent. It would take an incredible amount of energy, but hypothetically, it could be done.

And so Marshall, given years with nothing better to do, concocted his most convoluted but ingenious plan ever: after repossessing his body (by means of another, almost as convoluted scheme involving a young Spectraland native named Auravine), he would bring as many people as he could—millions, perhaps—over to Spectraland for an exclusive, one-time-only Biledriver reunion concert. Then, after gathering them in front of a large, custom-built amphitheater specifically designed to reflect Aura energy, he would set off a gigantic explosion, releasing everyone's personal energies into the air and turning him into the superwraith.

First, however, he'd known he would need to take control of Spectraland so that he could build his structure on the beach near Crownrock, and to do both he would need an army. But where would he get one? Fireflower had already protected the island's people from mind-control casts. But, ah—there was another option. A land across the sea that Blackspore had told him about, full of walking, talking bug-eyed freaks who would be perfect for the job. He would just need to get past those pesky Forbidden Tides...

His thoughts snapped back to the present. So there *was* Aura here in the Mono Realm after all, and he was now a part of it. It wasn't as strong as it was on Spectraland, but it was there nonetheless. He saw that he was drifting along above the Five-Point Province coliseum, where a team of Mono Realm workers was busy cleaning up wreckage from the battle. He glanced around to see if, perhaps, the "ghost" of that little traitor Auravine was lingering around as well, but, as he expected, it wasn't.

And why would it be? She didn't have the benefit of having died once already in a Songshell explosion.

He sensed that his body was nearby, possibly in one of the crevices in the coliseum's surface. He floated down to take a look. Sure enough, it was there, having fortuitously landed on a small ledge some ten feet above the rushing cryoriver below. He smiled—inasmuch as a ghost can smile—at his good fortune. He knew that in real life the bad guys got just as many breaks as the good guys, if not more.

From here, it would be relatively easy to pick up almost where he'd left off. Once he repossessed his body, the mind-control cast would go back into effect, and although he might not be able to secure as many followers as he had originally wanted, he would still have enough of them to make his plan work. As for right now, he just had to make sure that the coliseum workers pulled him out of the crevice before he froze to death. But even if he did die, he realized, feeling a good deal of smug self-satisfaction, he could always just come back and try again...

www.joelsuzuki.com